TIGER
HONOR

Also by Yoon Ha Lee
DRAGON PEARL

★ "Lee skillfully weaves Korean folklore into this space opera narrative, creating dynamic and relatable characters. With ghosts, pirates, and a rollicking space adventure, there's a little something for everyone here."
—*School Library Journal* (starred review)

★ "A high-octane, science-fiction thriller painted with a Korean brush and a brilliant example of how different cultures can have unique but accessible cosmology and universal appeal."
—*Kirkus Reviews* (starred review)

★ "Lee offers a perfect balance of space opera and Korean mythology with enough complexity to appeal to teens."
—*Publishers Weekly* (starred review)

"*Dragon Pearl* is a clever mash-up of Korean mythology and science-fiction tropes. With crisp dialogue, a winning protagonist and a propulsive plot, the tale is enormously entertaining."
—*New York Times Book Review*

"Who would have thought Korean mythology would make for such an intense and magical space opera! I loved every moment of it and want the next book NOW so I can explore all the Thousand Worlds with Min! This book is brilliant and gorgeous, and why didn't I have it when I was a kid?"
—Ellen Oh, author of *Spirit Hunters* and the Prophecy series

"I was so impressed by *Dragon Pearl*. The story is multi-layered, the world construction is impeccable—with an awesome intersection of tech and culture—and it is totally compelling to read. Min's nuanced feelings about her magic, her family, and her fox heritage are marvelously complicated. I loved her, and I know you will, too!"
—E. K. Johnston, author of the #1 *New York Times* best-selling *Ahsoka*

A *New York Times* Best Seller

Locus Award Winner for Best Young Adult Novel 2020

Mythopoeic Scholarship Award for Children's Literature Winner 2020

Kirkus Reviews' Best Children's Books of 2019

Chicago Public Library's Best of the Best Books of 2019

A Junior Library Guild Selection

TIGER HONOR

YOON HA LEE

A THOUSAND WORLDS NOVEL

RICK RIORDAN PRESENTS

Disney • HYPERION   LOS ANGELES   NEW YORK

First Edition, January 2022
1 3 5 7 9 10 8 6 4 2
FAC-021131-21323
Printed in the United States of America

This book is set in Janson MT Pro, Carlin Script LT Std/
Monotype; Penumbra Std, Goudy Trajan Pro/Fontspring
Designed by Tyler Nevins

Library of Congress Cataloging-in-Publication Data
Names: Lee, Yoon Ha, 1979– author.
Title: Tiger honor / Yoon Ha Lee.
Description: First edition. • Los Angeles ; New York : Disney-Hyperion, 2022. • Series: A
Thousand Worlds novel • Audience: Ages 8–12. • Summary: Thirteen-year-old nonbinary
tiger spirit Sebin must decide where their loyalties lie when their traitorous uncle hijacks
the battle cruiser that happens to be Sebin's first assignment in the Cadet Program.
Identifiers: LCCN 2021001107 • ISBN 9781368055543 (hardcover)
• ISBN 9781368066006 (ebook)
Subjects: CYAC: Loyalty—Fiction. • Gender-nonconforming people—Fiction.
• Hijacking of space vehicles—Fiction. • Shapeshifting—Fiction. • Families—
Fiction. • Space flight—Fiction. • Magic—Fiction. • Science fiction.
Classification: LCC PZ7.1.L4414 Ti 2022 • DDC [Fic]—dc23
LC record available at https://lccn.loc.gov/2021001107

Reinforced binding
Visit www.DisneyBooks.com
Follow @ReadRiordan

This book is for Cloud, my beloved catten, needy tortie, mighty huntress, who loved loafing in front of my keyboard while I was trying to write this book. Of everyone in my family, she *is* the most closely related to a tiger!

PROLOGUE

Juhwang Sebin, Cadet, 1728-99746.

Name, rank, and serial number. That's all I'm supposed to say if I'm captured.

Every member of the Thousand Worlds Space Forces knows that, even one as junior as I am.

It's a little ludicrous to worry about that, though, because the few people still active on this ship know who I am and what I've done. And those who put me here are my comrades. *You're nothing but a traitor* was the last thing Min said to me as she left me locked up in this cell.

The others don't need to be told what my name is, or any of that. They're perfectly aware that I'm a tiger spirit from the Juhwang Clan on the world of Yonggi, and that I'm responsible for the pickle we're all in.

Beyond that, there are more complications. I'm a prisoner on my own ship, the battle cruiser *Haetae*. We're still in transit through a Gate, and I don't know how much more time we have until we emerge on the other end.

I have, however, had ample opportunity to inspect the brig. The cell is approximately three meters square. Walls of bland gray metal, toilet and sink in the corner, physical bars instead of a force field. A smart precaution, considering that the last time I checked, half the power systems on the *Haetae* were knocked out.

In this cell there's a strip of faint lights running on backup power. I don't know how long they'll last. At least, as a tiger spirit, I have good vision even in dim illumination. I hope it's enough.

Just in case, though, I've memorized the layout of everything I can see, and I tried my best to memorize the maps of the ship that I was shown earlier, which included the restricted areas. I might be able to use that information—if only I can get out.

The other cells in this row are empty. Even if I couldn't see into them, my senses of smell and hearing would have told me that. It's almost a relief that it's just me here and not some additional unfortunates as well.

Besides, having to free other people would slow me down. Not a nice thing to think about, but everything has crystallized into hard practicalities. After all, if I don't stop the people who have fallen under the evil spell of a monster we all thought extinct, everyone on this ship is doomed.

I test the bars. They're specially reinforced to hold supernaturals like me. Goblins and dragons, to say nothing of tigers, are all stronger than the ordinary humans who make up the greatest part of the Thousand Worlds' population.

Brute-forcing my way out of this cell isn't going to work, even if I change from my human form into my native tiger shape. There's enough space for me as a tiger, barely, but claws wouldn't put a dent in this metal.

People have always seen my kind as excellent fighters. There's some truth to that. My family emphasized training and discipline when I was growing up.

But tigers aren't *just* fighters. In the oldest stories, we're known for our cunning, too. Some of us are more cunning than others. If I'd been smarter, maybe I could have avoided getting trapped in here by the people I thought were my friends. Who might yet be my friends, if I can free them from the monster . . .

There's only one person I can count on now, assuming he finds me before the monster subverts him—or returns for me.

While I'm trapped, I suppose I ought to reflect on how this all began, and how I started on the path that led to this cell. . . .

ONE

W hen the mail arrived, it should have been the best day of my life.

Mail—physical mail—came once a week at best. The Juhwang Clan of tiger spirits had made our home on the world of Yonggi for the past several centuries. Our ties to the land dated back to the steaders who settled this planet back when traveling between stars took decades, or even centuries. My grandmother, the Matriarch of the clan, claimed she could remember what the world had looked like before it was terraformed, when it was a ball of mud and toxic sludge. *Back then there* was *no mail*, she always said, her tail swishing ominously. *No food, no medical supplies, no fuel—nothing. That was before the Thousand Worlds came together, and you couldn't ever rely on anyone but family.*

But when our home security system announced that the mail had been dropped off, all I cared about was whether there was anything for me. I'd been obsessed with the mail for the past three months, ever since I'd applied to the Space Forces Cadet Program.

Normally you could only join the Space Forces at the age of fifteen, but due to raids at the Thousand Worlds' borders, they'd started recruiting younger cadets to accustom them—*me*, I hoped—to the rigors of space travel at an earlier age. They especially welcomed applicants with supernatural natures suited to the service, such as goblins, celestials, and tigers, like me. Even if I hadn't already been eager to join, the Matriarch would have encouraged it. *It's important for us to build our power base*, she'd said mysteriously.

Every time the mail arrived, I hovered over it in hopes of the coveted response, maybe even an acceptance letter. And every time the response failed to arrive, I consoled myself by reading more of the Space Forces handbook so I would be ready the next day, just in case.

My aunt Sooni was the only one who didn't laugh at the way I was fixated on the mail. *Aunt* was approximate—she was at least a hundred years older than me. (Tiger spirits don't age the same way humans do.) Aunt Sooni's understanding was the only thing that made it bearable to be the youngest in the clan.

We were in the middle of some martial arts exercises that involved shifting between human and tiger form to dodge attacks when the mail drop arrived. Aunt Sooni was an orange-and-black blur as a tiger, and a gray one as a human. I, too, was an orange tiger, unlike my favorite relative, Uncle Hwan, who visited when he could. *He* was a rare white tiger, and I often wished I had been born that color. It was because of Uncle Hwan that I longed to be accepted by the Space Forces—to someday become a battle cruiser captain just like him.

"Focus, Sebin!" Aunt Sooni called when I stopped in mid-exercise and turned toward the mailbox in my eagerness to pounce on the mail. "Remember discipline. Discipline is the most important thing. You have to finish the set."

I mock-snarled at her. She cuffed me lightly on the shoulder, not hard enough to hurt, but with enough force to remind me of her supernatural strength. Even in her human form, that of a short, stocky woman with touches of frost in her hair, she could wrangle a fellow tiger. I'd learned that the hard way.

With a growl, I condensed back into my human shape. At thirteen I was already taller than she was, if only by a mere inch. (Half inch, according to her. I always said we should round up, and she only shook her head.)

"All right," I said, resigned, because I knew Aunt Sooni was perfectly capable of snatching the mail and hiding it from me until I had performed my exercises to her satisfaction.

"Just for that," she said, and this time I knew to suppress my groan, "we'll add some high kicks. Go!"

Approximately four million kicks later, my legs burned with the exertion and Aunt Sooni declared herself satisfied with my efforts. "You know it's important to stay in shape," she said. "We have standards to uphold."

I wasn't so much concerned with the Space Forces' standards as my own family's expectations. We were the Juhwang Clan of Yonggi, after all, and, as the Matriarch liked to remind us, we had to be prepared in case our enemies moved against us, even if I'd never so much as witnessed an attack on the estate. Right now, that meant making sure I did all the exercises as perfectly as possible.

As much as my body hurt, I ached to sprint to the mailbox. My family had indulged me by letting me check the mail for the last month. *Normally I don't reward moping,* my mother's nonbinary mate, my nini, had said in their usual dry tone, *but perhaps a little is understandable under the circumstances.*

Still, I didn't want Aunt Sooni to think of me as an irresponsible tiger cub, so I walked at her side. It was a good chance to recover my breath, anyway. If I was accepted, I'd have to do more than just make a good impression on my family. I was determined to excel in the Space Forces, maybe even outshine Uncle Hwan someday.

To reach the mailbox, we had to cross the estate's outer courtyard. Both the inner and outer courtyards, each spacious enough for tigers to roam in, were bright with flowers, cultivated by my parents and some of the others from time to time. You wouldn't think that tigers would care about gardening. But, as my mother liked to tell me, we thrived in nature, whether that meant overgrown groves of bamboo or the graceful sweep of willow branches. The art of gardening consisted of arranging plants so they looked like they had grown in the wild, except more picturesque.

I appreciated the gardens, but I yearned to leave the planet and see other worlds. I could watch the holo programs, which depicted everything from fantastical ruins to the extreme temperatures on tidally locked planets in other systems, where one hemisphere was in eternal day and the other in eternal night. But it would be so much better to visit those places myself! And my best chance of doing that was getting into the Space Forces.

"Here we are," Aunt Sooni called as the mailbox came into sight. It was shaped like a miniature pagoda whose roof came off if you worked a cunningly hidden latch. I loved everything about it, even its absurdity.

More intriguingly, someone had left a package at its base.

That couldn't be for me, but I was curious about it anyhow.

Aunt Sooni, taking advantage of my distraction, added, "Race you!" and shimmered into her tiger form as she sprang into action. I did likewise, reveling in the fact that I became stronger and swifter in my native shape. As a tiger, you couldn't tell I was thirteen years old. I looked almost adult, complete with a fine orange pelt and deep black stripes, and a long, long tail.

Perhaps it wasn't strictly fair that Aunt Sooni had started the race before I'd had a chance to shift. But one thing my family emphasized was the importance of being adaptable. I remembered the last time I'd complained about the conditions of a training exercise being unfair. My mother had looked at me with disappointment and then explained that in time of war, *everything* might be "unfair." The enemy wouldn't give their opponent a fair chance, so a true warrior dealt with the situation instead of griping about it. From then on I'd kept my mouth shut and redoubled my efforts.

Spurred by the memory, I gathered myself for one great leap as we neared the mailbox. Even so, Aunt Sooni's own leap was more powerful than mine, and she arrived a second before I did. Her momentum carried her past the mailbox, and she swung back around, resuming her human form as she did so.

I changed back as well, trailing in her wake. "I almost had you!" I said, knowing that she wouldn't hear it as a challenge the way the rest of my relatives would.

"You did indeed," Aunt Sooni agreed. "Well done."

I ducked my head, trying not to let her see how much the words of praise meant to me. The rest of my family rarely gave out compliments. That didn't distract me from my purpose, however. I wanted to rise on my toes and reach for the mailbox, but I knew I had to await permission. Even Aunt Sooni had her stern side.

"Very good," she said, acknowledging my patience. "You may get the mail."

I had to restrain myself from lunging forward and picking up the package to shake it. The box was larger than I had realized, no more than a foot wide and only six inches deep, but almost half as long as I was. Aunt Sooni might not mind, but the other tigers would disapprove. *It's probably something completely unrelated*, I told myself as my heart pounded. I couldn't let Aunt Sooni see my hope—or my dread.

From time to time we got curios from Uncle Hwan, accompanied by brief but exquisitely calligraphed notes on expensive mulberry paper. More often the Matriarch received cryptic little parcels, which I wasn't allowed to ask about or show interest in. The Matriarch had made it especially clear that I was never to mention the existence of those parcels to any outsider who might happen to show up at the estate. I assumed this larger package, too, had to be kept secret.

I made myself step forward and calmly work the catch of the mailbox as though it were an ordinary task, as opposed to the one thing standing between me and my lifelong dream. The catch did its trick, and the roof of the miniature pagoda sprang open on its hinge. Inside was a letter, which I picked up as decorously as I could manage. I sucked in a breath when I turned it over and saw that it was addressed to one Juhwang Sebin and stamped in red ink with the seal of the Space Forces. A letter for me! I was in an agony of suspense wondering if it contained good news or bad.

Aunt Sooni's reaction took me by surprise. "Check to see if there's another one in there?" I could smell her own dread, as if she expected bad news. She could have nudged me aside and reached into the mailbox herself, but she was allowing me to save face.

I peered into the mailbox. She was right. I'd been so excited to find a letter for me that I hadn't thought to look for anything else.

"Huh" was all I could think to say when I drew out the second letter. It *also* bore the red seal of the Space Forces. But unlike my letter, *mine*, it was addressed in formal calligraphy to the Matriarch of the Juhwang Tiger Clan.

Then I knew. I should have figured it out sooner. The box contained a sword—an officer's sword. Like the one Uncle Hwan always wore on his visits. That, plus the letter, meant—No. It couldn't be.

I could only think of one reason why the Space Forces would return a captain's sword: because he was dead. My eyes stung. It wasn't the first time a member of the Juhwang Tiger Clan had died in service, but I'd hoped to follow in Uncle Hwan's footsteps and make him proud.

Not Uncle Hwan! I thought in dismay. The uncle who had always made sure to bring me something special every time he visited, whether it was a knife of my own or a cinnamon candy. The uncle who had told me stories about his adventures as an officer, fighting off pirates or saving his comrades from the Thousand Worlds' enemies.

"We must take this to the Matriarch right away," Aunt Sooni said. She pursed her lips as she regarded the package, her expression grim.

A memory flashed before me of the last time Uncle Hwan had visited the estate. He'd been resplendent in his Space Forces uniform, dark blue with shining gold braid, and along with his blaster he'd had a sword belted at his side. He'd let me look at the sword up close and then draw it from its sheath for one magical moment.

It was a masterwork, that sword. Even its sheath was finely ornamented, with gold scrollwork and symbols pieced together from mother-of-pearl. The hilt was wrapped in oiled leather, and a blue silk tassel hung from its pommel. I'd been disappointed to discover that the blade itself was blunt, and the corner of my uncle's mouth had crooked upward in amusement.

This sword represents my honor, he'd said. *It is my honor that gives it its edge, not the metal itself.*

I'd said I understood, although I didn't. Honor was all very well, but what good was a blunt sword against pirates or raiders from the Jeweled Worlds?

Now, as I looked down at the box, I trembled. Surely it couldn't contain Uncle Hwan's sword. "It can't be," I said to myself.

"That's not for us to find out," Aunt Sooni said briskly. Still, that acrid worry-smell came from her again. She hoisted the box with ease. "You can come with me, since I'm sure the Matriarch will want to hear your news, too."

We padded solemnly through the courtyard and to the separate building where the Matriarch kept her residence. From the outside, it resembled the mailbox pagoda, with its peaked roof and decorations in the traditional five colors of black, red, green, yellow, and blue. Someone's idea of a joke, although I had a hard time imagining the Matriarch had a sense of humor.

We stopped by the profusely blooming azalea bushes whose magenta blossoms masked the entrance to the pagoda. I craned my head back to squint at one of the thoroughly modern windows above us. I glimpsed a shadow moving behind it. The Matriarch liked to keep an eye on all the approaches.

"Matriarch," Aunt Sooni called out, "we have a package addressed to you, and a letter from the Space Forces." She used the most deferential language, on account of the Matriarch being the head of the family, and the oldest one here.

The wind rustled the azalea blossoms and their glossy leaves. For a moment, I wondered if the Matriarch had heard us. Even if she hadn't, we'd have to wait here until she acknowledged us. It was her way.

Then a hoarse voice with a hint of a growl in it said from above, "Come in, Sooni, and bring the cub with you."

I hated being called *cub* as if I were still a child, but the fact remained that I was the youngest tiger spirit in the family. Besides, I knew better than to object. I followed Aunt Sooni up the stairs to the foyer, where we both took off our shoes before continuing up more stairs into the pagoda proper.

The Matriarch sat cross-legged on an embroidered floor cushion, her back straight. Her long white hair had a single black streak remaining in it, and she had yellow eyes, which made her look impossibly tigerish even in human form. I had never seen her in anything but a hanbok, the old-fashioned dress of the Thousand Worlds. The jogori, or jacket, was a faded orange with subtle gold embroidery, and her chima, or skirt, was an equally faded black.

We bowed deeply. I was impressed by how Aunt Sooni managed it without dropping the box on her toes.

"Bring it here, Sooni," the Matriarch said in her growling voice.

Aunt Sooni did.

"Open it."

Aunt Sooni kept her fingernails sharp, as did all the elders in the family. Or maybe she'd turned them partway into claws. I wasn't sure which. I didn't have that kind of fine-grained control over my shape-shifting; most tigers didn't. She sliced the package's tape and opened the lid.

My breath caught when I recognized the sword.

"It's Hwan's," Aunt Sooni said.

The Matriarch's eyes flicked to me, sharp as a knife-cut. "So it is."

The Matriarch noticed my distress. Instead of rebuking me directly, she said to Aunt Sooni, "Sebin is disgracing themself."

I knew she'd meant for me to hear. I immediately lowered my gaze, flushing in shame.

The Matriarch opened the letter that Aunt Sooni gave her. Her eyes flickered. Then she looked at the two of us.

"Space Forces Command informs us," the Matriarch said, "that Hwan of the Juhwang Tiger Clan stands accused of treason and has disgraced his uniform. There is a warrant out for his arrest. He will be court-martialed upon his capture."

That can't be right! I wanted to cry out. Even though I was relieved that Hwan wasn't dead, this was almost worse. Uncle Hwan was the one who'd taught me about honor. He couldn't have *deserted.*

And if Uncle Hwan had been branded a traitor, what did that mean for me? Had my dream of serving among the stars just evaporated with the arrival of Uncle Hwan's arrest warrant?

TWO

The Matriarch had other things on her mind. "The Space Forces have insulted the clan's honor and threatened one of my agents. If I suffer them to cast out Hwan like this, the rest of my supporters will be next. This cannot be allowed to stand."

My heart almost seized. Did she mean I wouldn't be allowed to go, even if I got into the cadet program? Then I felt like a traitor myself for the thought. Shouldn't I care more about the clan's honor than my petty personal ambition to fight pirates and invaders?

The Matriarch harrumphed. "I can't believe Hasun allowed this to happen. I must have words with them."

I swallowed. My auncle, Rear Admiral Hasun, was one of the Matriarch's distant cousins. I wasn't sure of the exact relationship, as our family tree had unexpected branches on other worlds. Hasun was also the highest-ranking relative I had in the Space Forces, but the Matriarch outranked them within the clan. I didn't want their job, which sounded like sitting around strategizing and filling out paperwork. I hoped to have a starship of my own someday, maybe even a battle cruiser like Uncle Hwan's *Pale Lightning*. Then I realized that Uncle Hwan didn't have a ship anymore—there was no way Space Forces Command would allow a captain who'd been branded a traitor to keep one—and I felt worse than before.

Earlier, I'd wondered from time to time if people would say that I hadn't earned my cadet posting on my own, that my relatives had pulled strings to get me in. Now I faced the opposite problem. How would anyone take me seriously if they knew I was related to an alleged traitor? It wasn't the kind of thing I could keep hidden. The moment people discovered my clan, they would make the connection to Admiral Hasun, and now to Uncle Hwan.

"We will have to call a family council," the Matriarch declared. My heart sank, only to lift, cautiously, when she added, "The cub will attend."

Not for the first time, I wished she would address me directly instead of referring to me as *the cub* as though I were a peculiarly ambulatory statue. Or maybe an artifact someone had left behind from the days of the planet's colonization, kept out of obligation rather than any real affection.

Aunt Sooni, who could guess my thoughts, coughed politely. "Sebin is right here, Matriarch."

Then the Matriarch's words penetrated. I'd never attended a council before. They'd always been for the adults. She might call me *cub*, but perhaps she finally thought I was ready for more adult responsibilities—and a say in my own fate.

To summon the council, the Matriarch rang a bell that she kept in the pagoda. It had a low tone, not overly loud, but I'd heard it throughout the house and beyond in times past. For a human household it might have made more sense to summon everyone by paging their data-slates, but with our family, various members might be in tiger form, or sparring, or otherwise away from their slates at any given time. The bell, though old-fashioned, got the job done.

The ringing awoke a foreboding in me. As a cub, I'd often wondered if the elders were discussing some terrible fate for me. When I'd confessed my fear to my mother and Nini, the two of them had ruffled my hair, then said soberly that if I was the source of the trouble, I'd know it. Their words hadn't reassured me much.

Despite the Matriarch's insistence on honor above all things, I had grown up with folktales of tiger warriors who lured their prey closer through tricks. One that nagged at me was about a wicked tiger who had disguised herself as someone's grandmother in order to gobble them down. It was at odds with all the family stories of stern, brave tiger warriors who'd been celebrated by the Thousand Worlds. I'd never dared to ask about the disparity, sensing it would get me into trouble.

Aunt Sooni nudged me out of my reverie and guided me toward a seat near the door. "This is your place," she said, "since you're the youngest. Don't speak unless spoken to."

Her warning wasn't necessary. I had no intention of opening my mouth in a gathering of full-fledged tiger spirits. Clutching my envelope, I sat.

It didn't take long for my mother and Nini to arrive. They must have been training in the nearby gardens. I sometimes wondered what they were training *for.* My family always talked about the nebulous enemy as though they might attack at any moment, something I had never experienced. But I reminded myself that it was our family's duty to be prepared for any eventuality, even an unlikely raid on the planet.

My parents glanced at me with surprise before bowing to the Matriarch and taking their seats in front of me. I took the opportunity to study them as they passed. I'd gotten my sturdy build from my mother. My pale amber eyes and snub nose came from Nini. Like Nini, I wore my hair shaved at the sides, with bangs. I wished I could run to them for reassurance, but they would have chided me for weakness.

The rest of the family traipsed in, paying their respects to the Matriarch. There was Great-Uncle Myung, who had an artificial leg replacing the one he'd lost in the Space Forces. He'd served another eight years before retiring. Great-Uncle Chin-Mae accompanied him everywhere. And Great-Aunt Jung-Soo, who was the Matriarch's right hand, and who wore a hanbok similar to hers, except in simple blue and white.

There were eight tiger spirits here, including me. It made for a crowd. If we had shifted to tiger form, there wouldn't have been enough room in the pagoda for all of us. The clan included other members, but these were the ones with the right to sit in council. I knew that my presence was an exception to the usual state of affairs.

"Acceptable response time," the Matriarch said, looking at a clock on its stand. Its appearance was deceptive: It resembled a traditional water clock, but its bowls were empty of any liquid, and it sported an ordinary holo panel that told the time. Less than five minutes had elapsed since she'd rung the bell.

Everyone in the room stiffened. I did, too, by reflex. The Matriarch meant those words as a criticism. She had expected better, and the family had failed.

"But I have a more important matter to discuss with you all," she went on.

Everyone stiffened even more, which I hadn't thought possible. I held myself like a soldier at attention. My back ached from the tension. I reminded myself that I had to endure.

The Matriarch's description of Uncle Hwan's disgrace met with immediate growls, especially from Great-Aunt, who had been particularly close to him. "Hwan must have made powerful enemies," she said. "It's the only explanation."

"Hwan would never do anything to disgrace the family's honor," Great-Uncle Myung agreed, although his mouth twisted in distaste. He and Uncle Hwan didn't usually get along.

A snarl of outrage on Hwan's behalf started up in the back of my throat as well, and I hastily bit my tongue. Still, it was heartening to know that the family all agreed there had been some miscarriage of justice.

"Surely we can appeal to Space Forces Command," Great-Aunt said. "Admiral Hasun—"

"I will call Hasun right now," the Matriarch said, "and make it clear that they are to answer immediately."

I bit my tongue again. Hasun didn't serve in the field, despite their high rank, so perhaps they'd be available. By mysterious means, the Matriarch had arranged for Hasun to take a post on a starbase in-system, close enough that we could talk to them directly instead of relying on the couriers for faster-than-light communications. Hasun had apparently objected to this, calling it "high-handed," but the Matriarch's connections—whatever they were—were too powerful to be denied.

Hasun did something in logistics, making sure that troops were sent where they were needed, along with all the necessary supplies. I'd always expected the Matriarch to find the admiral's lack of a more warlike role disappointing, given the family's glorification of war. Instead, she made cryptic comments about how useful Hasun's position was for her schemes. For my part, I couldn't imagine wanting to work away from the front lines and the action, no matter how crucial logistics were. My family liked to emphasize the job's importance, even if it wasn't as *fun*.

Great-Aunt checked her slate. "It's 0300 hours where the admiral is," she noted, her voice neutral.

Ugh, three in the morning! Even my family didn't make me train at that hour. At least not often.

"Then Hasun is unlikely to have other engagements and will be available to take my call," the Matriarch said firmly.

Like everything the Matriarch owned, her slate had been embellished to give it a more traditional flair. She kept hers in a case that resembled a bronze-backed mirror, complete with etched ornaments in the shapes of clouds and various symbols for good luck and long life. It even had a faint green patina, although it didn't smell like real bronze but some kind of plastic.

The entire room fell into a hush as the Matriarch said in her imperious voice, "Connect me to Admiral Hasun of the Juhwang Tiger Clan."

"Your will, Matriarch," the tablet responded. My grandmother had always preferred a verbal interface. As for me, Aunt Sooni had taught me to set my tablet to vibration mode or simple visual alerts so I didn't disturb any of the elders. But then, the Matriarch ruled the clan. It was a different situation.

I kept still, thinking furiously. I'd only met Hasun in person once, before their promotion to rear admiral. They'd visited the estate and had a spectacular quarrel with the Matriarch. I wasn't sure why they'd argued, but their relationship had been frosty ever since. Hasun had never visited again.

The tablet chimed once. And again. And kept chiming. The Matriarch's expression didn't change, but I could smell her growing anger. It's hard to hide any strong emotion, especially from a room full of tigers.

Then a holo image blazed into life above the slate. I'd only seen their visage a handful of times, but I recognized Rear Admiral Hasun, if only because they had the family's deep-set eyes and flat nose. *Tiger nose*, Aunt Sooni liked to call it. Right now those eyes, a darker amber than mine, were bleary from lack of sleep. Hasun appeared in the blue Space Forces uniform, only slightly rumpled. I guessed that Hasun had changed into it for the call, since I couldn't imagine that they slept in it. For some reason, the fact that half their collar was sticking up made me like them more—that small evidence of imperfection, so little tolerated in my home.

"Matriarch Juhwang," Admiral Hasun said. "To what do I owe the pleasure of this call?"

Her eyes narrowed. "Don't pretend you don't know."

"You will have to be specific," Hasun said. Despite their deferential speech forms, I was impressed that the admiral hadn't rolled over and shown the Matriarch their belly. I rarely saw anyone stand up to her at home. "For the sake of clarity."

"For the sake of *clarity*," the Matriarch said, her voice lowering ominously, "I will ask how you could allow the Space Forces to declare Captain Hwan a traitor, whatever . . . peccadilloes may have been involved. Hwan is *useful* to me, Hasun."

Peccadilloes? I wondered what that meant. It struck me as

strange that the Matriarch didn't seem surprised by Hwan's disgrace.

Hasun lifted an eyebrow. "Matriarch," they said, "the situation is more serious than you realize."

I couldn't smell Hasun's aggravation through the holo, but I could definitely hear an edge to their voice. I wasn't the only one, either. Great-Uncle Myung's nostrils flared. Even Aunt Sooni, who was normally so cheerful, winced.

"How so?" the Matriarch barked.

I kept myself from shrinking back. *She's family,* I told myself. *She wouldn't do anything to hurt you.* Besides, I wasn't the object of her disapproval. Not at the moment, anyway.

"I wasn't on the board of inquiry that investigated Hwan's record," Hasun said dryly. "But, Matriarch, even in absentia, they found him guilty of high treason. It's not just a simple case of him taking more leave than he was entitled to."

I choked back an incredulous laugh. Uncle Hwan had never struck me as the type to relax, not even when he visited the family. The last time he'd been home, I hadn't been able to keep up with his strict training regimen, though he'd smiled and nodded approval at my fledgling efforts. I'd vowed to myself then that I would do better, and a part of me was disappointed now, however childishly, that I wouldn't get a chance to show him how I'd improved. The absurd image of my uncle swanning off to some pagoda near a carp-filled lake framed by graceful willows, perhaps while sipping a perfectly steeped cup of tea, presented itself to me.

Aunt Sooni must have scented my amusement. Without looking at me, she stepped on my toe. I kept from yelping in protest and forced myself to calm down.

I wasn't the only one who was frozen in place. The Matriarch's face remained a mask of severe dignity, but she stank of barely suppressed fury. Her eyes burned like star-embers, and if she'd turned to me I would have shrunk from her in sheer terror.

"Captain Hwan," the Matriarch said, "is not capable of bringing disgrace upon the *clan*, which is the only standard that really matters. He has served me long and well."

"*Former* captain," Hasun corrected. "The Space Forces regret that Hwan's actions reflect upon the family, but the board of inquiry's findings were airtight. He abandoned his duty to his crew and his ship to steal a magical artifact."

"If he went after the Dragon Pearl," the Matriarch countered, "he had good reason. He never made a move without my knowing about it."

The Dragon Pearl? Surely she was joking. It was a singular magical artifact, known for the ability to terraform worlds into splendor, or destroy them outright. It had been lost for some time. But wouldn't the Space Forces *want* one of their captains to secure such a valuable item?

I squirmed inside. The family's honor was important. But a member of the Space Forces also had an obligation to their crew and their chain of command. Even an admiral like Hasun ultimately answered to the councilors who ruled in the Pearled Halls. Surely the Matriarch wouldn't act in a way that caused a conflict? I opened my mouth to interject, then thought better of it.

"There's no misunderstanding," Hasun said. "I can't share more details, you understand, but what I saw was quite damning."

"Hasun of the Juhwang Clan," the Matriarch said, "are you telling me that your cousin is a traitor in the eyes of the Space Forces?"

"That's exactly what I'm telling you."

"You will fix this immediately. Hwan's disgrace will only embolden the clan's enemies."

This time my mouth ran away with me. "Matriarch," I blurted out.

Everyone in the room stared at me like I was a rabbit who had wandered in at dinnertime. My back prickled.

"Speak your piece, cub," the Matriarch hissed.

"It wouldn't be proper for an admiral to show favor to the clan," I said, making sure I spoke calmly and clearly. My heart was beating too quickly, and I knew that everyone in the room could hear it, but there was nothing I could do about that.

"Not openly, no," the Matriarch said. "Clan business is not for outsiders." It wasn't agreement.

"Cub?" Hasun wondered aloud.

There must have been some issue with the viewing angle. The Matriarch tilted her slate.

Hasun nodded. "Ah, I see Sebin. By the way," the admiral added, their expression softening, "congratulations."

"S-sir?" I asked, startled into a stammer.

"Courier service claimed the letter had been delivered," Hasun said. A wrinkle formed between their eyebrows. "Was there an error?"

"No, I received the letter," I said, aware of everyone staring at me. "I haven't had a chance to open it yet." I hadn't dared to. I didn't want to draw the Matriarch's ire down on me.

Too late. Her eyes, burning amber, looked as though they

were ready to reduce me to cinders on the spot. I realized now that the family council meetings were not a privilege, but a trial by fire. "Stand up and read us the letter," she said.

I ducked my head. "Yes, Matriarch."

The letter had a florid opening. I scarcely recognized *Our esteemed applicant, Sebin of the Juhwang Tiger Clan* as myself. Especially when my name had been calligraphed with such extravagant flair, in contrast to the more restrained style of the handwriting surrounding it.

But the rest of it . . . If my heart had been beating too fast before, now it was fit to burst out of my chest.

"'Space Forces Command wishes to inform you of your acceptance to our venerable institution as a cadet. Report to Camp White Pine at Starbase Borasaekbam for orientation and basic training at 0800 local time on the fifth of the tenth month, after which you will receive your first assignment.'"

The letter also included a travel warrant to cover the expenses of the journey.

"How interesting that the Space Forces Command rewards one of our clan at the same time that it declares an honorable tiger a traitor," the Matriarch observed acidly.

"It's a coincidence," Admiral Hasun said. "The committee wouldn't have denied such a sterling candidate."

I glowed to hear myself spoken of in such terms. It wasn't often that my family offered praise.

"In any case, I wish you all the best." Hasun signed off before anyone could get a word in edgewise.

"It does seem like a suspicious 'coincidence,'" my mother said into the uncomfortable silence, squelching my rush of joy. I wished she would smile at me, or say a word of congratulations.

But it wasn't her way, and I had to resign myself to that fact.

"Regardless," the Matriarch said, "we must make the most of the opportunity."

I didn't understand what she meant by that.

The Matriarch's burning stare returned to me. "You are young for this," she mused, "but you, too, may serve the clan. Stand straighter."

I did. I should have felt honored that she thought of me as useful. Instead, the lump of dread in my belly only grew heavier.

"Hold out your right hand," the Matriarch said.

I did so without question or hesitation. Either would have gotten me ejected from the meeting. I didn't want the Matriarch to think I was defying her.

"I don't know how Hwan could have been so careless as to allow those weaklings to corner him," the Matriarch muttered. "But Hasun has grown overly bold in their time away from the clan. They may send the most delicious hydroponically grown tangerines from their posting, as if I can be *bribed*, but it hasn't escaped my notice that they don't visit."

I wasn't sure what this had to do with me, so I kept my mouth shut. Still, I allowed myself a mote of hope. If Uncle Hwan wasn't dead, maybe I could help clear his name. Whatever it took.

The Matriarch took up a bronze-handled knife that she kept on her table. I shuddered. I couldn't help it. The knife smelled faintly of blood.

"You will swear to serve the clan in all matters," the Matriarch said. "Swear by the White Tiger of the West."

"By the White Tiger of the West, I swear to serve the clan

in all matters," I repeated obediently as my family looked on.

I knew this was a deadly serious oath, one that would exact a terrible price if I broke it. Four supernatural animals guarded the cardinal directions: the White Tiger of the West, the Azure Dragon of the East, the Vermilion Bird of the South, and the Black Tortoise of the North. When I was younger, I'd asked what accounted for *up* and *down* in space, the axis of a three-dimensional world, and I'd been told not to concern myself with such insolent questions.

While I contemplated the consequences of offending the White Tiger, the Matriarch brought the knife down on my upraised palm, leaving a gash. Blood welled up and dripped down onto the floor. I was keenly aware that I was bleeding amid predators, even if the predators were my own family.

"Remember your oath," the Matriarch said. "You will go out among the stars, meet comrades great and small, and learn the ways of a warrior. But above all things, the compass that guides you must be the way of the clan."

THREE

On the day I left home, only two people saw me off—my mother and Aunt Sooni. "The others don't hold with sentimental nonsense," my mother said, "especially your nini. Remember the clan's honor and you'll be fine." She patted my shoulder, although a part of me longed for a hug. I hadn't gotten one of those for some years now. "Besides, Nini has household business to take care of."

Under other circumstances I would have been dying of curiosity about this "household business." But today I was on my way to becoming a Space Forces cadet! It was difficult to concentrate on anything but the prospect of realizing my dream.

"Your hand isn't bothering you, is it?" Aunt Sooni asked, glancing at the bandage.

"It's fine," I said, wishing she hadn't drawn attention to it. Like all the adults, she had a scar on her hand where I now had a painful scab. But tigers heal quickly, and I didn't expect it to be more than a passing nuisance. It certainly wasn't worth wasting any medical gel on. The household did have some first aid kits—I'd been drilled in their locations and use since I had enough hand-eye coordination for it—but my family would have scoffed if I'd used one for something this minor. Besides, the whole point of the Matriarch's slice was to leave a scar.

We passed through the house, and I savored the details, knowing I might not see them again for some time. It might lack the fancy tapestries and paintings of the newer, richer families of merchants and explorers, but there was a genteel grandeur to the worn walls. They sported blaster scorch marks from past bandit raids and the immense grooves of claws where local predators, now only seen in zoos, had attacked the house. I could recount the story of every mark and scar, the legends behind the silk scrolls and their depictions of archers on horseback and tiger warriors.

Together we exited the house and walked to the front gate with its drapery of wisteria. I wrinkled my nose, not because of the fragrance—the perfume was intoxicating—but because I was usually the one responsible for trimming it back. Who would take over the task while I was gone? I could have asked, but I didn't want my mother and Aunt Sooni to think that I was reluctant to leave.

"Bring honor to the family," my mother said gruffly, giving me one last pat on the shoulder before walking back toward the house.

That left Aunt Sooni. She leaned in and adjusted the pins on my collar, which I tolerated. Around home we didn't usually wear them, but I was going to be among strangers and mine would let people know that I was nonbinary.

"I wanted to give you something for luck," she said. She produced a small silver knife. Traditionally women had used them in self-defense, although these days anyone might carry one as a charm against bandits or burglars. "To keep you safe."

If it came to a fight, my own fangs and claws were likely to be more effective than such a small blade. The whole thing was hardly longer than my hand. But it came from Aunt Sooni, and it was the only gift I had for the journey ahead.

I bowed to her in the proper formal fashion, even though she'd only enforced the courtesies when other people were around. "Thank you," I said. "I'll remember."

We looked up as an AI-piloted hovercar decelerated smoothly before the front gate. "There it is," Aunt Sooni said. Someone in the household—I wasn't sure who—had arranged for transportation. "Time to go."

"Good-bye, Aunt Sooni," I said. I drank in the sight of her face one last time, then turned away. I didn't look back as I opened the gate.

The journey from Yonggi to Starbase Borasaekbam, where I had been summoned, passed in a haze. I took the recommended medications to ease my acclimation to space travel, and spent the rest of my voyage reviewing the regulation handbook. It came as a relief to my head and stomach when the starship that had transported me finally docked.

I drew in a deep breath, then exited the docking bay. People walked briskly past me, following lanes marked by patterns. Aunt Sooni had explained to me that some spaceports used patterns combined with raised textures for the benefit of those who were blind or color-blind. Indeed, I spotted a couple people moving with the aid of a cane or robot guide.

Under other circumstances, I would have enjoyed taking in the sights. I had imagined that all spaceports were alike, but if the base on Yonggi and this one were anything to go by, I couldn't have been more wrong. While my homeworld's spaceport had resembled a military fort, with vigilant turrets, Starbase Borasaekbam breathed of elegance. Someone with a gardener's soul had designed it, from the high ceilings and skylights to the alcoves with moss gardens and glass-domed terrariums. My instincts insisted that I could be ambushed at any moment, although I couldn't imagine that the starport would neglect security. Still, I could see the architect's priorities, and one of them had been beauty.

A jumble of smells assaulted my nose from all directions. Humans and other tigers were familiar, but the rest I'd only learned through the scent training my aunt had subjected me to. Goblins, dragons, celestials, and more. And the crowds! I'd never seen so many people in one place before. It left me feeling vulnerable and exposed. But I couldn't show weakness in front of these strangers, so I stiffened my back and kept my face a mask.

The letter had come with additional instructions, which I had memorized. I was to report to the Crescent Annex in the starport. Since my slate wasn't recognized by the local network's warden program, I lined up at one of the kiosks, relieved that no one recognized me. Ambivalence bit my heart. I wanted to be proud of my tiger heritage, and anyone who noted my amber eyes and my sturdy build would be able to guess it, even if they didn't know my clan specifically. It seemed like cowardice to consider being discreet about my family connections.

The queue moved along quickly, and I asked the kiosk about the layout of the starport and how to get to the annex. A message popped up asking if I wanted to alert Ensign Hak Bada of the Space Forces that I had arrived. I said yes. The question was only a courtesy. Word would get to them regardless of my response.

"Are you done yet?" an irritable voice asked from behind me.

I'd taken less than five minutes, but I didn't want to argue and cause a scene. "Sorry," I said, and ceded the kiosk to the person in line behind me.

I followed a lane marked by one broad stripe and two narrow dotted ones. The moss and terrariums weren't the only greenery. There were also indoor groves of bamboo that towered above me, ringed with paper lanterns sporting the symbols for *good fortune* and *long life*. A master geomancer must have been involved in the creation of this place, to ensure that good luck flowed to all of its corners. For the first time, I wondered if geomancers and soldiers ever quarreled over layout.

The Crescent Annex's entrance was marked by an immense painting of pale stars dripping from a crescent moon, like a river-fall of light. Hard to miss. I shot the painting a curious glance, then continued to the checkpoint to present myself to the guard.

"Are you Juhwang Sebin or Baik Jee?" the guard asked, narrowing her eyes at me.

Interesting. There was someone else arriving at the same time? I should have expected as much. After all, I wouldn't be the only one reporting for training.

"I'm Juhwang Sebin," I said, with the appropriate amount of deference.

She took a retinal scan to verify my identity and had me sign in. "Ensign Hak is waiting for you in Room Crescent

Eight," she said. "Down the corridor, fourth door on the right. Don't dawdle."

"Thank you, sir," I said.

The guard sighed. "I'm not a 'sir,' I work for a living." At my puzzled look, she shook her head and said, "You'll figure it out eventually."

The Crescent Annex's interior was, in contrast to the rest of the starbase, austere to the point of sterility. All the walls were matte metal, and the black doors reminded me of waiting maws. Fortunately, they were also labeled with plaques. I found the fourth on the right, confirmed that it was Room Crescent Eight—and whirled when I heard rapid footsteps behind me. I dropped into the crouch of a fighting stance just in case.

The person who'd startled me held up their hands—*his* hands. My sharp eyes picked out the information from the pins on his collar. He was a short, skinny kid with a beaky nose dominating his thin face, his short-cropped hair indifferently combed. But he was smiling at me, and he smelled friendly.

"Sorry, sorry!" he said. "You must be the other cadet? The guard told me I'd just missed you."

He was breathing hard, and I could hear the thudding of his heart. He must have run to catch up. What disturbed me was that I hadn't detected him until he was right behind me. I'd gotten distracted. Inexcusable.

"I'm Sebin," I said, giving him the slight bow owed to a peer rather than an elder or authority figure. I thought about adding, *Sebin of the Juhwang Tiger Clan*, but I hesitated, and then the moment had passed.

The boy returned the bow. "I'm Baik Jee," he said. His

smile widened into a grin, and I couldn't help but smile back. "Come on, let's not keep the ensign waiting!"

I reached forward to knock on the door. Jee did so at the same moment. We rapped on the door together.

"Juhwang Sebin and Baik Jee, I presume," a crisp voice came from behind the door. "Come in."

I glanced sideways to see if Jee had a reaction to the revelation of my clan, but he didn't so much as blink.

The door slid open. Jee entered first, and I followed.

Ensign Hak stood at her desk despite the presence of a large chair. It could have held two of her, and the ensign was a big-boned woman. I could smell a trace of goblin heritage, which explained her size. Goblins were known for their strength. Their famed wrestlers could even take on a tiger, Uncle Hwan had told me.

"You're on time," she said with a trace of disappointment, as though she'd been looking forward to upbraiding us. "Sit down, both of you. This will be the most exciting and most typical part of your Space Forces experience—filling out forms."

Jee groaned. I felt the same way, although I knew better than to show it. "What kinds of forms, sir?" Jee asked.

"Recruitment paperwork," Ensign Hak said. "Mess this up and we'll boot you." She snickered when Jee and I gaped at her. "No, that's not true. But it *will* cause problems up and down the chain, and trust me, you don't want to run afoul of military bureaucracy."

The ensign shoved two slates at Jee and me. "I've allotted an hour for this," she said. "If you finish faster, you'll have more time for settling into your assigned bunks . . . to say nothing of your first day of orientation."

"What happens during orientation, sir?" I asked, pushing my luck.

She frowned at me but said, "Evaluations."

Jee groaned again.

"Do you have a problem, Jee?"

"No, sir!" he said hastily. "I just thought they already had my test scores."

"Oh, everything's on file," Ensign Hak said. "However, there are military occupational specialty tests that the Space Forces prefers to administer itself. In short, we want to know whether you're going to be a marine or a mechanic."

I'd known about this intellectually, but I hadn't considered the implications. Uncle Hwan had often emphasized the importance of every member of the crew. *Don't ever think the engineers do less than the command staff,* he'd said. And that made sense—if the ship broke down, all the orders in the world did no good.

But what if the test results meant that I would be assigned as an Engineering candidate, or Communications, or Marine, rather than Command? I couldn't give up my dream of having my own ship someday because of a *test score.*

With that thought, I settled into the task of filling out the forms as quickly and accurately as I could. Name: easy, although I winced every time I had to declare myself a member of the Juhwang Tiger Clan. There was even a section for me to give the old-fashioned hanja characters for my name, as opposed to the Hangeul alphabetic script. Fortunately, I'd memorized those during my calligraphy lessons with Nini, although I couldn't read any other hanja. I wondered if that had been a mistake on my part. I'd done my best at all my studies, but the parts I'd paid the most attention to had been—surprise, surprise—the stories of starship battles.

The form asked other questions about my lineage, which I answered with a growing sense of dread. I had to provide vital statistics like height and weight, and answer health questions like whether I had any allergies or dietary restrictions. It made sense. The Space Forces welcomed recruits of all kinds, from humans to dragons, tigers to celestials, and they needed to be prepared.

Jee was still working. I peeked at his slate. He was a slow writer, with meticulous handwriting. Under *Additional Information*, a field I had ignored, he mentioned that he was a human but one of his parents was a goblin, and they'd adopted him. I made a note to myself not to ask him any awkward questions about his family. I didn't want to make him uncomfortable.

I returned my attention to my own slate. One last question remained, and I contemplated it with a frown. *Why do you wish to join the Space Forces? Answer in one sentence.*

It was so straightforward, so direct, that it struck me as a trap. I'd expected them to ask me what *I* offered *them*. I wasn't sure what I could say to persuade them to put me on the Command track. And why would they only give me one sentence to answer?

I wondered if it would count against me if I made no mention of Uncle Hwan, even indirectly. After all, anyone reviewing this questionnaire would know about the connection. Best, then, to face it head-on.

I tapped my chin with the stylus, then lowered it and wrote, as crisply and clearly as I could manage, *I wish to show that a tiger can serve with honor.*

That didn't mention that I wanted a ship, but no one was going to hand over command of a ship to a thirteen-year-old anyway. I had to play the long game. I didn't want a ship *right this minute.* (Well . . . maybe a little.) I wanted to prove myself and *earn* that ship after I worked my way up through the ranks, so that my family and Uncle Hwan would be proud of how I'd upheld the clan's reputation.

I handed in my slate, which Ensign Hak accepted with a grunt. She eyed Jee and said, "You have eight more minutes."

"Sorry, sir!" Jee said, and scribbled only marginally faster than he had earlier.

I chafed at having to wait for Jee. But showing impatience would be unkind, and it gave me the opportunity to study him further. He took his time with each question, brow furrowed in thought. So maybe he wouldn't be the best teammate when quick action was necessary, but there were other situations where that kind of deliberation could be an advantage. Uncle Hwan had always said that you had to look for what your crew were good at and make the best use of their skills and tendencies.

I didn't know what the ensign, or Jee for that matter, would have said about the fact that I relied so much on things that Uncle Hwan had said for guidance. The fact was, though, Uncle Hwan was the only starship captain—ex-captain—I knew personally. I'd grown up with stories of his exploits, from the way he'd fought off an advance force of invaders at Jamjari to his exploration of the dangerous star-tides of the Ssang-yong binary system.

Uncle Hwan served as my lodestar. In the past I would have been proud to talk about how he'd influenced me growing up, despite his infrequent visits. Now I would have to settle for having him as my secret guide.

Jee turned in his slate with a full forty-seven seconds to spare. I knew this because Ensign Hak made a point of declaring it sarcastically. Jee only ducked his head and smiled at her. Nothing seemed to dent his good cheer. I could learn a thing or two from him.

Ensign Hak gave both forms a cursory looking-over, then nodded. "Right," she said. "I'll have to escort you down, since neither of you have the security clearances to enter the Training Annex."

"Of course, sir," Jee said. "Will we be patched into the local network as well?"

She looked at him warily. "Why are you so interested? You want to work in Security, too? Or"—her eyes narrowed—"try some hacking?"

"None of that, sir!" he said too quickly. "Communications. I want to work in crypto."

I regarded Jee with new respect. You had to be good at both math and languages for that. I did fine with the former, but I didn't want to pursue it any further than I had to. Still, who wouldn't want to work with codes and ciphers?

For whatever reason, Jee's statement made the ensign sigh. "Of course you do." She had stowed the slates in her desk and come around it to lead us out of the office when the door suddenly opened.

That's funny, I thought. *Shouldn't it be locked against intruders or random interruptions?*

The newcomer, a tall, lanky figure, exclaimed, "Hak-youhavetocomerightnow!" all in one breath.

FOUR

I peered at the newcomer, then at the shorter, fine-boned person in their wake. Both were clad in gray hanboks, although I didn't see any insignia to tell me who they were or what they represented.

Rather than snarling at the intruders, the ensign snapped to attention and bowed deeply at the taller one. I did likewise. Jee, on the other hand, regarded the two with a nonplussed expression.

The tall one was on the far end of middle age, with cheekbones so sharp you could have used them to slice wood. Now that I had a chance to look more closely, I also noticed that this one was wearing ugly yellow utility boots at odds with the elegance of their hanbok.

The shorter one wasn't actually short, and I managed to catch a glimpse of the collar pins that told me she was a girl, maybe sixteen years old or so. It was hard to tell. Her hair was shoulder-length, and she had a sharp, pointy face. Her shoes, while practical, weren't as conspicuous as the utility boots.

"Investigator, please slow down," Ensign Hak said with the

merest hint of exasperation. "You know no one understands you when you talk that fast."

"You have to come right now," they said, "and that means you, too, Cadets Sebin and Jee."

I stared at them. It was one thing to follow orders from a known and trusted authority, another to do whatever a stranger said. That was another rule my family had instilled in me. "Excuse me, sir," I said, since I figured I should at least use polite address, "but who are you?"

Ensign Hak paled, but the tall newcomer wagged a finger at her. "I'm Special Investigator Yi, and this is my associate, Kim Min. I'llexplainonthe— I mean," and they took a deep breath, "I'll explain on the way." They turned on their heel and strode out without waiting for a response. Min followed them smartly as if she were used to this. Perhaps she was.

"Well, what are you waiting for?" the ensign barked. "Go with them!"

We hurried after the two. Yi was already halfway down the hall, aided by their great stride, and Min kept pace by trotting. I had long legs for my age, but I didn't want to leave Jee and the ensign behind. It wouldn't have been proper.

Hak and Jee double-timed it, so I needn't have worried about them keeping up. When we were just behind Yi, Ensign Hak hissed under her breath, "That's *the* Special Investigator Yi! They were the one responsible for uncovering the conspiracy between Councilor Jung and the Crested Raiders! Don't tell me you've never heard of them."

I hadn't. My family had been strict about what I was allowed to watch on the holo shows. Most of the time, I'd been too busy with chores or training anyway. But Jee was nodding emphatically, his eyes wide. And even I knew that special investigators were appointed by the councilors of the Pearled Halls to solve crimes that the Thousand Worlds' ordinary inspectors weren't equipped to handle.

"Does the special investigator usually take an interest in cadets?" I asked, since that seemed like a safe question.

"They do not," the ensign said in a low voice, scarcely audible even to my tiger hearing. "They—" But before the ensign could finish her sentence, Yi and Min slowed down so we could catch up. Hak clamped her mouth shut, to my disappointment.

I only gathered the most cursory impressions of the rest of the Crescent Annex as we passed through it on the way to the training wing. Lots of right angles, and none of the confounding gardens or high windows that would make great haunts for snipers. Aunt Sooni had taught me marksmanship, mostly by hunting drone targets with a blaster, so I could develop my aim and reflexes. I'd asked her about laser rifles, but she said it was best to focus on my natural advantages, by which she meant hand-to-hand and tiger-form combat. But that didn't mean I hadn't been taught to be aware of the places where snipers could lurk.

We passed into the part of Starbase Borasaekbam that served as the base proper. This had a different look again from the harmonious gardens of the main starport and the Crescent Annex with its bland walls. Soldiers stood watch at the entrance, but Special Investigator Yi flashed a badge at them and we were admitted without question. Since I trailed behind Yi, I couldn't see what the badge was, not even its shape. I noted in passing that soldiers farther back were monitoring us on holo.

Paradoxically, the soldiers' precautions put me at ease,

maybe because it reminded me of home. Back at the estate, there was always a family member on security duty. Sure, we had cameras and an AI keeping an eye on the grounds, but the Matriarch had always said that the task was too important to entrust solely to a machine. Here, the one thing that bothered me was that the soldiers accepted Yi's credentials so readily.

Don't be silly, I thought as I lengthened my stride to keep up. Yi and their associate Min had sped up again. Surely the Space Forces screened for reliability and loyalty, and never mind the accusations against my uncle.

The naval base had walls painted heaven-blue, accented by spectacular murals featuring starships and binary stars or glowing spiral nebulae or, in one case, a holo of a pulsar. If I allowed my mind to drift the tiniest bit, I could imagine that I was walking out among the stars.

"Got to get you to the docking bay for pickup," Special Investigator Yi said as we approached another checkpoint.

"Investigator?" I asked, frowning. Despite the promises of an explanation, we hadn't received one yet. "What about our training?"

"There's a complication," Yi said. They glanced at Min. "Do we have time for a briefing?"

Min consulted a slate, then nodded. "The ship's been delayed as you wanted—I mean, as you predicted."

Yi looked around, then led us toward a door. The blue light on the outer panel indicated that the room wasn't in use. "This will do."

Is this a kidnapping? I wondered. But that was ridiculous. I hated how much I was on edge for no good reason, even though my instincts were screaming at me that something wasn't right.

I'd noticed Min's stumble in her response to Yi, and I wondered what it was that she hadn't said. The threat, if a threat it was, must be subtle. I doubted that anyone—especially a high-profile special investigator—was going to disappear us in the middle of a naval base.

There had to be a logical explanation. For example, it would be rude, if not inadvisable, to have a classified conversation in the middle of the hallway where anyone could overhear us. Even other cadets like, well, Jee and myself.

Min entered first and swept the room with a sensor wand. "It's clear. No bugs."

Only then did Yi motion for us all to enter. Yi came in last and shut the door behind them. They put their palm to the pad on the door, locking it. The pad lit up red. "Secure enough for my purposes," Yi said. "Cadets Jee and Sebin, ordinarily you would undergo an orientation and training course over a few weeks before setting foot on a battle cruiser. But in this instance we can't wait quite that long."

"But you can spare the time you're taking for this briefing?" Jee asked, his brow furrowing.

Yi's mouth curled in a sardonic smile. "Good point, Cadet." Their eyes flicked toward Min, and she nodded. "The truth is, there's been a delay in resupplying the battle cruiser *Haetae*. No one's going anywhere until the food stores are topped up, so that does give us enough time for this briefing."

I glanced sideways at Ensign Hak at the *whoof* of her exhalation. "No one would want a ship to set off with inadequate stores," she agreed. Her face had gone gray.

I'd grown up planetside, but everyone knew that starships relied on frequent resupply. Even though bigger ships had hydroponics to grow some of their own food, that couldn't account for the needs of the entire crew. A ship that ran out of provisions was vulnerable, especially if it also took damage to its stardrive.

"*So,*" Yi went on, "we might as well make good use of the delay. After resupply, *Haetae* has orders to respond to an emergency call from the colony of Norandol in the Fortress Sector."

I winced. "Border trouble?"

I'd studied maps of the Thousand Worlds from a young age. Some of my earliest memories were of being quizzed on the different sectors and their strategic significance on a holo map that zoomed in and out. The Fortress Sector was one of the Thousand Worlds' most dangerous regions. It bordered not one but two of our rivals, the Phoenix Empire and the Sun Clans. Starbase Borasaekbam was located in the adjacent Cinder Sector, and also heavily defended as a result.

Min pulled out a slate and summoned a map for our benefit. Jee peered at it closely, and Min stepped back so as not to impede his view. This at least told me where Norandol was. It must be a minor colony. Probably mining, from the name, which meant *yellow stone.* I'd never heard of it, and my parents had made sure that I knew the worlds of major strategic interest.

"There's no one else in a position to help Norandol," Yi said. "The Space Forces are in the middle of a major action in the Fortress Sector, so ships that wouldn't ordinarily be called there have to step in. The *Haetae* is the closest."

"What's the emergency?" I asked. It was the duty of the Space Forces to come to the aid of any of the Thousand Worlds. But I knew that it wasn't always possible to help everyone, and that Space Forces Command had its own priorities.

"Resources," Yi said. "Min, if you'll bring up that terrain map?"

Min obliged. I wondered if Yi ever did anything for themself. Then again, given the importance of a special investigator's duties, maybe it made sense for Yi to have a lackey devoted to taking care of boring administrative affairs.

The original map shimmered into starry confetti, then re-formed into a close-up of a slowly rotating planet. As I'd guessed, Norandol looked distinctly unpromising, with terrain in varying shades of brown and only a few glittering seas. It also featured several impressive mountain ranges delineated by hard shadows.

"Norandol is subject to dust storms," Yi said, "although with luck anyone on the surface can use weather-magic to escape the worst of the effects. It's due to one of those dust storms that the planet's most interesting feature was uncovered—Gate crystals."

Jee sucked in a breath. I clenched my teeth. The crystals powered our stardrives. Interstellar travel relied on a steady supply of them. I'd never worried about the Thousand Worlds having enough of them, mainly because they kept that sort of information from ordinary citizens.

"Investigator Yi," I said uncertainly, "shouldn't this be classified . . . ?"

"You're going to be on the ship same as everyone else," Yi said, and Min nodded emphatically.

My unease crescendoed. I was sure that ship captains didn't share every detail of their missions with their crews. And cadets on a training cruise wouldn't need to know something like this . . . would we?

The smart thing for me to do would have been to clam up

and keep an eye out for further developments. But I had to find out what was going on. "I'm not seeing why it's so important to bring a pair of cadets along," I said.

Jee grimaced at me as if to ask, *Do you* want *them to leave us behind?*

"If you don't make this journey with the *Haetae*, you could be stuck on the base for some time, the way things are going," Yi said, their eyes crinkling in apparent bemusement. As if they'd heard Jee's thought, they added, "You don't want to be cooling your heels here for months, do you?"

"Of course not," I said automatically, even though Yi had sidestepped my question. I made myself smile. Probably not very convincingly, since dissembling wasn't my strong suit, but it satisfied Yi. Min, on the other hand, slitted her eyes at me. She didn't say anything, though, and I wondered what I could do to ease her suspicions.

"Now that that's settled," Yi said, "it's imperative that the *Haetae* go to Norandol's defense. Back when it was just a struggling mining colony, the raiders from the Phoenix Empire and the Sun Clans left it alone. Now, though, we need to get there before they make their move."

"What exactly is the threat against Norandol?" Jee asked.

"An unusually unlucky solar flare caused their magical wards to fail," Yi said, "and they lost a third of their hydroponics. Which is why it's so important that the *Haetae* be fully supplied, *and* ready to fight off any interlopers."

I nodded, not trusting myself to speak. On the one hand, Yi had an answer for everything. Maybe my superiors were thinking ahead. After all, if the usual training couldn't be carried out due to a military emergency, it made some sense to involve cadets in dangerous situations. If the Space Forces didn't, they could run out of new blood. And I certainly wouldn't mind jumping right into the action.

On the other hand, I didn't like this. I should have felt flattered that Yi had trusted Jee and myself with this information. But it seemed slapdash, and that bothered me. Perhaps my upbringing in the Juhwang Tiger Clan had made me more sensitive to security matters. After all, Jee didn't seem to think anything was amiss. And Min kept looking at me with those considering eyes, as though she found my reaction curious.

Min's tablet chimed. She glanced at it, lips pursed, then at Yi. "Looks like resupply is complete."

I noticed this time that Min was barely deferential to Yi despite his status. I didn't approve, but if Yi wasn't going to call her on it, there was nothing I could do. Besides, it wasn't any business of mine how Yi handled their associate.

Still, there was one thing I was determined to do by the book. Maybe Yi liked playing things fast and loose. Maybe my new captain would be the same way. I hoped not, but I had to be prepared for anything.

"I'd like to be sworn in, then," I said. Technically I wasn't officially a member of the Space Forces until that happened, and neither was Jee.

Min spoke up. "Is there *really* time for this?" she demanded.

I decided I disliked her. It wasn't too unexpected for an investigator's assistant to take the rituals of the Space Forces for granted. But her opinion wasn't the one that mattered. Those rituals were important to *me*.

"Someoneontheshipwillswearyouin," Yi said, back to speaking in that rapid-fire voice again.

"But—" I protested. This *felt* irregular. I'd read the code of conduct and the handbook for recruits. I even had parts of them memorized. But neither of them told me what to do if I was being ordered around by a special investigator who came from another ministry entirely, that of Domestic Security.

I'd thought myself so clever for spending all those days reading the handbook ahead of time. I'd been so sure that it would stand me in good stead if the Space Forces accepted me. Now I realized that the gaps could be just as important.

Yi and Min were still looking at me. "Understood," I said. Inwardly, however, I swore to find out what was really going on.

FIVE

The next hour passed in a blur. When I looked back on the preparations later, I was surprised they took that long. Back home, my parents always had a small bag packed for me in case we had to evacuate the family estate at a moment's notice. "It's the emergency you *don't* predict that's dangerous," Nini liked to say. Later, when I was older, they showed me the estate's stockpiles and how to pack emergency supplies for myself. If something did go wrong, I could stuff everything in a bag and be on my way in under fifteen minutes—under ten if things really got bad.

Other people, even in the Space Forces, didn't appear to have this level of preparedness drilled into them. I wondered if my family was unusual. I hoped not. It had always been impressed on me that I would have to prove myself to the Space Forces, not the other way around.

You're getting ahead of yourself, I thought as I filled out another set of forms at a worn table. I wasn't sure why we couldn't have gotten this out of the way when we were dealing with the first set. The lieutenant who'd intercepted us on the way to the

Haetae's docking bay, a dour-faced man, had insisted that we couldn't board without the proper papers, since neither Jee nor I had a naval ID yet, and Yi didn't want to go scrambling for a senior officer to override the guards.

Jee, less inhibited, had asked the lieutenant, "Is there a reason we couldn't have done this earlier, sir? Some of the questions are even the same as on the form we've already filled out."

The lieutenant sighed. "The regs are the regs, worm egg."

"Sir?" Jee looked confused.

The lieutenant pursed his lips. "Remember, there are three kinds of people in the Space Forces—officers, noncoms, and worms. Guess which one you are?"

Yi shook their head as if at a tired old joke. "You're not even sworn in yet, Jee. Hence worm *eggs*."

"Anyway, hurry up with those forms," the lieutenant said, tapping his stylus against my side of the table.

I kept myself from twitching in response. "Done," I said, handing him my slate. I tensed up when he glanced at it, wondering if he'd comment on my relationship to Uncle Hwan.

The lieutenant typed rapidly once we'd finished the forms, then nodded. "Congratulations, you've passed the security check," he said, although he didn't sound congratulatory at all. He had us pose for ID photos. The desk beeped several times, then spat out cards, and he passed them over to us.

I fought to suppress my grin. An ID of my own, with my new rank on it. Cadet. Or my rank once I was sworn in, I supposed. This was extremely irregular.

"Ship's stores can provide uniforms," the lieutenant went on. "We did have a couple sent down, but no one thought to check your sizes and they're, uh . . . One looks like it was made for a seven-foot giant, and the other, well, besides being made for someone who didn't meet the minimum height requirements in their human shape, it has holes in it, and I don't mean the ones your body parts are supposed to go through."

Min looked severe. "We'll have to write this up in our report."

The lieutenant laughed in her face. "Please. You Domestic Security types may swan around in your fancy outfits"—my gaze swept involuntarily to Yi's ridiculous utility boots—"and you may get all the fancy tech toys, but you don't have jurisdiction."

Still, I smelled his aggravation. It suggested that Yi and Min had more power here than the lieutenant wanted to admit.

"Now, Min, don't vex our colleague," Yi murmured.

That only made the lieutenant's aggravation smell stronger. He had the sense not to provoke a confrontation, though.

Once the paperwork was taken care of, we were finally escorted by the lieutenant, with Ensign Hak in tow, to the *Haetae*'s docking bay. Yi flashed their badge at more guards, with the same result each time.

"You're expected, Investigator," one of the guards said to Yi. "Good hunting out there."

Yi smiled benevolently. "Much appreciated. I never turn down good luck."

I didn't know how many docking bays the naval base contained and sensed that it was better not to ask. We passed through enclosed walkways, each with their walls painted heaven-blue and adorned with fortuitous symbols like peach blossoms, until we reached the one we wanted. After one final check of my new credentials, the guards allowed us through.

I'd thought I was prepared for the sight of a battle cruiser, even one groundside. I was wrong. My breath caught at the sheer size of it.

The *Haetae* was vast, all black and silver and aggressive angles. Painted on the side was a haetae, its namesake, a creature with the body of a lion, scales, and a horn jutting out of its forehead. Haetae were supposed to protect people from disasters, especially those due to fire, and to bring law and order. It was a fortunate name for a starship.

I'd spent long hours poring over different warship classes, committing their appearances to memory. With its triangular silhouette, the *Haetae* must've belonged to the Kestrel class, capable of atmospheric flight as well as maneuvers in space. I was just as impressed by its armaments, which included missile ports and gun turrets. When someone got around to swearing me in, I would be part of its crew.

Someday, I swore to myself, *I'll be a captain, too.* Maybe not of a ship this impressive, but I had to start somewhere.

"Look at those scramblers," Min said in an aside to Jee and me, interrupting my daydreaming. "They help protect the base from aerial and orbital surveillance."

I was annoyed that I hadn't noticed them earlier. Someone had installed them at regular intervals around the bay.

"Do you work with a lot of technology?" I asked. I was obviously fishing for information. But if I had to work with Min in the future, I wanted to know her capabilities. I had the feeling I'd be seeing a lot more of her once we were underway.

She smirked at me, and my dislike of her intensified. "It's part of the job. I'm good at tech. But there should be plenty of people in the crew qualified to take care of that, don't you think?"

"I'm sure," I said, as blandly as I could manage. She wrinkled her nose at me.

The *Haetae*'s main boarding ramp stood open. Someone in an ensign's uniform, presumably the officer of the deck responsible for boarding, was waving at us to hurry up.

Yi swept ahead with Min walking by their side. I hoped I'd be able to get a good look at Yi's badge when we checked in. Jee and I brought up the rear, clutching our IDs.

Ensign Hak exchanged a few words with the officer of the deck while I sniffed surreptitiously at the latter. Human, like Jee. Still, I couldn't underestimate her. Among other things, she had a blaster belted to her side, and I bet she knew how to use it.

The officer of the deck turned to Yi and Min. "IDs, please."

This time I finally got a glimpse of Yi's badge, even if from the back. It was a circle with a rim that flashed gold. Perhaps aware of my curiosity, they tilted it, and my eyes widened. Not just Domestic Security, but a member of a special task force. Min had a similar badge, without the gold rim, presumably because she was lower-ranking.

I suppressed a stab of envy. Not that I had any interest in working for Domestic Security. Among other things, you didn't get a *ship* that way. But Min looked fairly young, only a few years older than I was, and she was already accompanying a special investigator on an important mission. Whereas I was likely to be chopping vegetables or scrubbing the deck for weeks at a time.

Don't get impatient, I chided myself. It was important for every member of the crew—even a would-be future captain—to become familiar with the ship's workings and maintenance.

Besides, I was no stranger to hard work. And I was sure that hard work was what it would take.

We were next. Jee saluted the officer of the deck clumsily and I tried not to criticize him in my head. My family had shown me how to execute a salute with my hand held to my brow at the proper angle. Jee must not have had the benefit of that early training. I'd have to take him aside and show him how if no one else got to it first.

The officer of the deck inspected Jee's ID. His smile looked goofy in it, but she only grinned. "We all look terrible in our ID photos," she remarked. "You're good. And you?"

I presented mine for inspection. The woman's lips moved as she looked at my name. Then her eyebrows lifted. "You're not related to . . . ?"

I lowered my eyes despite wishing I could stare her into silence. It would have been improper on more than one level, though. I was going to be a cadet, and she was an ensign. She was doing her job. And beyond matters of rank, at thirteen I was definitely her junior.

Ensign Hak caught the other ensign's eye and shook her head minutely. I wasn't sure why Hak had intervened, but I silently thanked her. Surely Hak already knew of my connection to Uncle Hwan. At least *she* hadn't made an issue of it earlier.

"I'm sure the captain knows," the officer of the deck muttered, giving the ID a faint scowl. Then she waved her hand at the ramp. "Up you go."

I couldn't calm the juddering of my heart as I walked up the ramp, trying for dignity and probably failing. Jee didn't even do that much. He gave a little hop and skip as he crossed from the ramp onto the deck of the ship proper. Ensign Hak accompanied us, her expression amused.

"That's right, Cadet," Ensign Hak said. "Enjoy that shiny excited feeling while it lasts."

"What do you mean, sir?" Jee asked as he looked around, wide-eyed, at the airlock. It could have accommodated some twenty people. Every inch of it shone.

Ensign Hak snickered. "You'll find out. Ah, Special Investigator, I'll have someone of a more elevated status escort you and your assistant to special quarters." She raised her voice. "Lieutenant Rhee! We've got that special guest we were holding for, sir!"

Wait a second, I thought. Hadn't Yi said that the *Haetae* had been delayed because of a resupply issue? Something didn't add up. This time, though, I kept my thoughts to myself.

The lieutenant appeared. "Special Investigator, what an honor," she said, bowing obsequiously. "We have the most luxurious guest cabins available for your use, and . . ." Her voice trailed off as Yi and Min followed her.

Strangely, the lieutenant's exaggerated deference eased the earlier stab of envy I'd felt. I didn't want to be a cosseted *guest* on the *Haetae*, after all. I wanted to be a working member of the crew, no matter how junior.

"You two," Ensign Hak said briskly, "come with me. The first item on the list is to get you in proper uniforms. It's a pity the ones at the base were no good."

Hak adroitly picked her way through the maze of corridors, which were wide enough for four abreast. We fell in behind her. "We'll have to visit the quartermaster," she added.

A tone sounded from the intercom. "All hands, prepare to lift off."

Hak kept us moving. Evidently the *Haetae* was more advanced than the transport I'd taken to get here, with an anti-gravity system that meant we didn't need to be strapped in for launch. I felt a humming through the deckplate that increased and then leveled off, but no sense of movement.

I snatched glances at my surroundings as we went. The ship gleamed like a knife newly forged. I scarcely spotted any scuffs on the deck. Everything had been meticulously polished. A good sign, even if I was going to take part in the meticulous polishing soon. Still, the bulkheads were austere, with no decorations like there had been in the starbase, just numbers and letters labeling the passageways.

I memorized our path, although my usual reliance on landscape and scent cues wasn't going to help me much. I hoped we would receive maps later. It wouldn't make sense for more senior crew members to have to escort a couple of cadets everywhere, after all.

Other crew members passed us, whether they were walking in the same direction only to peel off at the junctures, or heading in the direction from which we'd just come. I struggled to keep my attention on our route instead of being distracted by all the strangers. Especially since, once the initial dazzlement wore off, I felt increasingly as though I'd been abandoned in enemy territory.

It wasn't an irrational response, but I disliked myself for it anyway. Sure, the officer of the deck had spotted the connection between me and my uncle. But she hadn't opened her mouth about it, thanks to Ensign Hak. And Jee hadn't noticed anything wrong.

The captain will know, I thought. Not that I even knew who our captain was.

Ensign Hak had reached the quartermaster's office.

Quartermaster Yang was a poised woman who wouldn't have looked out of place on a recruiting poster. After we saluted, Hak pointed at Jee and me and launched into an explanation in sign language. I recognized a couple of the simplest signs—*urgent, clothes.* The government's official news channels included sign language interpreters, and I'd been curious enough to look up a few words, mostly to compare it to the military tactical sign language I was learning from Aunt Sooni. I wondered if sign language was in common use on this particular ship. I hadn't heard of any such thing on Uncle Hwan's battle cruiser.

The quartermaster signed back to Hak, then motioned to Jee and me. Jee and I stepped up after a moment's hesitation. "Sir," I said to her, making sure I faced her so she could read my lips. To be honest, everything I knew about reading lips came from Great-Uncle Myung, who had taught me that it was handy when spying, but I figured it couldn't hurt.

Yang smiled but shook her head and pointed at her eyes. "You can talk to me normally," she said aloud. "Hak's just showing off. My contact lenses turn everything into text I can read—that was the only way they'd let me into space. Right, I need some measurements from the two of you."

After our measurements were taken, the quartermaster disappeared into the back. Jee asked Hak in an undertone, "Do we get to learn sign language, too?"

Hak said, "If you have the free time and inclination, it never hurts. My mothers are Deaf, so I grew up with it. I'm convinced that's why they assigned me to this particular ship—so Yang has someone to talk to in her own language."

The quartermaster emerged with two full kit bags. "'These should fit. Now out with you. I have to double-check inventory.'"

"Thank you, sir," I said directly to Quartermaster Yang, determined not to offend the person who controlled my *clothes*, to say nothing of our food supplies and armaments. I wasn't under any illusions that cadets would be allowed to engage in live-fire weapons training, but a tiger could dream.

Yang smiled again and waved us off.

"I'll show you to your bunks so you can get changed," Hak said, "and then the senior cadets can orient you."

Jee perked up. "How many of us are there, sir?"

"Just two more at present," Ensign Hak said as she herded us along. "Namkyu and Euna. You'll like them."

"Of course I will," Jee said with a confidence that made me smile. He was the kind of person who made friends with everyone. I hoped I'd get along with the other cadets, too.

"Cadet bunks are on level three," Hak added casually. "We'll have to take an elevator to get there." She indicated one down the hall, and we picked up our pace.

"We'll get a map at some point, sir?" I asked. I was trying to get a sense of the ship's layout as a whole, and mostly what I had so far was *It's really big*. I had a good memory, but there were no cues like unusual rocks and interesting trees, or scent marks and trails laid down by other tigers to help me.

"Yeah, the older cadets will fill you in," Hak said. "It's in your training materials, and—"

An alert chimed from the intercom system, and Jee jumped. "The ship is preparing to Gate," said a low, stern voice. "All hands prepare for Gating."

"Relax, kid," Hak said. "The *Haetae* is more modern than even most Kestrel battle cruisers. It just came out of the shipyard last year. It's not like the old days, or some of the older ships, where you'd have to strap into a gel couch. You'll scarcely notice the Gate effects."

Jee's face fell. I knew I had a similar expression, despite my less than pleasant experience on the way to the starbase. We didn't want Gating to be *ordinary*. We wanted Gating on our first battle cruiser posting to be *special*.

Ensign Hak took pity on us. "I suppose a couple minutes' delay won't hurt," she said. Instead of heading straight for the elevator, she diverted us to a viewport.

A broad-shouldered spacer was already there, presumably off-duty. "Move over, will you?" Hak said with steely geniality. "First-timers."

The spacer sighed. "Of course, sir. We shouldn't ever disappoint the *first-timers*." But as they ambled aside, they winked at us.

Jee and I pressed our noses to the viewport. I didn't want to lose my dignity in front of the crew, but this was going to be my one and only *first Gating*!

We would probably have to Gate several times to reach our final destination. Each planetary system's Gate connected it to a few nearby ones, so it was a matter of playing connect-the-dots to get from one location to another.

The first thing I noticed was that we were already in space. Liftoff had occurred so seamlessly that I had barely noticed the transition. I assumed that magical technology had smoothed the *Haetae*'s accelerations as it lifted off from the starbase. We were already far enough beyond the atmosphere that the stars shone cold and clear, without the haze or twinkling effect you'd see from groundside.

An iridescent glow washed over the glitter-jewel stars in

their field of black. I almost forgot to breathe. It was beautiful in the way of pearl and abalone, beautiful in the way of unimaginable treasure. Yet it also woke a deep sensation of foreboding in my chest, as though the glow hid unnamed dangers.

"Good," Hak said, a soft tinge to her voice. She wasn't unaffected by the sight, either.

All that, and we still hadn't been sworn in. *Maybe it's an omen,* I thought, but at the time I'd meant it as a joke.

SIX

J ee and I were still agape at the fading shimmer of light as the ship completed its journey into Gate space. I could have lingered at the viewport forever, watching the staticky gray otherspace outside. Intellectually, I knew how deadly it was to living organisms. The ship would have robot assistants for any repairs that might need to take place to the exterior.

Normally I wouldn't have worried about the odds that we'd need to make repairs while in transit. However, Special Investigator Yi had spoken of trouble brewing at Norandol, our destination. I might not be one of the ship's officers, but I knew better than to assume that the operation would go smoothly.

Ensign Hak, for her part, frowned at a communication that had just come to her wrist unit. "Time to get you two dressed and sworn in," she announced. "C'mon."

I followed her after one last glance at the window with its eerie gray expanse of nothingness. Despite the strangeness, it was oddly alluring. A reminder that we'd left the starbase behind and were on our way—in space.

I thought I might be acclimating to the ship's recycled air. The ecofilters theoretically kept the air sweet and pure, but I smelled traces of sweat, grease, even the leaves of plants. That last must have been coming from hydroponics. A ship this size would grow some of its own fresh vegetables. A sudden wave of longing for home washed over me, even though I'd hardly been away for a week.

The cadets' bunkroom was on the third level. Hak knocked peremptorily on the hatch, then keyed it open without waiting for a response. "Anyone in here?" she asked as she walked in.

A girl with a sallow face and long hair pinned up into a bun rose hastily, setting down a sketchbook. I glimpsed a cartoon of a girl with a blaster in each hand facing down a tentacled horror. It was pretty good art, too.

"Just me, sir," the girl said, standing at attention and saluting. I peered at the name tag on her uniform, right next to the pronoun pins, and saw that this was Euna. "Er, Namkyu went to the rec room. I don't know when they'll be back."

Euna had an unearthly smell of night air that suggested descent from celestial maidens. The other scents in the room reminded me of earth and deep waters. Perhaps Namkyu was an imugi, one of the great serpents that dwelled in the depths. The stronger ones sometimes ascended to become dragons. Either way, imugi and dragons both brought good luck.

I longed to sit down with Euna, someone of my own rank and age who had been here awhile, and talk with her about the *Haetae* and its crew. If nothing else, she might be able to give me some idea of how widespread knowledge of the Norandol situation was and how others might react to my family. But I couldn't interrogate her in front of Hak, and Jee would look at me askance, too. Maybe I could pry some information out of Euna later.

The room itself was cramped, with two double-high bunks on each side and two small desks bolted to the deck. The desk Euna had sat down at displayed a spiny potted plant of a type I had never seen or smelled before. On the other rested an anatomical figure, its organs and meridians labeled in tiny script, except its head was on backward. That one smelled of imugi, and I wondered about the absent Namkyu's ghoulish sense of humor. Two desks for four people—I supposed we'd have to share.

"All right," Hak said, oblivious to my musings. She pointed at my kit bag. "Change and make it fast. The sooner you're sworn in, the sooner you can help with all the work that goes into making a battle cruiser run."

Jee broke into a smile the way he did anytime someone addressed him. "Like decoding secret messages, sir?"

Euna blinked, and Hak laughed, not unkindly. "More like scrubbing decks or applying grease to the guns, kid."

"Maybe there are secret messages scratched into the decks," Jee said, even more hopefully.

That only made Hak laugh more. "Not on Captain Chaewon's ship! If she found anyone defacing her precious baby, she'd feed their carcass to the plants in hydroponics."

While they bickered in a friendly fashion, I ducked behind the privacy curtain and changed my clothes. I couldn't stop my hands from trembling as I did up the buttons and zippers. A uniform of my own! And one that fit properly. Apparently Quartermaster Yang knew how to do her job.

Sure, it was only a cadet uniform, dark blue without the gold braid that distinguished officers. Wearing this would cement my place at the bottom of the crew's hierarchy. But that was the point. Everyone would recognize me as part of the crew. Someone who belonged here.

What's wrong with you? I asked myself. After all, I'd belonged back home, too. The Juhwang Tiger Clan was close-knit, to the point where I'd scarcely interacted with anyone outside the household. Maybe that was the issue. Here I was surrounded by strangers, and I didn't know them well enough yet to feel that we were comrades.

I did up the last button on my shirt. Then I pinned my name tag and pronoun pin—*they/them*—in place. It bemused me that people would use the tag and pins to get to know me, rather than my personal scent.

"Let's have a look at you two," Hak said after Jee and I had both changed. I stood still for her inspection, conscious that I could be penalized for an upturned collar—a memory of my auncle Hasun's collar flashed before me, except no one was going to upbraid an admiral!—or a scuffed shoe. Hak's lips compressed when she spotted something I'd missed. My gut tightened in dread, but all she pointed out was that one pant leg's hem was folded up in the back. Relief washed through me at the unexpected mildness of her comment.

Jee had managed to misalign his shirt buttons, so Hak made him redo them. He emerged flushed but presentable. Euna was trying not to grin. I bet she had undergone the same many times. She'd done a quick sketch of Jee looking flustered and one of me as well.

"Don't get into any trouble," Hak said to Euna, who nodded too quickly, covering the drawings with her hand. To Jee and myself, Hak said, "Time to present you to Captain Chaewon. She'll want to meet the newest members of her crew."

I blinked, not sure whether to be alarmed.

Ensign Hak noticed my expression as she ushered us out. "The captain takes a hands-on approach," she said. "In an emergency, even the lowliest member of the crew could be vital to everyone's survival. The captain believes in being prepared."

It sounded nice. In reality, though, I was sure I would spend my training cruise learning about the workings of the ship and chopping vegetables or checking hydroponics for mold. I didn't want to volunteer for those tasks, exactly, but I knew my duty. I might as well appreciate my meeting with Captain Chaewon, since it could be my only one.

Although I was keyed up about the prospect of seeing my captain in the flesh and having to make a good impression, I remained alert to my surroundings. Aunt Sooni would have been proud. I noticed, for example, how Jee was strolling along without a care in the world. I couldn't tell whether he was always like this. For that matter, I didn't know whether the other cadets would share his carefree approach to life.

He'll learn, I told myself. Wasn't constant vigilance what the Space Forces wanted of us, after all? It was hard not to judge him, even though I liked him. If something went amiss, I would be depending on him and our other shipmates. Of course, they would have to depend on me, too—it went both ways.

"Halfway there," Hak said as an aside.

I almost didn't hear her. I stopped dead, nostrils flaring. The others had continued almost three yards ahead of me before they noticed I wasn't keeping up.

"Sebin?" I heard someone saying as if from an otherworldly distance.

I should have reacted. It was Ensign Hak's voice. She was an officer, and senior to me.

It didn't matter. My nose knew what it had encountered—Uncle Hwan's scent mark. I was standing right in front of it. He'd touched this particular alcove, and recently, too.

Like all cats, tigers could mark their territory with their personal scent. The entire Juhwang Tiger Clan estate had trees that the Matriarch ritually marked once a month, delimiting the extent of our territory. The scent lasted longer than you'd think, even when storms blew through. It was part of our tiger magic, Aunt Sooni had told me.

But what could Uncle Hwan be doing on the *Haetae* if he was considered a fugitive and a traitor? And why had he scent-marked *another captain's ship*? Just the thought of his challenging Chaewon's dominance like this made my hair want to stand up on end.

He must need me, a voice whispered in the back of my head. This wasn't just a challenge to Captain Chaewon, I realized, but a signal to other tigers of our clan. He was calling on me for assistance.

"Sebin!" Hak snapped.

I faced her. I was sure my face had gone white, that all the blood in my body had evaporated.

Hak had stopped and turned around and was now glaring at me. "*Cadet* Sebin," she said, with an emphasis that we both knew meant *This is not the time to make a poor impression.*

Maybe I was just imagining Hwan's scent, with its distinctive notes of pine and embers. I'd heard that traveling through Gates sometimes caused hallucinations. Gate-sickness was common enough that they had medications for it, although the meds weren't entirely reliable, either.

I dragged my mind back to the present. I knew my uncle. I knew he had been here, impossible as that seemed. He was signaling me, and . . .

"Sir," I said reluctantly, "there's someone on this ship who isn't authorized to be."

My gut clenched as I said this, and the scar on my hand ached suddenly. I'd sworn an oath to the clan. Uncle Hwan was *family*. I was supposed to be loyal to my kin.

"Cadet," Hak said with a glower, "we don't have time for your flights of fancy. Security would have caught any stow-aways, and there's obviously no one here right now."

I slumped miserably and quickened my pace to catch up with them. Shouldn't Hak be taking this more seriously? She might only have a human's sense of smell, but she had to be used to crewmates who had keener senses.

Hey, Jee mouthed at me, *you okay?*

I smiled at him despite the leaden sensation in my chest. *I'll be fine,* I mouthed back. Maybe I could warn Captain Chaewon instead. She might take me seriously—assuming he hadn't already gotten to her.

We continued walking down the final corridors on the way to the captain's office. Jee kept shooting me worried glances, but I had no attention to spare for him. What could my uncle's presence mean? And what would he want of me?

Perhaps, and my breath caught with sudden hope, he wasn't a disgraced fugitive after all. Maybe this was all part of some secret plan. I didn't know what that might look like, but it wasn't completely implausible that Space Forces Command might want to ferry an accomplished captain out of sight so he could take part in some special mission.

Don't let your imagination run away with you, I thought. Still, calm settled over me. There must be some rational explanation. Either Ensign Hak knew and couldn't tell me right now, or she didn't know and I'd find out later. All I had to do was exercise some patience.

The captain's office, when we arrived, stood out from all the other entrances. The hatch displayed the Space Forces logo, a flower, and a spear, above a scroll that said CAPTAIN CHAEWON OF THE *HAETAE* in energetic calligraphy. I wondered if she'd done the lettering herself, or if that task had fallen to someone else.

"Captain, it's Ensign Hak with the new cadets," Hak said in a respectful voice. "No one got around to swearing them in, given our precipitous departure."

"Enter," said a smooth soprano.

The hatch slid open. Hak guided us in and demonstrated a painstakingly perfect salute. Jee and I imitated her.

The first thing I noticed was not the captain but the overwhelming sense of calm that radiated throughout the office. Shelves bolted to the walls featured a variety of succulents, some with pink-tinged fleshy leaves, so different from the azaleas and forsythias and cosmos of my family home. A master of pungsu jiri, the art of geomancy, must have arranged everything from the placement of the desk and plants to the symmetrically aligned plaques and honors that festooned the walls, all in service of bringing good fortune to the captain in particular and the ship in general. The only things out of place were several tacky, brightly colored spaceport banners of the type you'd expect as tourist souvenirs.

Captain Chaewon was a sturdy woman with a square-jawed face. She smelled human with a trace of tiger heritage, and she held herself with a steady confidence that made me want to trust her. Her hair was iron-gray. She had risen to greet us, and I was impressed by her perfect stance, like a statue of a warrior of old. A sheathed sword hung from her waist. I thought back to the sword that the Space Forces had sent home, and the matter of Uncle Hwan.

"Greetings, cadets," she said. "It is my pleasure to welcome you aboard the Space Forces battle cruiser *Haetae*, which will be your home for the next six months, if not longer. I am Captain Chaewon." She paused to look us both over, then nodded.

I let out my breath in a tiny sigh before I could stop myself.

"It's time to swear you to the service of the Space Forces," she continued. "Understand this—whatever oaths or duties you may have undertaken before, this one supersedes it. Loyalty to family is important, as is loyalty to your homeworld. But as a member of the Space Forces, your foremost duty is not to these, but to the Thousand Worlds as a whole."

I was entranced by the gravity of her words, although I kept my eyes properly lowered. I'd always thought in terms of personal honor, or family honor, rather than the good of the Thousand Worlds. I wondered how Uncle Hwan had felt when he was sworn in, and who had accepted his oath. It was one of the things he'd never told me. Maybe I'd get a chance to ask him more questions after all.

The captain drew her sword. Its polished metal gleamed in the light shining from the ceiling. I stared at the ring pommel in fascination. I'd seen ones like it before, naturally. All the adults in my family owned swords. But those were real weapons intended for combat, in case we needed to fight in our human forms and our firearms' batteries ran out.

The captain's sword, on the other hand, was clearly ceremonial. It might have worked as a weapon if she clubbed someone over the head with it. But, like Uncle Hwan's sword, it had no edge, and the weapon was so heavy it would take someone with a goblin's or tiger's strength to wield it effectively in combat.

Captain Chaewon handled the weapon skillfully enough. "Cadet Baik Jee," she said imperiously. Jee saluted. She extended the sword to him. "Put your hand on the point of the blade."

He did so, and the point made a dent in his palm without drawing blood, another sign the sword was for show. Unless—and the thought nagged at me—honor was the real weapon.

The captain began speaking again. "Swear that you will serve the Thousand Worlds with courage and honor. Swear that you will defend its people to the fullest extent of your ability. Swear that you will respect the chain of command and serve your superiors loyally."

"I swear it," Jee said in a choked-up voice, and then, more loudly, "I swear it, Captain."

Captain Chaewon flicked her wrist in a way that my eyes couldn't follow. Jee yelped, and blood dripped onto the deck. I could smell its iron tang as well as Jee's alarm.

"Let this be a reminder to you," Chaewon said, "that honor may seem simple, but it always demands a price. You must be ready to pay that price, whatever it is." She twisted her hand again, and a blue flame sprang up and consumed the traces of blood on the blade. I could have sworn that it wasn't sharp, but clearly I'd been wrong.

The captain turned to me. I steeled myself for the bite of the sword. But before she could speak again, we were interrupted by a percussive boom that thundered through the bones of the ship. It was so deep that I didn't hear it so much as feel it reverberate through my body. An explosion?

The lights flickered, then went out, plunging us into darkness.

After a moment during which I could only hear my own frantic heartbeat, other lights flared on, fainter and harsher. Powered by backup generators, presumably. Alarms pierced the air, almost deafening me.

"Sir—" I started to say. The scar on my hand throbbed.

The captain was no longer paying attention to Jee or me. "Get them out of here," she told Hak. "I have to reach the bridge." She strode past us before I could get a word in edgewise—or tell her about Uncle Hwan's scent mark.

So much for making a good first impression.

SEVEN

Ensign Hak paled, then shooed us out of the captain's office. "You need to hole up with the other cadets," she told Jee and me.

All my fur would have been standing on end if I'd been in tiger form. As a human, this translated into an uncomfortable prickly feeling, as though my skin were about to burst into fur. I would have felt safer as a tiger, protected by my greater size, tough hide, and natural weapons. I itched for a blaster like the one Hak had.

"Come on," the ensign said. I lengthened my stride. Hak could walk very fast when she put her mind to it. Jee almost broke into a jog to keep up.

Another boom reverberated throughout the ship. The lights flickered again. Just as I thought they'd come back on, they fell into darkness with a near-subliminal whine. Jee stank of fear. I couldn't blame him. I didn't feel sanguine about the situation, either.

Still, my job was to follow Ensign Hak's instructions so she could fulfill her duty and get back to her assignment, whatever it was. Maybe the other cadets would fill me in on what to do. And to think my vision of the orientation had been boring—not like this at all.

We'd gotten down the corridor and just turned to the port side at the T-junction when a barrier slammed shut behind us. At the same time, another one came down at the other end of the hall. We were trapped.

That's odd, I thought. Despite the overwhelming smells of cleaning agents and scoured metal, each corridor did have its own unique odor. Even without my excellent memory for the path we'd taken, the smell, with its slight hint of green-tea cookies and a dissonant bitter note that had come from Euna's plant, would have identified this passageway as the one with the cadets' bunkrooms.

"Well, that's not ominous at all," Jee said under his breath.

"Keep it to yourself, Cadet," Hak said, clearly rattled. "There should have been an additional alert before they sectioned us off. . . ." I heard her scrabbling for something, and then she flicked on a flashlight. It was a relief to be able to see again.

I looked at her, questioning. "Why did they barricade the corridor, sir?" I asked.

"Could be a few different things," she said as we continued to make our way to the bunkroom. "Security measure in case of boarders, although that shouldn't be possible while we're Gating. Emergency measure in case of hull breach. But no one should be able to attack us while we're in transit, either, and the captain hasn't made an announcement. . . ."

I remembered how precipitously the captain had left us to get to the bridge. If she was so busy she hadn't even had the opportunity to give the crew guidance . . . I shivered. I didn't like what that implied.

"I'm going in," Hak announced. She keyed the door open.

This time two cadets stood and saluted. We'd met Euna earlier. The other one, a spindly kid with narrow eyes and dirt on their hands, had to be Namkyu. They were holding a flashlight of their own.

"Ensign Hak," Euna said, "w-what's going on? We heard the alarms, but we keep waiting for an announcement and there hasn't been any and we don't know if we should report to duty stations or if we should—"

Hak cut off her stream of words with a stern look. "Your job is to await further instructions."

Namkyu spoke up. "Are these the new cadets, sir?" They eyed me uncertainly. I smiled back, but it felt stiff. I was too nervous about the situation to relax.

Jee and I introduced ourselves. Namkyu still smelled wary, and I wondered why. We'd have to sort it out over time—if we got the chance.

"So we stay in the bunkroom until we hear something, sir?" I asked, to be absolutely sure. I itched to be part of the action, but orders were orders.

"That's right," Hak said. I heard Euna groan under her breath and hoped that the ensign's hearing wasn't as sensitive as mine. "If there's an emergency, contact Lieutenant Han-gyeol for instructions. Otherwise, stay put. I'll have to use the override to get past the barricade so I can check in with . . ."

I watched glumly as Hak spun on her heel and exited. Then we all looked at one another. The alarms continued to bleat.

They were already giving me a headache, not that I wanted to admit it.

"Is there anything we can do while we're 'staying put'?" I asked. I hated to be idle. "What does your usual schedule look like?"

"You're all business, aren't you?" Namkyu observed. But their hostility had eased, which reassured me. They nodded at me in a cordial fashion. "Normally we'd be in class right now. We've been learning about the Gate drive and its basic functions. I'm tracked for Medical, which is why I've been studying with my friend Guts"—Namkyu gave the anatomy doll a friendly pat—"but we're all supposed to know the fundamentals."

"I want to do Weapons," Euna volunteered. "My reflexes are fast, and I'm good at the kind of math you use for targeting, but I know there's a lot of competition for it. My parents said that if I was going to waste all my time playing shooter games, I might as well get something out of it." Her eyes shone—literally—with a bluish light, and I remembered that she was part celestial. "I'm to be trained in extravehicular work, too, since I don't need a spacesuit to survive in a vacuum. Haven't had a chance yet, though."

"Here," Namkyu said grudgingly to Jee and me. "Let me show you two your bunks. Euna has the bottom one on the left, I took the one on the right. Preferences?"

"I want left," Jee said, then glanced at me. "If you don't mind, Sebin?"

"Of course not," I said.

It was eerie discussing something as mundane as bunk assignments when the ship was under attack or malfunctioning or whatever was going on. At the same time, this scrap of normalcy gave me an anchor. This might not be the peaceful introduction to the *Haetae* that I had envisioned, but I could start establishing a routine so that I felt like I belonged to the ship and its crew.

The bunk looked no worse than the plain mat I'd slept on at home. I didn't imagine that I'd spend much time in this room—not anytime soon, at any rate. Even as I thought this, Jee pulled off his boots and sat down at one of the desks.

"Does this sort of thing happen often?" he asked just as the secondary lights came back on, even fainter than before.

Namkyu turned off the flashlight. "Gotta conserve the battery," they explained, patting Guts again. If their smell hadn't given it away, I would have realized then that Namkyu was more nervous than they wanted to let on.

"Life in the Space Forces," Euna said with an admirable nonchalance. Then she spoiled the effect by adding, "We've never been damaged while Gating before. They say it's rare."

"Like how rare?" I pressed.

She hesitated. "It's not like I'm an expert, but no one can attack us from the *outside* while we're in Gate space. Which leaves either sabotage or maintenance failure."

A nervous laugh rippled around the room. None of us wanted to think about the former possibility. But the latter wasn't great, either. "Was the *Haetae* docked for repairs before this mission?" I asked.

"Only routine maintenance," Namkyu said, their mouth twisted in a sour grimace. "Mind you, it's not impossible some technician messed things up. If that's the case, an inquiry will reveal the truth. You'd think with the scrubbing we've done all over the ship, though, we'd have noticed something awry before now."

Jee was swinging his legs and kicking the desk, which was going to be a very annoying habit if he did that while I was trying to sleep. "Do we have slates that are cleared for use with the ship's networks?" he asked.

Namkyu's eyebrows rose. Then they went over to a cabinet and drew out two slates. Namkyu handed one to Jee and the other to me.

We crowded around to see what Jee was going to do. "Find out what's happening on the bridge," Euna suggested, leaning in eagerly. Her eyes were glowing again. I guessed it happened whenever she was excited.

My conscience twinged. "Are you sure that's a good idea?" I asked. "We should stay alert in case there's a need for us." I realized how ridiculous that sounded even as the words left my mouth.

Euna tossed her head. "That's not likely," she scoffed. "They've got experienced senior crew up there. What could we contribute?"

"Euna, your eyes," Namkyu said mildly. "Keep that up and you're going to lose the bet, and then you'll have to take my laundry shift."

She sighed. "I keep forgetting about that. I gotta wear contacts to keep the glow from giving away my position!" She fished in her kit bag and pulled out a lens case. Once she inserted the dark contacts, they did, in fact, dampen the glow.

"It's not like there are hostiles on board," I said. I hoped it was true.

Jee's mouth crimped, but he recovered quickly. "Well, we can help by figuring out what the situation is," he reasoned. "That way we won't be caught unawares by whatever's going on."

"You're right," I said, as uneasy as I felt about hacking into the ship's computer. Who knew how good Jee was at it, after all? And we didn't want to distract the bridge crew from the emergency, whatever it was. But I didn't like the thought of remaining stuck here doing nothing, either. And I felt I should back Jee.

I pulled up a map of the ship on my own slate and studied it despite my headache, committing as much as I could to memory. Silently, I thanked Aunt Sooni for helping me work on my visualization skills, even if scent trails were so much easier to keep in my head.

"I'm in!" Jee announced after some furious typing.

We all jostled for a view of the slate.

"And to think my nini said I should spend less time playing video games and more time doing sit-ups," Euna said with a grin. "I always told them, why not both? Video games for work, sit-ups for pleasure, that's what I think."

The mood turned somber as we took in the scene on the bridge. The camera was focused dead center on the captain's chair. Normally this would have been reassuring . . . but the chair was empty. In the on-off strobing of the red lights, I glimpsed her fallen form. I couldn't tell whether she was still alive.

"Well," Jee said after a stunned moment, "that can't be a good sign."

That had to be the understatement of the century.

"No wonder we haven't heard from the bridge," I said. "Who's the executive officer?"

"The ship's XO is Commander Ae," Euna said. "They should be in charge if the captain's knocked out."

I could tell she didn't want to face the possibility that the captain wasn't just knocked out, but dead. I didn't either, to be honest.

"Can you move the camera around?" Namkyu, more pragmatic, asked Jee. "Or switch to another one?"

"Sure," Jee answered. The camera jerked around and spun dizzyingly before slowing down. I winced and looked away before it worsened my headache. "Hold up," Jee added. "I can get us a panorama."

"We should notify Lieutenant Han-gyeol and Ensign Hak," I said. "Given that comms seem to be down, they might need this information."

Jee squirmed. "We'd get in trouble for hacking the bridge cameras."

"The safety of the ship comes first," I pointed out. "We can sort out the rest later."

Namkyu heaved a sigh and fiddled with Guts some more. "What do you think, Euna?"

She studied me, then nodded decisively. "Sebin is right. This is too big for us to keep to ourselves. Worst case we get a slap on the wrist and they tell us to play board games while they deal with the big bad, whoever it is. Because, you know, the most important skill we can develop in a crisis is rolling dice."

"Sounds legit," Namkyu said. Jee nodded, too, though he was obviously reluctant. "Who's oldest?"

We compared our ages. Namkyu was the oldest, then me, then Euna, then Jee. The hierarchy should have been based on who had served the longest, which would be Namkyu and Euna, but since we were all the same rank, we had to rely on age instead. It was good to get that figured out.

"Better for you or Euna to report in anyway," I said. "Jee

and I are new, so people won't recognize us." Uncomfortably, I recalled the fact that I hadn't been sworn in, either. But that didn't seem to matter right now.

"Sure thing," Namkyu said. They addressed the ship's computer system. "Cadet Namkyu to Lieutenant Han-gyeol, please."

I took note of the formality level that Namkyu used when addressing the ship's computer. That was something I'd never asked my relatives about and Uncle Hwan hadn't mentioned. I used a medium-polite formality level if I had to speak to the estate's systems, but it hadn't occurred to me that the convention might be different in the Space Forces.

"Lieutenant Han-gyeol is not available," the computer replied in its smooth voice.

A crease formed between Namkyu's brows. "Where is he?"

"Lieutenant Han-gyeol is not available," the computer repeated.

"Is he all right?"

"Cadet Namkyu, you are not authorized for that information."

The skin on the back of my neck prickled. "What about Ensign Hak?" I asked.

"Yeah, try her," Euna agreed. "I mean, we just saw her moments ago."

Namkyu did so.

"Ensign Hak is not available," the computer said in that same smooth tone, which I was starting to find ominous.

"What's her status?"

"Cadet Namkyu, you are not authorized for that information."

Namkyu had picked up Guts and was twisting its head around and around in their aggravation. "Authorized or not, we need to get through to *someone*."

The computer didn't have a useful answer to that, either.

I thought furiously. There had to be a way to yank *some* information out of the system. "Is there *anyone* we can contact?"

Euna's laugh held an edge of nerves. "We know the bridge isn't going to be any help."

Another reverberation juddered through the deck. The emergency lights dimmed further. We stared at one another. I was sure the others' pallor was mirrored in my own face. The red light washed over their visages and turned them into grue-some masks.

"We can't just do *nothing*," Euna fretted. "Jee, do you see anything else useful? Is there anyone moving around on the bridge?"

"I'm trying to get a better view," Jee said, frowning at his slate. "I'm getting a lot of static, though."

"Maybe you could go through a list of all the people you know," I suggested to Namkyu.

The lanky cadet was looking increasingly frazzled, but they nodded. They began querying the computer in a rapid-fire voice, cutting it off every time it repeated the worrying refrain of *not available*. I did my best to memorize the names. There were a lot of them, and it was harder without personal scents or faces to attach them to, but I thought they might be useful later.

"Uh, guys?" Jee's wavering voice broke my concentration. Namkyu ignored him and continued talking to the computer. "I hate to mention this, but the camera feed just got cut."

"What do you mean, cut?" Euna demanded. Then she caught sight of what was on Jee's slate and blanched.

I craned my head to get a better look. Jee was right. But he hadn't told us everything. Not only had the video feed vanished completely, it had been replaced by a single screen of text:

INTRUDER ALERT
INTRUDER ALERT
ALL HANDS PREPARE TO REPEL INTRUDERS

"We're not intruders!" Jee said, although he smelled guilty.

"I don't think it means us," I assured him. "Someone must have boarded at Starport Borasaekbam, if not earlier, and gone undetected somehow."

"Then we have to link up with someone else," Euna said, frowning. "We're sitting ducks here. We don't even have real weapons like the rest of the crew."

"But we're safe . . . right?" Jee said slowly. He glanced from Euna to me and back again.

"It's not our job to be safe," Euna said. "It's our job to *do something.*" She reeked of impatience.

"That's not what Ensign Hak said!"

I didn't want them to start arguing. "Jee," I broke in, "does the system have any idea *where* the intruders are? Or who they are, for that matter?"

He bent over the slate again, only to pale further. "The system's shut down."

"What?" Namkyu asked sharply, having finished going through their list of contacts.

"The video system," Jee said. "It's down."

"The bridge video's down?"

"No," Jee said. "I mean it's down everywhere. I can't even access the feed for the corridor outside this room."

"So . . ." Euna said, working through the implications, "anyone could be wandering around out there and we'd have no idea who they were."

Jee winced. "Since you put it that way . . ."

"That's not likely," I said, since I didn't want him to lose his nerve. I made a note to myself to be extra reassuring for his benefit. "We didn't see anyone else on the way here, and then it was barricaded."

"Only authorized parties will have the overrides to the barricades," Namkyu added.

I nodded. "The only person who could be in the corridor now is—"

My calm, reasonable train of thought was interrupted by a percussive bang just outside. Everybody jumped, myself included.

"Does anyone have *any* weapons?" I hissed, because if we were about to be invaded I didn't want to go down without a fight.

The smell of guilt wafted from Euna. "Technically, I shouldn't, but . . ."

"You'll need it," I said. "Get it ready, whatever you have."

As for me, I backed away from the others to give myself room, not that there was much of that, and flowed into my tiger shape. In the jumbled moment of transformation, I heard the others' exclamations and smelled their fear. I rumbled at them reassuringly before realizing they might perceive it as a growl.

The bang came again. Then, to everyone's horror, the hatch opened with a shriek.

EIGHT

I leaped for the hatch.

Or rather, I would have if there hadn't been three people in the way. In my heightened state of excitement, I hadn't made allowances for the tight quarters. I surged forward, yes. But even though Jee, Namkyu, and Euna hastily flattened themselves to either side of me, I got stuck. I'd interrupted Euna's attempt to arm herself with whatever weapon she'd snuck on board. And in the meantime, we formed a ridiculous clump of flesh.

The hatch finished opening, admitting someone I recognized by her scent—Min. She was still clad in the gray hanbok. Her eyes widened as she looked us up and down.

I snarled at her, more out of embarrassment than hostile intent. Then I regretted it when I smelled Jee's raw fear. I needed to be more careful of my comrades. I owed him an apology.

Min drew out a blaster and pointed it at me. "Leave the cadets alone!" she shouted.

Whoa! I didn't want her to char my hide! I returned to

human form, leaving the others blinking in bewilderment. To my relief, the tiger magic restored my cadet uniform. I hadn't been sure it would recognize it as the proper attire.

"Sorry, Jee," I murmured, heat rushing to my face. "Didn't mean to scare you."

"No problem," he said. His smile was wobbly but good-natured.

Min didn't lower the blaster. "Sebin?" she asked cautiously.

"It's me," I said. "Sorry about that," I added to the others. "I thought we were under attack."

Min grimaced. "You thought right. There have been explosions that might have . . . Where *is* everyone?"

"What are you doing here?" I countered. "Why aren't you with Yi?"

"I asked first."

"We were hoping to find out," Jee said before our conversation could degenerate any further. "All we know is . . ." He gestured eloquently at the flashing red lights. "Where's your superior?"

Min's grimace deepened. "Yi was called to the bridge. Before they left, they told me to check on all of you."

"Jee," I said, "did you see any trace of Yi on the bridge before the cameras cut out?"

He shook his head. "It was too dark to see clearly," he said in an uncertain voice. "Maybe I missed them."

At last Min lowered the blaster, although she didn't holster it. "What do you mean, cameras?"

Jee shot me a glance that meant *We're in for it now.* I nodded reassuringly at him. He said, "We hacked into the ship's security feed." At Min's raised eyebrows, he added defensively,

"We weren't able to get in touch with anyone. It seemed like a good idea to find out what was happening before we decided what to do next."

I hated that he was justifying himself to Min. All the same, we weren't supposed to be hacking into our own ship. I wondered where Jee had learned those skills, and then decided I didn't want to ask him in front of Min.

"Maybe the special investigator will know what's going on," I said.

"Special investigator?" Namkyu asked. They'd put Guts down at some point, this time with its head on correctly. "You mean it's true that we were waiting for one to board the ship before we took off?"

I didn't need a keen sense of smell to detect Namkyu's suspicion. "I doubt the investigator was the saboteur."

"Yi would never—" Min said hotly, then checked herself. "Listen, let me call them for instructions. I bet Yi has some clue why the ship was attacked while in Gate space."

This time she did tuck the blaster into its holster. While she put in the call on her data-slate, I considered the possibilities. I couldn't think of a reason why Yi or anyone else would want to sabotage the ship they were on, which struck me as a dangerous endeavor. Surely the saboteur was long gone.

Then I remembered Uncle Hwan's scent mark, and my gut clenched. Should I bring it up now? Or wait until we found an authority I could report it to?

Min's next words made it clear that the latter wasn't an option, not at the moment. "I can't reach Yi," she said tautly. "I've got to find them."

"Wait a second," I said. "If the bridge crew has been taken

out, it's not going to be safe for any of us to wander around alone. We should stick together."

Her voice sharpened. "My duty is to the special investigator."

"Why do we have a special investigator on the ship in the first place?" Euna wanted to know.

The conversation was derailing at a time when we needed to take action. "We can ask Yi when we find them," I said. Maybe we'd get more information. I wasn't sure whether to share what Yi had told Jee and me about our mission in the Fortress sector. Surely the other cadets already knew about it? Regardless, it wasn't my place to give out that info.

"Captain first," Namkyu said. "We have to see if she's still alive."

"How good's your medical training?" I asked.

Namkyu held out their hands and smiled wryly. "Healer's touch," they said. "I learned to realign gi"—the breath of life and luck that animated all things—"from my grandfather. And I always carry a basic medkit. I'm qualified as a first responder."

"With all the practicing you do on that creepy doll," Euna quipped, "you should be ready to repair real people."

"Yi will be able to help us," Min argued.

"Look," I said, "the special investigator was headed to the bridge, right? We'll go there first. Yi and the captain are probably in the same location anyway. There's no conflict."

Min hesitated, then nodded, her mouth tight. "Okay."

"I don't suppose you have any more blasters where that one came from," Euna asked her, "or a personal shield?"

"Sorry," Min said. "Just the one blaster."

Euna grimaced. "Then I'm going to have to make do." She

fished in her kit bag, retrieving something that looked like an overgrown flashlight.

"What's *that*?" Jee asked.

"A glare pistol," Euna said. "Good for blinding people if they don't have eye protection, although it doesn't cause permanent injury. I'm immune to it because of my celestial heritage—bright lights don't bother me."

"That's good," I said. "But we'd better get moving."

"I'll take point since I have the *real* blaster," Min said. "Sebin, as a tiger, you have good senses. You should guard the rear."

No one argued. Min pulled out her blaster again, so soon after she'd put it away. Jee took a sheltered position in the middle of the pack, clutching his slate like a talisman. Euna stood to his left, Namkyu to his right. I brought up the rear.

I wondered if I should change back into tiger shape, but I didn't want to alarm any crew members we ran into. It was generally understood that crew should maintain human guise. Ships weren't designed to accommodate the varied sizes and shapes of supernaturals in their native forms. Besides, if we ran into a threat, it would only take me a moment to shift.

I hated the fact that we were entering a dangerous situation with the scantest of intel. If only Jee had been able to keep the video feed up longer! I didn't like the implications of the interruption, either. Was there a virus of some sort in the system? Or worse, was the intruder still aboard, actively preventing us from gathering more information?

I wasn't the only one who had that thought. "Jee," Min said in an undertone as we walked toward the bridge, "can you keep monitoring the computer system? To see if any users are active?"

"Sure," Jee said, clearly nervous, "but there's a risk they'll see me nosing around."

"We'll have to chance it."

I disliked the way Min was taking charge. She wasn't one of us. But it would have been petty to pick a fight over it. Especially since I would have made the same call.

We had an immediate problem—leaving the bunkroom was easy, but the way to the bridge was blocked by the doors that had slammed down earlier, and we didn't have the access codes that Ensign Hak had referred to. I looked at Min, although she couldn't see me behind her. I raised my voice and asked, "How did *you* get through the barriers, Min?" If she could replicate that trick . . .

No such luck. "I was assigned to that cabin," Min replied, pointing down the hall. Three hatches away from our own. "I didn't have far to come. Investigator Yi has the one next to it, but they were called away before the barriers came down."

"You weren't given the ones for special guests?" Euna asked. "Those cabins are normally for, well, cadets."

Min shrugged. "Yi's request. I didn't ask why."

Maybe Yi wanted to keep an eye on us, said a whisper in the back of my head. But why? All I knew about the *Haetae*'s special mission was what the special investigator had told me. If Yi didn't trust us, they could have kept quiet in the first place.

Unless, perhaps, there was a deeper game going on. But I kept that thought to myself. No need to fall prey to paranoia until I had more evidence.

"Jee," I said, "can you see what's on the other side of the barrier? We're depending on you."

Jee smiled, some of his usual cheer restored. "I'm ahead of you. Unfortunately . . ." He showed us his slate.

It was the same story as before. Not only was the camera feed nonfunctional, the warning message still flashed at us.

"So there could be a yawning vacuum on the other side and we'd never know it," Euna said, shifting her weight from foot to foot. "Fun times for me, not so great for the rest of you."

"I doubt it . . ." Namkyu said, although they sounded unsure.

By then we had reached the barrier proper. Namkyu put their ear to it and listened intently, then shook their head. "I don't hear anything on the other side."

"Sebin," Min said, "you try? You have good hearing, don't you?"

I nodded and took my place next to Namkyu. I heard the faint padding of footsteps, so soft they would have been inaudible if I hadn't been concentrating hard. "There *is* someone on the other side."

"We should signal them," Jee suggested, "before I start messing with the computer."

I shook my head. "I'm not sure they'd be able to hear us. Besides, what if they're hostiles?"

"It wouldn't work anyway," Namkyu said dryly. "Those barriers are designed to stand up to heavy assault. You could shout yourself hoarse, maybe, or batter yourself against them, and then I'd have one more patient. But we have to get to the other side one way or another, Jee, so you might as well get started."

"I always knew that apprenticing with that cousin of mine was going to get me in trouble," Jee grumbled.

I was desperately curious about Jee's family, which sounded

more and more on the lawless side, but I didn't want to distract him right then.

"Stand back," Jee said. "Just in case."

Just in case what? I wanted to ask.

Jee tapped urgently at his slate. The barrier groaned, then began retracting into the ceiling. The first thing I heard was a yelp of alarm. Min's blaster was trained on the widening gap.

Air swirled into the corridor. I smelled the person on the other side before I saw anything but their feet. In all fairness, I wasn't sure whether I recognized the scent first, or the distinctive yellow utility boots. It was Yi, and they had their own blaster, a sleeker model, trained on Min.

"Don't shoot!" Min cried. "It's me, Special Investigator."

Yi gave her a searching look, then took the rest of us in with a glance. "And your friends?" they asked, with just a hint of reproof.

Briefly, I explained to Yi that we hadn't been able to contact anyone who could give us instructions—until now.

"It's just as well we linked up, then," Yi said, nodding firmly. "And I see you're able to manipulate the barriers."

Jee flushed. "That was me."

To my relief, the special investigator didn't chide Jee.

"Should we look for more reinforcements?" I asked.

"No time," Yi said. "Besides, there aren't any that I know of. The other cabins are empty. Someone swept through here before I did." Yi gestured behind themself, and we saw some fallen figures. "An explosion knocked out a number of on-watch crew. Whoever did this was fast, determined, and ruthless. I've tried contacting the off-watch crew, but I can't get through to anyone."

Namkyu paled. They briefly explained their earlier efforts to reach someone in charge and the computer's insistence that they weren't authorized for it. Yi nodded in grim understanding.

"How many crew does the *Haetae* have?" I wondered. Something I should have asked earlier.

"A battle cruiser this size normally carries a crew of four hundred," Yi said. "Granted, the *Haetae* is a bit understrength, but still. We have to be wary of any opponent who's able to take on that many people—and prevail."

Jee was sweating profusely. Euna was frowning, and Namkyu kept biting their lip. Even Yi's normal composure looked shaken. The only one who didn't seem to be fazed was Min. I hoped she was taking the situation seriously. For my part, I was coming to grips with the fact that this first mission might well be my last.

We headed to the elevator that would take us to the bridge. I winced every time we spotted scorch marks on the bulkheads or deck, or came upon a fallen crew member, and I could tell Namkyu wanted to stop to examine the latter. Uncle Hwan had taught me it was important never to leave one of your own behind, yet that was exactly what we were doing. When I asked Yi about it, though, the investigator said, "No time right now. The best way to help them is to take back control of the ship."

The elevator was locked down. I looked at Jee to get it moving again, and he nodded. "This could be a bad idea," he muttered. "We might be heading straight into an ambush."

"We can't leave the bridge undefended," I said.

Yi cut a glance at me. I smelled not alarm but surprise,

as though I'd upended some unspoken preconception on their part. "Cadet Sebin is quite right."

"I'm almost done," Jee said, tapping the data-slate. A few seconds later, the elevator opened.

We got in. The combination of tight quarters, five of us, and the on-off blinking of the red lights made the trip nightmarish. Each time the lights dimmed, I imagined that hungry ghosts would emerge from the shadows to engulf us. But at least ghosts were one thing we didn't have to contend with.

Still, I couldn't help shivering. The air here was colder than I had expected, colder than in the rest of the ship. I wondered if it meant anything.

I must have said this out loud, for Min looked sharply in my direction. "Trouble?" she asked.

I shook my head. "Nothing important."

Min's attention shifted when the elevator shuddered, then stopped.

"Are you kidding me?" Euna demanded. "Of all the times for an elevator failure . . . Too bad I can't fix the problem by shooting the controls."

"I don't suppose anyone's a mechanic," I said glumly.

"I am," Min said, surprising me. "Let me look at the control panel. There's got to be a manual override for this thing."

We reshuffled ourselves to give Min access. She produced a toolkit, removed the screws holding the panel in place, then got to work.

As Min tinkered with the wires, Jee said, "It *could* be a coincidence." His face was screwed up in worry.

"I'm not sure I want to assume anything is a coincidence right now," Yi said.

We looked at each other. "Maybe someone's trying to prevent us from reaching the bridge," I said slowly. "Which makes it all the more important to get there, and soon."

"I'm doing my best," Min said through gritted teeth. After an uneasy pause, she added, "I don't think this is a mechanical failure. Someone hacked the control system."

"You can tell all that from a panel?" Jee asked.

"I have my ways."

I couldn't see her face, but she was hiding something. I hoped it wouldn't get the rest of us into trouble. Yi didn't press her further, though, so I would have to accept that for now.

"That means it's up to me," Jee said.

I itched to claw my way out of the elevator. While close quarters didn't ordinarily bother me, it was different being trapped. Caged. Every moment we were stuck in here could make a difference.

It could be worse, I told myself. At least we weren't being gassed, with no spacesuits or alternate air supplies to protect us—never mind that Euna was immune. I didn't know if the *Haetae* had any such countermeasures against intruders. I was guessing the captain would have activated them if she'd gotten a chance.

"I wish I'd spent more time learning to do things with computers besides gaming," Euna said as she peered over Jee's shoulder.

"Give him some space," I said.

Jee shot me a grateful look. Euna backed up as much as she could, which meant she collided with me. I suppressed a growl. It wasn't her fault.

"Okay," Jee said, "that should do—"

Abruptly, all the lights in the elevator blinked out, even the red strobe. I could feel the elevator accelerating upward.

"That wasn't what was supposed to happen," Jee said breathlessly.

"It's progress," Min said.

Namkyu turned on their flashlight. "You don't need to glow for us, Euna," they added teasingly. Euna elbowed Namkyu, but she was smiling.

At that moment I was more grateful for that narrow beam of light than I could have expressed. I could see well at night back home, with the stars and moons to provide light, but not in total darkness. All cats require some illumination. While my excellent senses of smell and hearing meant that I wasn't completely unaware of my surroundings, I still valued my sight.

The elevator jolted to a halt. "Is this the bridge level?" Euna asked in a hushed voice.

Jee checked something on his slate. "Yes," he said. He didn't sound as certain as I would have liked.

"Cameras still down?" I asked. Not that they would help us if the bridge was also awash in darkness.

"Yeah," he said.

"Special Investigator," I said, "I'll go first when we open the door. I can shift into tiger form and get an idea of what's out there as well as shield the rest of you. Min, Euna, you cover me with your weapons. Euna, don't hesitate to fire the glare pistol if you need to. I can navigate by scent."

"Sounds good," Min said.

"It's a plan," Yi said.

"Here goes nothing," Jee said.

The elevator opened.

NINE

I surged forward, shifting into tiger shape as I did so. It was a relief to be freed from the confines of the elevator, and to *move*. The human part of me urged caution, reminded me that motion wasn't always the most useful kind of action. But I was past caring.

The bridge's emergency lights still shone, unlike the elevator's. That was a relief, too, except for what they revealed.

The video feed that Jee had pulled up earlier had given me a general idea of what to expect. I recognized Captain Chaewon's fallen form, although her smell didn't reveal whether she was dead or merely unconscious. The rest of the bridge crew had also been taken out. Counting was harder when I was a tiger. I didn't know how many people usually crewed the bridge, but perhaps a dozen people lay unmoving.

That was when the ambush came.

"Sebin, watch out!" Min cried. She shot over my shoulder at a darting movement. Whatever it was, her red bolt of fire missed.

I roared as I leaped toward the target. As a tiger, I could

cover almost eight yards horizontally in a jump. The morbid thought occurred to me that this way I wouldn't have to creep around the bodies of the fallen.

But the enemy was a tiger, too. And one much bigger than me. It was white. Could it be—?

More blaster fire blazed ahead of me. Almost all of it missed. Our opponent had inhumanly quick reflexes. Supernatural reflexes—like mine, but better. Still, Min scorched the attacker with a well-aimed shot to the side of the head.

I circled the intruder, snarling. Suddenly I was assailed by a strong, familiar smell. That of Uncle Hwan. And not just his typical smell, but with the additional earthen undertones of a tiger asserting authority in his own domain.

What was more, Uncle Hwan was also circling—dodging—avoiding any direct attack on me, as though he didn't want to hurt me. "Sebin! You belong with me," he rumbled in the language of tigers, which the others wouldn't be able to understand. "Come!"

The scar on my paw began to ache, a reminder of the oath I had sworn to the Matriarch. I dropped into a crouch and moaned in confusion. Then I resumed human shape. "Uncle?" I whispered.

In the ruddy light, the white tiger appeared flame-tinged. The sight should have terrified me. Instead, I found it awe-inspiring—a tiger in his prime, utterly assured as he faced down his enemies.

Except those enemies were my comrades.

"Look out!" This time it was Euna with the warning. Searing light flashed from her glare pistol as she fired, blinding everyone but, presumably, Euna herself.

I couldn't see anything but purple afterimages. I resorted to tracking location by scent and the movements of air currents, just as I'd promised Euna. Uncle Hwan must have done the same.

Too late I realized that Uncle Hwan had cornered Yi, and the investigator was in serious danger of being mauled. Yi wielded a blaster of their own—I could hear the high-pitched whine every time they pulled the trigger—but its fire only seemed to enrage Hwan. I heard the investigator scramble for cover, only to trip and go sprawling. Uncle Hwan roared and snapped at Yi. I could both hear and smell the saliva dripping from Hwan's powerful jaws.

For once, the strictures that had guided my life didn't tell me what to do. But I knew I couldn't let Yi get chomped, even if the person doing the chomping was my uncle. I shook off my confusion, and changed back into a tiger. "Uncle, you can't!" I cried in the language of tigers. I interposed myself between Uncle Hwan and Yi.

Hwan roared ferociously. My ears flattened against my skull, but I couldn't back down. I roared in return.

"I'll be back for you later," Hwan said, "when the odds are better. You'll understand soon, Sebin." His footsteps receded.

I resumed human shape. By now my vision had started to return, although everything was hazy and ringed with the purple afterimages. The earsplitting wail of the alarms made it impossible to gather my thoughts.

That was the only reason I didn't notice sooner that the others had surrounded me instead of chasing down Uncle Hwan.

I blinked fuzzily at Jee, who avoided my gaze, then at the investigator. Yi and Min both had their blasters trained on me. Euna was frowning. "What's going on?" I asked.

"You have some explaining to do," Yi said coolly. "Namkyu, we've got Sebin covered. Go check on the captain and the rest of the bridge crew."

"Of course," Namkyu said. They rushed to Captain Chaewon's side, rummaging in their medkit as they did so.

I would have liked to watch Namkyu at work, not least because I was terrified that the captain had perished. And at my uncle's hands, as impossible as that seemed. Was he really the renegade that the Space Forces had painted him to be, despite a long and honorable history of service?

That question would have to wait. First I had to figure out why my comrades had turned on me. "Explain what?" I asked, genuinely confused.

"You recognized the saboteur, didn't you?" Euna said accusingly. "I saw the whole thing. You were *talking* to that other tiger. You *knew* it."

Yi sucked in their breath. "This is serious," they said, as if I didn't know that. "Very serious. Sebin, what do you have to say for yourself?"

I tried to put myself in the others' heads. It was dawning on me that I was in a lot of trouble. They must have mistaken my confusion at seeing my beloved uncle here, and as an attacker, as collusion.

"I did recognize him," I said slowly, knowing that this would only condemn me further in their minds.

Yi's eyes bored into mine. Min was scowling, and Euna shared her expression. Jee continued to avoid looking my way, as though he were ashamed of me.

"Cap—I mean, Hwan of the Juhwang Tiger Clan," I said. And because Yi was still waiting with that accusatory expression, and Euna's eyes were starting to glow even through her contacts, I added, "My uncle."

"You realize that aiding a saboteur, and one who attacked the crew, is a crime subject to court-martial," Yi said, their face stern.

I blanched. "It's not a crime to be *related* to someone!" Besides, what if they had misunderstood the whole situation? Uncle Hwan might have come to assist Captain Chaewon on the bridge and thought that *we* were the intruders. I still didn't know how he'd gotten onto the ship, but I knew he had an explanation, even if he wasn't here to give it. Too bad anything I offered would be pure speculation. And given the way the others were looking at me, they wouldn't be interested in any of my theories, or be willing to give my uncle the benefit of the doubt.

"Perhaps not," Yi said, although their tone made me think otherwise.

"Special Investigator," Namkyu called, sounding worried. "I hate to interrupt, but . . ."

The muzzle of Yi's blaster didn't waver from me, but they nodded to indicate that they were paying attention to Namkyu. Min was frowning slightly, her eyes darting back and forth as if she couldn't decide what the biggest threat was. Jee and Euna, less disciplined and also not armed with blasters, turned to regard Namkyu.

Brushing their hair back from their face, a nervous tic, Namkyu continued, "Captain Chaewon is alive, but she needs further medical attention. I think some kind of drug knocked her out—either that or a strike to her gi. She has a broken arm, too. She needs time in one of the healing pods if the sick bay is still intact."

"That's good. She should recover," Yi said. "The others?"

I could have taken advantage of the distraction to spring free of the circle, but that would only have confirmed my guilt in the others' eyes. Even so, I was sorely tempted. I didn't like being treated as a hostile, and I liked the thought of what might come afterward even less. Would they throw me in the brig?

If only I'd had more time to talk to Uncle Hwan and find out what he wanted from me. I had always loved his visits when I was growing up. Meeting him on a battle cruiser should have been a dream come true. Instead, he'd attacked us. I dreaded the possibility that he'd been responsible for the mayhem on the bridge. The circumstances had turned what could have been a happy occasion into a frightening one.

I could smell my own nervous sweat, along with the others' paranoia, as Namkyu moved around the bridge. Despite the morbid sense of humor they'd displayed back in the bunkroom, they worked with a quiet thoroughness. I caught myself wishing Namkyu would hurry up instead of leaving me in suspense. All the same, I recognized that they currently had the most important job of anyone here.

Please be alive, I wished for the crew. It bothered me that, aside from Captain Chaewon and her XO, Commander Ae, I didn't know any of their names. Aside from the interrupted meeting with the captain, I hadn't gotten a proper introduction to anyone but the other cadets.

"My bad luck strikes again," Min muttered under her breath, so quietly I wasn't sure I'd heard her correctly. A breath of cold air gusted from her.

Surely it wasn't just her misfortune? There was a lot of bad luck going around on this cruise, my own included. Unless she was cursed or something?

It can't be that, I thought. The special investigator couldn't be so foolish as to travel with a cursed person, as opposed to taking her to a shaman to *un*curse her. I didn't know a lot about curses, only that bad luck could follow someone for any number of reasons—failing to make the proper ancestral offerings, offending a shaman, running afoul of ghosts, improper use of geomancy.... With all the possibilities, it was a wonder anyone had *good* luck.

At last Namkyu finished their rounds. "Everyone's alive," they reported. "That renegade Hwan must have known this was the only way we'd show him mercy. That, or he didn't want to risk being haunted by a crowd of vengeful ghosts."

I sagged in relief. I'd been afraid they would accuse Uncle Hwan of killing the crew. Ghosts or no ghosts, he never would have done that. Things still looked bad for him—and me—but at least no one would be condemned for murder.

That you're aware of, a nagging voice in my head interjected. After all, we didn't know what had happened elsewhere on the ship. I remembered the fallen crew we'd passed before, devastated by whatever attack had crippled the *Haetae.*

They can't be dead. I clung to that thought. Surely I would have felt—and smelled—that much death. And yet... I remembered the booms that had reverberated through the ship. Who knew how many people had been hurt?

"We'regoingtohavetosplitup," Yi said, resuming their normal rapid speech.

I forced myself to focus. I couldn't afford to miss a single word.

"Getting medical care for the bridge crew is our second priority," Yi said.

"Only second?" Namkyu demanded.

Yi looked at them dourly. "There's a fugitive at large on

the ship, and possibly more with him. Who knows what other damage is being done right this moment? The ship needs the guidance of the next person in the chain of command. Who is not me, unfortunately, since I'm not Space Forces. We'll have to find—"

"That's ridiculous!" Jee exclaimed, cutting them off. "This whole situation is crazy!"

I bristled at Jee's outburst, even though he hadn't been addressing me. Discipline was the backbone of the Space Forces! My family had been very clear on this point. It was why they had prepared me for service with such rigid household rules.

"Nevertheless," Yi said, "unless we receive definite information that there is no one left on the ship besides yourselves, that is how we have to proceed."

I blanched at the implication. I hadn't thought that far ahead, and I kicked myself mentally. I should have been prepared for even an emergency that dire. The chain of command extended down through the lowliest cadet. But for us to be in charge of, well, anything, everyone else on the ship would have to be unavailable. I couldn't imagine one enemy taking out so many people singlehandedly, which meant there had to be multiple hostiles.

Yi kept speaking. "Agent Min," they said, and with a jolt I was unpleasantly reminded that Min, for all her apparent youth, had more pull than we did as cadets. "Take Cadet Sebin to the brig and get the truth out of them. The rest of us will attend to matters on the bridge."

"Special Investigator," Min said, "are you sure there will be security staff down there to let us in? Normally that would require an officer's authorization."

She knew the regulations well, I had to give her that. I was impressed that Yi would entrust her with me without giving her any backup. I wondered if she had capabilities she hadn't shown us yet.

"You'll figure it out," Yi said with a meaningful look. "Go."

"You're coming with me," Min said to me as Yi and the others scrambled into action.

"Just you?" I asked, not bothering to hide my skepticism.

"Blaster fire might not kill you immediately in tiger form," Min said, "but it would sting. I don't want to have to hurt you. Come on."

I blinked at her, trying to concentrate on her words. My head felt as though stars were swirling at the edge of my vision. Suddenly what Min was telling me made sense. She was my friend, wasn't she?

An uneasy voice murmured in disgruntlement at the back of my head, then quieted. I had no reason to suspect that Min had anything but my best interests at heart. As long as I cooperated, we'd get this cleared up.

Behind me, I heard Jee asking, "Are you sure that's safe? Not to question Agent Min's competence, but . . ."

"Don't be fooled by her unprepossessing appearance," Yi replied. "Min has special defenses . . ." I couldn't hear the rest of the sentence.

I wondered what those defenses were, but by then Min had herded me out of the bridge and toward the elevator.

"No need to pay attention to any of that," Min said soothingly.

I quieted. If Min said it wasn't important, I didn't need to worry about it. Obediently, as though in a trance, I drifted after her. I felt myself smiling, and I couldn't say why, although that didn't bother me, either. After all, Min hadn't mentioned that it was a problem.

"I can't believe how much of the crew is locked down," Min commented to herself as we emerged from the elevator. "Hwan must have hacked into the anti-intruder systems and used them to gas the on-duty crew unconscious. What irony."

The barriers rose at our approach. Jee must be looking out for us. I said this out loud, and Min glanced sharply at me, then nodded. "In order to get around, Capt—I mean, the fugitive Hwan must also know how to hack the access codes," she said, eyeing me as though she thought I might shed some light on the situation.

I noticed her slip and blurted out, "You know my uncle?" Perhaps she would help me clear his name.

That's ludicrous, a colder part of my awareness scoffed. *Why would she do that?* But I dismissed the thought as uncharitable.

The muscles around Min's eyes tightened. A tiny shift, but one I noted immediately, intent as I was on her reaction. "Don't worry about it," she said, with a bit of an edge.

I remained slightly tense. This was something I needed to keep an eye on. But she clearly didn't want to talk about it, so I didn't press her.

Still, I couldn't help noticing that we passed unimpeded through all the corridors. Once in a while I heard a faint scuffling from behind the hatches to either side, as though crew members were hiding. I was tempted to call out and ask for information. But Min strode onward, giving no sign of doing any such thing, so I held my tongue.

She'll have an explanation, I told the lurking cynical part of myself that thought this expedition was a bad idea. *I just have to trust Min.*

The eerie emptiness of the ship reached an abrupt end when we reached the brig. There were two security officers slumped at their posts, also unconscious. I almost stepped in front of Min to shield her in case anyone recovered unexpectedly, but she gestured for me to stay back.

"Time to do my thing," Min muttered.

Trust Min.

I looked around. All the cells were empty. I didn't know what the *Haetae*'s record of disciplinary actions was, but I liked to think that the brig was used as a last resort.

Like when someone's accused of treason, my annoying backbrain supplied.

Min made a call using her slate. "Special Investigator, could you have Jee unlock one of the brig cells?"

A pause, then, "It should be done," Yi replied.

Indeed, one of the doors opened. The cell almost looked enticing.

Min led me there. "In you go," she said. "It's for your own protection."

"It's for my own protection," I repeated. I couldn't help it. I was smiling again. The bars would keep me safe from all but the most ferocious of enemies.

I walked into the cell, then turned around to face Min, wondering what she had in mind.

The door snapped shut with an ominous click. Min stared at me from the other side of the bars. This time there was no trace of friendliness in her voice. "Now, Sebin," she said, "you're going to tell me everything you know about the traitor Captain Hwan."

TEN

I stared out at Min. My lips curved into that smile again. "What do you mean?" I wasn't trying to be obstructive. I needed to know what she was after so I could answer her as completely as possible. "He's my uncle. I've known him since I was a cub."

Min bit her lip, and I smelled her impatience. "I mean his plot to sabotage the *Haetae*."

"I don't know anything about that," I protested. Her brows drew down, and I hastily added, "I can't believe he's gone renegade."

She slitted her eyes at me. "You're telling the truth?"

"Of course," I said, injured that she doubted me. Why would I lie to Min of all people? I had to convince her that I wanted to cooperate. "I tried to warn Captain Chaewon, but—"

Min inhaled sharply. "You tried to warn the captain about what?"

I stood straighter, glad to have found something of interest to her. "It was before I was sworn in," I said. My scar ached, but I ignored it. "We were interrupted by the alarms going off."

Min's nod indicated that I should continue.

"Earlier," I said, "I smelled my uncle's territorial mark in one of the corridors. I thought the captain should know, just in case she wasn't aware, but I never got the chance to tell her."

Min smelled even more strongly of suspicion, although I couldn't tell why. After all, I was doing my best to be honest. "You didn't think to mention this to anyone else?" she asked.

"I wasn't sure what was going on," I confessed. "I'd heard that some people suffer strange hallucinations during Gate transitions. This is only my second time on a starship. I couldn't be certain it wasn't a figment of my imagination."

Min huffed. "You could have told Special Investigator Yi."

"I was so worried about the status of the bridge that it didn't occur to me," I said. That was the truth. "Besides, I don't think my uncle would stoop to sabotage!"

"Wake up!" Min shouted. Her voice reverberated in the confines of the brig. "Who else could it have been?"

"He's my *uncle*!" I shot back. I had to make her see there had been a grave misunderstanding. "He's never harmed me. I don't know what's going on with the board of inquiry, but I can't believe he'd turn his back on a long and honorable service as a Space Forces captain. And he could have taken all of us out easily a few minutes ago if he'd wanted to, but instead he ran. There's got to be more to this."

"'Long and honorable service,'" Min repeated derisively.

My hackles rose. "It's true," I insisted.

"You clearly don't know your uncle as well as you think you do."

I frowned. "What do you mean?" A nagging tendril of doubt insinuated itself into my thoughts. After all, there was no reason my uncle should be on the *Haetae*. I'd never heard that the captain had authorized him to board the ship. So at minimum he was a stowaway, and one wanted by the authorities, even if I didn't know why.

"Your *uncle*," Min said, her voice sharpening on the word, "attempted to steal a powerful artifact and use it for his own ends instead of turning it over to the proper authorities in the Thousand Worlds. He wanted to destroy his enemies rather than use it peacefully to terraform worlds so they could become fertile and prosperous."

Chills went down my back. There was only one artifact she could be referring to. "The Dragon Pearl?" I whispered.

I'd never thought much about the Dragon Pearl before, dismissing it as a legend. Even if it had really existed, it hadn't been spotted in centuries, ever since the shaman Hae had vanished with it. I hadn't heard of it turning up lately, but then, I'd also lived an isolated life on the family estate, so that didn't mean anything.

On the other hand, the Dragon Pearl was said to have the power to transform entire planets, whether into uninhabitable wastelands or lush biospheres strewn with forests and meadows. I could easily imagine it being used as a weapon. My blood chilled as I thought of the Pearl devastating a settled world. I didn't know if it could kill the inhabitants outright, but it wouldn't take much experimentation for someone to find out.

"The Dragon Pearl," Min affirmed with a sharp nod.

"You're not saying it's on the *Haetae* and Uncle Hwan came here to steal it?" I asked, guessing wildly.

"As if the Thousand Worlds would leave such a valuable artifact lying around," Min said, sniffing. Still, I caught a whiff of regret. "And as if I'd tell *you*."

"How do you know all this?" I asked, ignoring a twinge of hurt at her scorn.

Min's mouth thinned for a moment. "Let's say I've had run-ins with Hwan before. I thought I'd seen the end of him, but obviously I was wrong."

I bristled at the blunt way she spoke his name, without an honorific. Even if he had been stripped of his rank. "You're wasting your time here," I said. "I didn't have anything to do with the sabotage. You should let me out so I can help. Every pair of hands"—or paws—"might make a difference when we don't know who the enemy is."

"Listen to yourself," Min said. The smell of frustration strengthened. "You may not have been aware of helping him, but Hwan took advantage of your presence."

"That doesn't make sense," I objected.

"He was clearly signaling *you* with this scent mark," Min said. "Not just leaving his smell behind, the way all of us do, but deliberately marking a place territorially, like a cat."

I nodded reluctantly. "But anyone with a good sense of smell would have picked that up."

"Not everyone would have recognized it," Min said.

A niggling thought pushed its way to the forefront of my consciousness. "Did *you* recognize it?"

"Don't be ridiculous," Min said. "I'm human. My sense of smell isn't that good."

"Of course," I said. I didn't know why I'd thought otherwise. If Min claimed to be human, she had to be telling the truth.

I heard a buzzing from . . . Min's pocket?

"Oh, of all the—" Min checked herself, then pulled out her slate. Her brow furrowed, then she muttered a curse and withdrew so she could read whatever the message was in private.

I blinked slowly, trying to get my bearings as Min drifted

out of sight. I listened to her footfalls. She moved lightly for a human. But then, some humans had that kind of physical control. I assumed it was part of her training as a Domestic Security agent.

Min was talking in a low voice. I strained to hear her but could only recover fragments and snippets. "... Hwan's plans ... before the next ... as you say."

I shook my head and flexed my fingers, wondering what Min had in store for me. The longer she was away, the more a haze lifted from my brain. I'd followed her so meekly, without questioning her. I'd been so sure she had nothing but the best intentions. I wasn't the distrustful sort, but that wasn't like me.

She's your friend, whispered one voice in my head, while another insisted, *Something's wrong.*

The last shreds of fog lifted. She'd done something to me! I didn't know what. Some kind of trick. How could I have fallen for it? I'd even trapped myself in this cell, where I couldn't retaliate.

Anger boiled inside me. But I couldn't let Min know. As much as I was tempted to shift into a tiger and charge the bars of my cage, I knew that wouldn't make a difference. No— better to feign cooperation and try to wring some concessions from her.

How did she do that, anyway? Then I shuddered as the answer occurred to me. Min must be a gumiho, a fox spirit. Fox magic was the only kind I'd heard of that had that effect on people. It was called Charm. Foxes had been driven off, possibly even exterminated, not only due to their versatile shape-shifting powers, which they inevitably used for trickery, but because of their ability to Charm people into doing anything. I had thought there were no more gumiho in the Thousand Worlds, but what better way for tricksters to hide themselves than by letting everyone think they had vanished?

I had to get word to Jee and the others. Especially to Special Investigator Yi—

I stopped cold. What if Yi already knew their assistant was a gumiho? I didn't have any definite proof, but the fact that Yi had been so comfortable sending Min with me, and without backup, was telling. As was Yi's confidence that she could get answers out of me, even if she hadn't believed a word I said.

I was still thinking furiously when Min returned. Cold horror gathered like a lump in the pit of my stomach. I didn't know of any defense against Charm. Perhaps such things had once existed, but gumiho had been considered extinct for so long that I'd never heard of countermeasures for their powers.

Perhaps I could fool Min by pretending to be under her thrall, so she would grow overconfident and lax in her use of Charm. For the first time, I wished I'd paid more attention to history and religion lessons. I'd never been much interested in either, except as they pertained to battles.

I looked up and gave Min my most dazzled smile, or my best guess at one. It should have worked.

Instead, Min's breath huffed out in an exasperated sigh, and suddenly I couldn't look away from her face. I'd doubted her . . . but why? She hadn't done anything suspicious at all. There had to be some reasonable explanation, as with Uncle Hwan.

"You figured it out, didn't you?" Min said in a hard voice.

"Figured what out?" I said. But I knew.

She lowered her voice. "That I'm a fox spirit. That we weren't exterminated by people like you. That we *survived*."

My eyes widened. I should have been paying attention. Instead, I spotted a faint shape coalescing next to her, with features very like hers. This one was a Space Forces cadet, with a uniform like mine, except he had long, unkempt hair and legs that trailed off into shadows, as though he had no feet. His name tag read CADET KIM JUN, and he was shaking his head, lips moving although I couldn't quite hear the words. A cold wind gusted past me.

"A ghost," I breathed.

Min flinched. "Jun-oppa!" she snapped. The address she used told me that he was her elder, despite his lowly rank—her older brother, in fact.

The ghost spoke. "Sebin doesn't mean us any harm," he said. "Leave them alone, Min."

She pursed her lips. "I don't think Sebin's quite as innocent as you think, Jun."

"If you let me out, I can help," I said again, determined not to give up.

"At the very least," Min went on, "the fact that Sebin knows about you and me is a problem. Now I have to persuade them to keep quiet."

Jun shook his head. "If you hadn't used Charm in the first place—"

"I had no choice!"

"It's fine," I assured Jun. "I don't mind."

I'd never seen a ghost face-palm before. I was impressed that his hand didn't go right through his head. Then again, I'd never met a ghost before, period.

I wondered abstractedly why the ghost's presence didn't bother me. It should have freaked me out, given that the dead only lingered in the mortal realm when they had unfinished business. In all the old tales, that usually resulted in bad luck for any people they haunted. Indeed, the Matriarch had summoned a shaman once a year to placate any spirits that might be hanging around the estate. I wondered now what my family did that might attract unruly ghosts.

Still, Jun didn't seem particularly otherworldly, other than the fact that I could see through him and the way his legs trailed off into a misty nothingness. Then I reconsidered. I had attributed it to a quirk of the life-support systems, but a chilly breeze circulated around him. The cold made me shiver with its intimation of winter and the cavernous dark of the dead.

Jun's nose twitched, and then he sneezed. I hadn't known that ghosts could do that, either! "You should stop now," Jun chided Min. "After all, it's not like Cadet Sebin can *do* anything to you from in there. I think we've gotten as much information out of them as we're going to at this point."

Min was seething, but she nodded. Still, she hadn't finished arguing. "I can't believe how accommodating you want to be," she said, her tone sullen. "After all the things that Hwan did to you, too—"

My ears would have pricked if I'd been in tiger form. Did my uncle do something to hurt Jun? Could he possibly have caused . . . the cadet's death?

A different possibility occurred to me. What if Jun had been one of my uncle's crew members? Jun could have died during a legitimate mission. That would explain his lack of animosity toward Uncle Hwan, or me.

"Min, you have to let go," Jun said after a worried glance in my direction. "I don't like being dead any more than you like me being dead. Dwelling on it will only worsen our luck."

Was *this* why the cruise had been such a disaster from the outset? Because the ship was carrying around a ghost, with all the bad luck it implied? That would explain a lot, actually.

Jun glanced at me again and added, "Maybe we should have this conversation elsewhere."

"Then I can't keep an eye on them," Min said. She shook her head. "If your control hadn't slipped, I could afford to turn my back on Sebin. As it stands, we can't risk them telling the others about you."

"It's not like the others are here, or likely to head here any-time soon," Jun pointed out.

Crystals of frost had started forming in the air. And this time Jun's voice echoed hollowly in a way it hadn't before. And his teeth . . . I stared in fascination at the way his teeth length-ened and distended his mouth. Maybe he wasn't as friendly as I had assumed.

Nevertheless, Jun drifted away from my cell, and Min trailed after him.

Is he her keeper, or the other way around? I wondered.

I tried to eavesdrop, but no luck. Since they were aware that I had tiger senses, they spoke so softly even I couldn't over-hear them.

In my pants pocket I stroked the hilt of the knife Aunt Sooni had given me, but I didn't take it out. It wouldn't be of any use in this situation. Thinking of my aunt brought me some comfort, though.

Another, more disquieting thought occurred to me. Jun had mentioned bad luck. What if the so-called sabotage wasn't my uncle's fault, but Min and Jun's? Jun didn't *sound* like he wanted to take the ship down with everyone in it. Still, maybe ghosts didn't have a choice in the matter, just as tigers didn't have a choice about having stripes and a tail. However benign his intentions, the fact remained that Jun's presence posed a threat to the ship—a ship that was already in trouble.

The mist cleared from my thoughts again. Even if Special Investigator Yi knew that Min was one of the reviled gumiho, Yi might not know about the ghost. At least, I surmised that Min had been keeping Jun's presence a secret until he unexpectedly manifested in front of me.

I didn't know Min's story, or Jun's. If they were sister and brother, I could think of many reasons why she'd want to protect him. Just as I wanted to give Uncle Hwan the benefit of the doubt, whatever he might be up to. But the fact remained that the ship's welfare came first.

Even if I couldn't get out of here, I needed to contact whoever was in charge.

Had Min and Jun left? I didn't know, but I had to chance it. "Excuse me!" I bellowed, projecting for all I was worth. I had to hope that someone had regained consciousness and was in a position to help me. "Is anyone there? I have an urgent message for whoever's in charge!" I would have sounded more credible if I could have named someone specific, but I didn't want to confuse the issue by asking for Captain Chaewon when she was probably on her way to sick bay.

"I told you Sebin was untrustworthy!" I heard Min hissing, presumably at her brother, and my heart sank. "Nice try, Sebin," she yelled back to me. "You're nothing but a traitor." Then I heard her departing footsteps.

ELEVEN

That was how I wound up in the brig on the first day of my very first cruise, after making it into the Space Forces. How my dream of starting as a lowly cadet and working my way up through the ranks to earn my own ship was smashed before it even began. After everything that had befallen the *Haetae*, I would be lucky if my superiors condescended to let me scrub the decks for the rest of my life—or worse. And that was assuming we survived.

I gripped the cell's bars. The lights kept flashing red, giving the entire brig a surreal aspect. I wished I could squeeze my eyes shut against the painful assault of light. Open them to a world that made sense.

But wishing never made anything so, unless maybe you were a shaman, and even shamans had to enact the proper rituals and appease the spirits. The only path left to me was action.

My world had narrowed to the cell's confines. Min and Jun had left me here, easy pickings. I wondered again who had attacked the ship. Even if Uncle Hwan were responsible, which I doubted, surely he couldn't have acted alone. And if he wasn't to blame, the perpetrators could be anyone.

I stared at the bars as though the heat of my desperation could melt them. Alas, no tiger had that power. I changed into tiger shape and smashed against the bars, to no avail. They held fast.

That was just as well, anyway. If the ship came apart that readily, I would have had serious qualms about its spaceworthiness. I knew intellectually that space was a hostile environment for all but those of celestial blood, like Euna. These days, even people descended from heavenly attendants preferred to go into a vacuum clad in spacesuits and full oxygen tanks, and they didn't venture into Gate space at all. Here, trapped by metal walls, I realized how fragile a battle cruiser was. The starship was all that stood between us and the hostile environment outside.

"I'm going to make this right," I said to the silence. I couldn't hear any guards talking or scuffing their heels against the deck, which would at least have reassured me that I wasn't completely alone. "Whatever it takes. Even if it means I never get a starship command."

It might be too late to salvage my reputation, or that of the Juhwang Tiger Clan, but that no longer mattered. One of the legendary gumiho was on board, and I had to get out of here and warn the others before she Charmed them, too.

I gathered myself again and smashed into the bars. They held firm. I could feel the bruises smarting beneath my hide, tough as it was. They didn't hurt too badly—yet. I was sure that would change once the adrenaline wore off.

Fight smarter, I told myself. A battle cruiser's brig would be equipped to hold even crew members with supernatural strength like dragons or goblins or tiger spirits. Crashing my way out of this prison wasn't going to happen. Which left—

Before I could complete my thought, a draft gusted into my cell. I stiffened. I'd had enough time in here to acclimate to the normal patterns of air circulation, which was to say not very much at all. If anything, the air down here was stifling when there weren't people moving about. Had Min and her ghostly brother returned? Maybe I could trick them into letting me out. . . .

Then the scent reached my nose. I cringed from the bars, crouching down low in preparation to—I wasn't sure. Bow like younger to elder, perhaps, or spring into an attack? It could have been either. For the smell belonged to Uncle Hwan.

"Sebin," Hwan rumbled as he came into view.

Uncle Hwan had come for me, just as he had promised. It was all I could do not to melt in relief.

I had seen Uncle Hwan in his human form many times before, but not like this. Not as an interloper. On his visits home, he'd always appeared in uniform. I'd never questioned that. After all, as a member of the Space Forces, he was entitled to it.

Now, however, Uncle Hwan was clad in a gray shirt and slacks that did little to hide his impressive physique. Even if I'd been an ordinary human, a stranger, I would have recognized him as a tiger, and not just from his amber-tinged eyes. The only embellishments were a communicator that winked gold at his wrist and the telltale bulge of a blaster beneath his shirt. I had no doubt he could retrieve the latter at a moment's notice.

The one thing that marred his physical perfection was a bandage along the side of his jaw. I remembered Min clipping him with her blaster. I clenched my teeth. I would make her pay for that.

"Uncle?" I asked, just to be sure. "Is that you?" Ordinary

tigers couldn't speak, not in any of the human tongues. As a tiger spirit, however, my supernatural nature allowed me to speak to another of my kind, just as Uncle Hwan and I had conversed on the bridge.

"Of course it's me," Hwan said.

I resumed human shape. Sure enough, I ached all over from banging into the bars of the cell.

"I see that Min and her compatriots didn't waste any time making false accusations against you, when they are the ones endangering this ship," Hwan added.

How does he know that? I wondered. The ship's surveillance system?

Still, I considered his words. Min's use of Charm had proven she couldn't be trusted. She had to be up to something more sinister after all, even if she wasn't the one responsible for the ship's sabotage.

Are you sure he's telling you the truth? one side of my mind asked, while the other countered, *Would your own uncle lie to you?*

Besides, everything Min had done had convinced me that she was the real enemy. For all I knew, Uncle Hwan had come aboard the *Haetae* in an attempt to stop her. That made more sense than Min's wild accusations.

"You have history with Agent Min, Uncle?" I ventured.

Hwan laughed harshly. "She's going around as a Domestic Security agent these days? *That's* new."

"What do you mean?" Was she an impersonator? That possibility hadn't occurred to me, but it made sense. A fox spirit would not only be able to take the shape of another person, or an invented one, but also persuade people that she was the real deal. The prospect made me sick. On the other hand . . . "Are you sure they didn't recruit her on the strength of her abilities?"

"It's possible," Hwan said, scowling. "Some fool might have thought of her as an asset, without considering the ways in which she's a tremendous liability. She infiltrated the *Pale Lightning* on my last cruise and masqueraded as a member of my crew. *She's* the reason I was ousted from my rightful place as its captain. In the course of her adventures she stole the Dragon Pearl, which I was attempting to secure for the clan's use. Who knows what she did with it. . . ."

"And the sabotage of the *Haetae?*" I pressed. If my uncle was involved in any way, I needed to know.

Hwan's voice lowered. "It's only temporary. I couldn't allow a *fox spirit* to take control of a fully operational battle cruiser."

I hid my shock. So he'd done it after all, even though I had to admit he made a compelling argument. I decided to keep him talking, hoping he'd let more information slip . . . even if I didn't know what I would do with it.

"Surely putting the ship in danger puts you in danger as well," I said. I didn't have to feign my concern. After all, I was on the ship, too. But he knew battle cruisers inside and out. And no matter what, Hwan was still my uncle. He was the only one I could trust now.

"The danger is within acceptable parameters," Hwan assured me.

I shivered. *Acceptable parameters* sounded like it could excuse an awful lot. "But why—"

A snarl escaped Hwan. I remembered the way my parents would growl when I questioned them, and I thought I'd pushed him too far. But instead he said, "The Space Forces thought they could take my ship from me. That I would accept being stripped of my captaincy. But no tiger of the Juhwang Clan would simply let them do it." His lips drew back into a slow smile. "So I decided to take a ship for my own."

"You wouldn't," I breathed in disbelief. "You can't just *take* a ship." A moment later it occurred to me that contradicting my uncle wasn't a smart move, not if I wanted him to let me out of here.

"Can't I?" Hwan said, raising an eyebrow. "It's as good as done."

As good as . . . "By yourself?" I asked, eyes widening in awe. It wasn't as much of an act as I would have liked. I couldn't help but be impressed by the way he had so efficiently taken out the ship's bridge crew—its nerve center.

"Allies await me on the other side of the Gate," Hwan said. "The question is, Sebin, will you be one of them? You *are* family, after all. Hold out your hand."

I did. The scar throbbed painfully. He held his hand out as well, displaying a faint matching scar of his own.

"I swore by the White Tiger of the West," I whispered.

Hwan's voice dropped to a persuasive purr. "You've trained so diligently since you were a cub. It would be a shame for all that potential to be wasted."

"But Uncle," I said, "what can you possibly do with a single battle cruiser? You'll be hunted by the Space Forces. And won't you need a crew?"

Hwan grinned ferociously. "Remember what I told you, Sebin. A captain frequently acts alone. Joint actions are rare. A single captain and his crew could still accomplish great deeds and bring glory to the clan by fighting raiders. And I have allies who will reveal themselves in due course. In time, still others will join our banner. Imagine it!"

I could. I did, in fact, remember the stories he'd told me of desperate battles at the border, where it was just Captain Hwan and the *Pale Lightning* against the brigands who dogged the Thousand Worlds' borders. He'd always prevailed in the past, so why not now?

Besides, pragmatically speaking, he was offering me a way out. Not just from the brig, but from the dead end of my naval career—after only one day!—thanks to Min's interference. Why not?

"Well, Sebin?" Hwan asked.

"I would be honored," I said, trying to hide the tremor that went through my legs. Hwan might be my uncle, but he was still a tiger. I knew better than to display raw fear in front of a fellow predator, especially one older and deadlier than I was. "I could learn much from you." The scar on my hand ached all the way down to the bone.

"You could indeed," Hwan said. "Let me get you out of there."

I didn't want to know what had happened to the two guards slumped on the deck at the checkpoint. Had Hwan dispatched them on his way in? *Please don't be dead*, I thought as we approached them. He'd left the crew on the bridge alive, hadn't he? I wasn't sure what that signified. It could be simple pragmatism—avoiding their vengeful ghosts, or the knowledge that the Space Forces would stop at nothing to destroy him if he went so far as to kill his former compatriots.

I wasn't done with questions, but I limited myself to one. "Captain," I said. I saw by the gleam in his eyes that he was not unaffected by the appeal to his ego. Besides, he really had been a captain not so long ago, and he was going to resume his role, if not in a conventional manner. "Just one more question."

I'd caught him in an indulgent mood. "Ask, and then we must hurry to secure the ship."

I felt a twinge of guilt. But surely my uncle wouldn't cause permanent harm to anyone unless they provoked him.

Is that your real motive for going along with him? asked a cynical voice in the back of my head. *Protecting people? Or do you just like to feel important?* "What are you going to do with Min?"

"Min?" Hwan smiled. "I have uses for her. Think about it, Sebin."

Uses for her. The words echoed in my mind as I trotted after my uncle. I had a long stride, but so did he, even as a human, and I didn't want him to think me weak. That had been a running theme in my childhood. As much as I loved my family, from my parents to Aunt Sooni and the various elders, I'd always gotten the impression that the weak were to be pitied at best, scorned at worst.

As we left behind the two guards, I sneaked a glance at them to see if they were still breathing. To my relief, I saw their chests rise and fall slightly. I hoped they'd receive medical attention soon. Interestingly, Hwan didn't seem concerned about further resistance from anyone.

"How did you . . . uh, put them out of action?" I ventured, hoping he'd indulge another question.

"The ship has defense measures against boarders," Hwan said. "Knockout gas. But it can be turned against the crew, if they're not prepared."

"And I wasn't affected because . . ."

Hwan smiled warmly at me. "I would never let any harm come to you. I knew exactly where you were holed up."

So Min had been telling the truth about that, if nothing

else. I remembered her muttering about the gas. My thoughts turned to my uncle's cryptic comments about how he could use her powers.

Unlike other supernaturals, foxes weren't physically intimidating in their native forms. However, they made up for it with the versatility and strength of their magic. Min and Uncle Hwan hated each other, so she would never willingly cooperate with him. But what if my uncle could gain control of her somehow, and compel her to use her powers for his benefit?

Tigers didn't have Charm, so I didn't see how that could happen. But it might explain why he hadn't simply killed the unfortunates who had gotten in his way. Hwan could only have snuck a limited number of allies aboard using his inside knowledge of battle cruiser layout and security protocols. Therefore, he might need to rely on the *Haetae*'s existing crew, and Min could be his key to dominating them.

No wonder the Domestic Security Ministry was so desperate to corral him. Hwan was uniquely positioned to cause devastating damage to the Space Forces. If he ever sold military secrets to the Thousand Worlds' enemies, like the Phoenix Empire or the Sun Clans . . .

I shied from the implications. He wouldn't go that far. No, he was betting on being able to control Min. I could see the plot now. Once he had secured her cooperation, he could have her use Charm on his behalf. Unless someone in the crew had a secret defense against it, everyone would be helpless to resist Min's magic. Presumably that would buy him enough time to reach his mysterious allies and replace everyone with a crew that was actually loyal to him.

Which left the problem I had wondered about earlier. How

did Uncle Hwan intend to control Min? What was his secret weapon?

I didn't realize I had said this out loud until I heard Hwan chuckle darkly. "A good question," he said. "You are right to be wary, Sebin, considering the malevolence of a fox spirit's magic. Your quickness of thought will be an asset."

I glowed at his praise, something I had rarely received at home.

"Fortunately, my colleague has found a countermeasure," he added.

Colleague? I hadn't seen or smelled anyone.

The question must have been evident on my face, for Hwan said, "You'll meet her soon. In the meantime, we must stay out of range of Min's power. Which, for now, means staying out of sight."

That was the first good news I'd heard all day. Sort of. At least Min's magic had limits. I'd had some terrible vision of her being able to Charm the entire ship at once. But if so, surely she would have done so already.

We eventually reached one of the *Haetae*'s cargo bays. "What are we doing here?" I asked as Hwan punched in the access code. We both slipped inside.

My tiger eyes adapted easily to the dim light. The red alarms flashed even here. All I could see were barrels labeled MATTER PRINTER PARTS, THIS SIDE UP, and DO NOT INGEST.

I heard a slight metallic tap. I also noticed that each of the barrels had a perforated panel. Breathing holes. Beneath the stink of metal and circuitry, I could smell people.

Uncle Hwan had figured out a way to smuggle collaborators on board after all.

TWELVE

I lost my voice for a second as I surveyed the cargo bay, counting and calculating furiously. How many people had Uncle Hwan snuck aboard? And where had they come from? I hadn't heard of any mass defections from his original ship, the *Pale Lightning*, but then again, that was the sort of thing that the Space Forces would have kept quiet.

A rustling noise interrupted my count. A small figure stepped out from shadows I hadn't even seen. They were wrapped in layers of silk. The golden embroidery on their clothes should have made them easy to see. Instead, I hadn't so much as smelled them.

Now that I was aware of their presence, though, My nose tickled with the unsettling sensation of magic. Crouched by the figure's side was a shaggy tan dog. Its ears pricked as it came forward to sniff at me and Uncle Hwan.

"This is Shaman Sena, my partner," Hwan said. "She can stop the gumiho." He inclined his head to her.

The dog barked imperiously.

"And Shield, of course," Hwan added, gesturing at the dog. "A Sapsali. He has powers against evil spirits and ghosts."

The dog's tongue lolled out in a grin.

I bowed deeply to Sena. My previous encounters with shamans had been glancing at best. My parents had sequestered me in my room on the yearly occasions when the Matriarch invited them over to banish unlucky influences, and Aunt Sooni had tried to distract me with board games. I'd peered curiously from the window as the shamans chanted and danced and spoke for the ancestors, but I'd come to the conclusion that I didn't want to mess with people who crossed over so easily into the realm of the dead.

Great-Uncle Myung had reinforced my decision by telling me that a shaman wouldn't hesitate to turn my stripes green if I annoyed them. The threat had impressed me so much that I had never dared try to talk to one before. I was half tempted to turn tiger right now and check the color of my stripes, just in case.

"Who is the youngling?" Sena asked. Her voice was cold and raspy. I could smell her displeasure.

"Cadet Sebin," Hwan said. "My kin. They will be assisting me."

"If you insist," Sena said.

Shield, less easily mollified, growled at me. I wasn't usually afraid of smaller creatures, but this wasn't merely a dog—it was a *shaman's* dog. And as a Sapsali, it had magic of its own.

"It's time," Hwan said crisply, gesturing at the barrels.

Sena nodded.

Time for what? I almost asked.

The answer revealed itself soon enough. About half the barrels split open, as though they were monstrous eggs. The image was more apt than I realized, for the barrels transformed into metal carapaces armoring the enormous humanoid figures within. Soon I was confronted by a unit of some forty-odd soldiers of a type I had never seen before.

"These are your allies, Captain?" I asked in a hushed voice.

"Mercenaries outcast from the Sun Clans," Hwan confirmed. "They have joined their destinies with mine in exchange for a place on this ship."

I stared at the mercenaries, transfixed. Each one was encased in a spiky gray-black metal helmet and armor, cleverly articulated around the joints so they could move without impediment. It made them resemble giant horned beetles. I wasn't sure whether the transformation from barrel into armor was magic or technology, or some eldritch combination of the two.

Hwan wasn't going to depend solely on Min to Charm the entirety of the *Haetae* into submission. He also had a strike force to back him up. I had to admit it was a clever plan—I would have done the same in his place.

Hwan said something to the mercs in a foreign language. One of them responded likewise. I was starting to wonder how much I didn't know about my uncle.

I had little opportunity to ponder the question before Hwan snapped out more words—I didn't need a translation to recognize orders when I heard them—and the mercs formed up into squads of five each. They moved out, marching in effortless cadence.

A flicker of unease passed through my mind. I knew that going rogue and hijacking a ship was a capital offense in the Space Forces. Conspiring with foreigners to take over said ship—they wouldn't forgive that, either.

But what if the alternative was leaving the ship at the mercy of a fox spirit? Especially one who might be after a powerful artifact like the Dragon Pearl for her own purposes? I recalled her smell of regret when she'd spoken of it. Perhaps, and my spirits lifted at the thought, Hwan could redeem himself to the Space Forces if he foiled Min's plans. I just hoped the mercs, whom I knew nothing about, would cooperate.

"Are you sure you can trust them, Hwan?" Shaman Sena asked. She spoke to him as an equal, not as though she were a subordinate. That made sense—he'd introduced her as a partner. And a shaman was an authority in her own right, even though her purview was the supernatural world rather than the military.

"The mercenaries have their own code of honor," Hwan said.

I wasn't the only one who noticed the evasion. "Do you know if the gumiho's magic will work on them, too?" Sena said. "If it comes to that?"

"There's no reason it shouldn't," Hwan said, but I detected a thread of unease. "Power is power, whatever the form."

That gave me the unpleasant realization that I knew nothing about foreign magic. I couldn't tell whether this was because my family had limited my access to information about other systems, or whether it wasn't common knowledge within the Thousand Worlds, period.

"What happens now, Captain?" I asked. I wasn't sure I wanted to remind Hwan and Sena of my presence, but I didn't want to waste time, either.

"Now we hunt the gumiho," Hwan said.

My legs shook, and I wasn't sure whether it was dread or anticipation. Min had used Charm so casually on me. I never wanted to go through that again. "How . . . ?" I asked, reluctant to reveal my fear of falling under Min's sway, even though Hwan would be able to smell it.

Sena had noticed my hesitation. "You've had a run-in with the fox spirit? Can you track her?"

Hwan laughed dryly. "Sebin could, but it will be faster to locate her through the *Haetae*'s surveillance system. So far nobody has figured out how to undo the emergency override."

I filed that bit of information away in case it became useful later. I didn't see how, since it wasn't like anyone had entrusted *me* with the override to the override, assuming one even existed. But maybe something would come up.

Hwan pulled out a slate and entered commands. A holo image formed above the screen. It showed Min and Special Investigator Yi conversing in hushed voices as they walked down one of the many identical corridors. I was grateful for the fact that all the hallways had painted labels. This one was on level five. Even so, Hwan had the slate project a map next.

"Excellent," Hwan said, perusing the diagram. "We can trap them in this section of the ship." He pointed at the area they were passing through. "But we'll have to move fast to catch up with them."

The shaman nodded. Even the dog, Shield, bobbed his head as though he had understood what Hwan was saying.

We made an odd group as we hastened to the elevator that would take us to level five. Hwan led the way. While I was tall for my age, in his shadow I felt smaller and more helpless than I ever had before. It wasn't a sensation I was accustomed to, and I disliked it intensely. For the first time, I wondered what life was like for the smaller and more vulnerable—not to say *prey*—denizens of the Thousand Worlds.

He's my elder, I told myself. *I will learn from his example.*

We got into the elevator. Sena had to coax Shield into it. Hwan cleared his throat and glowered when Sena resorted to extending an extremely stinky dog treat. To my mortification, my mouth watered at the smell of meat, even if it was desiccated, and I tried not to think about how long it had been since I'd had a square meal. There was no way I was going to complain to my uncle about being hungry. I wanted to earn his approval.

Shield lunged for the treat, then gnawed happily on it, mollified.

As the elevator swooshed and I felt the telltale acceleration, I closed my eyes for a long moment. I allowed myself to imagine an alternate universe where my training cruise was going completely as planned, and I was doing something soothing, like wiping viewports clean. I'd generally been responsible for menial chores at home, because my parents insisted that it built character. I'd never thought I would miss doing them.

"What if they're ready for us?" Sena asked.

"They're not as ready as we are," Hwan responded, and that seemed to satisfy her. "You'll protect us. The gumiho is the biggest threat."

This intrigued me. I wasn't used to the idea of powerfully built Uncle Hwan relying on anyone else for protection. But then, I'd experienced Min's Charm. He was right to be wary.

As the elevator doors opened to level five, I racked my brain for anything that explained Hwan's unusual confidence. Maybe it was the dog. Could a Sapsali really be that effective against foxes?

For once I envied the more scholarly types. While I'd had the obligatory calligraphy practice and lessons in tactics, my family hadn't encouraged the study of magic or folklore. I'd had a guilty fondness for the adventure stories that Aunt Sooni told me at bedtime, but other than that . . .

This time, Sena took the lead. She left an almost electric thrumming in her wake, as though the very air molecules were singing. Perhaps they were. I was fuzzy on the details of how shamanic magic worked. Hwan strode half a step behind, close enough to spring into action if he needed to intervene. I brought up the rear, conscious of the fact that Shield was pacing me and not his master. Keeping an eye on me, I expected.

Hwan consulted the slate once more for Min's location. By then, however, I'd picked up her scent trail. Which meant my uncle had, too. I marveled anew at the way she smelled entirely human. Part of her shape-shifting magic, I guessed. Even in human form, most supernaturals, or people with some supernatural heritage, carried a whiff of otherworldliness around with them. No wonder people dreaded foxes so much. They could practice their malevolent schemes without going detected.

I wondered how many foxes remained in the Thousand Worlds. Min couldn't be the last of her kind—or could she? And if she was, could I really blame her for hiding her nature? But that didn't excuse the way she'd bewitched me with Charm.

"Slow down," Hwan whispered, barely audible.

The shaman strolled ahead as though she hadn't heard him. I started to call out a warning, then swallowed a yelp as Hwan clamped his hand over my mouth. I stilled.

"That was for you, Sebin," he said into my ear. "She has ways of protecting herself that people like you and I can only dream of. Stay out of sight in this corridor. Move when I signal you. Blink twice if you understand."

I blinked twice.

Uncle Hwan released me and dropped into a waiting

crouch. Although he appeared deceptively relaxed, I knew from sparring with Aunt Sooni that even in human form a tiger spirit could spring from that position into a deadly pounce with a moment's notice, or draw and fire a blaster. I'd also seen Hwan demonstrate his superior aim against the estate's target robots. I almost felt sorry for Min.

I could hear Min and the special investigator conversing, even though their words were muffled. Then they fell silent as the shaman walked toward them. Sena made no effort to soften her rather stompy footsteps.

One of the dubious advantages of existence on a starship was the controlled airflow. At the moment, Uncle Hwan and I were upwind (so to speak) of Min and Yi. Even if they suspected our presence, our smells wouldn't alert them.

"Stop right there," Min's voice called from around the corner. "Who are you?"

The shaman didn't answer. Instead, Shield growled, then burst into ear-shattering barking.

"What the—?" Min said, sounding shaken. Then: "We're not enemies—"

"Now," Hwan snapped. He shifted into his true shape of an immense white tiger and charged.

I became a tiger myself and followed, wondering what was going on.

Min was still talking, but I didn't feel compelled to obey her, or even to listen. Nor was I convinced that she was my best friend, or that she meant well. This time around, I felt remarkably clearheaded.

I did have to give Min credit for being quick-witted, though. She grasped that her fox magic had failed her and drew her own blaster. "Special Investigator, *run!*" she shouted. I could hear Yi's retreating footsteps as Min provided covering fire.

Hwan leaped toward her. Min scuttled backward with astonishing nimbleness, firing at his head.

Afterward, I couldn't say what made me jump in front of him. Habit, except I'd never been shot at before. Reflex, maybe, or family ties. I'd known all my life that I might be required to give up my life in the line of fire. I just hadn't expected that it would come so early.

The blast took me squarely in the forehead. Later I would learn that this had been pure bad luck—or maybe good luck from Min's viewpoint. While it would take more than a single blaster bolt to *kill* a tiger, it stopped me. I howled and fell to the deck, thrashing.

"I knew you were with him all along!" Min yelled, incandescent with fury. To be honest, by that point I only understood that she was angry. The pain blotted out any hope of coherent thought. And it didn't help that Shield was still barking his head off. I listened without really following what was going on.

"What did you do?" Min demanded.

"It's not about what we did," Hwan said after changing back to human form, his voice hellishly self-assured. "It's about what we're *going* to do."

Sena stooped and offered Shield another treat. It reeked, but in a delicious way, and it wasn't a meat I recognized. I might have started drooling at that point, because self-control was quite beyond me.

"Most people have forgotten how to protect themselves from gumiho," Sena remarked in her dry voice. "But some remember the old lore, and I happen to be one of them."

"'Happen to,'" Min said, sharp with scorn. "Tell me, what's the secret?" Her voice sounded distorted, almost like . . . the yipping of a fox?

Sena shrugged. "It's the dog. A dog can always smell a fox. And once Shield has recognized you, your powers are stripped away."

"But how can you understand me?"

"A simple translation spell," Sena said scornfully. "I am used to having to converse with all kinds of spirits, even your kind."

The pain receded. I sniffed the air. This time, as opposed to previously, I detected a pungent odor that could only be fox. It was not dissimilar to that of the dog.

My eyes focused. Min didn't just smell like a fox. She *was* a fox, crouched defensively with the blaster lying uselessly in front of her forepaws. She had a rust-colored pelt with black ears and black legs, and her white-tipped tail was tucked between her hind legs.

"If you think losing my magic makes me any less your enemy, Hwan," Min growled, "you are extremely mistaken."

Hwan scoffed. "How you feel about me is immaterial. But what about your brother, Jun?"

Min stopped growling. A whine escaped her. "You wouldn't."

I squinted. Next to Min I saw . . . another fox? Except unlike her, this one was translucent. A ghost. And not just any ghost, but the brother I had witnessed her talking to in the brig.

"You know exactly what I'm capable of," Hwan said. "Just so we're clear, if you don't put yourself and your powers at my disposal, I will have the shaman send your brother to his final rest."

THIRTEEN

Min's ears flattened against the back of her skull. "You're the one who got him killed in your quest for the Dragon Pearl." But she must have realized that Hwan would be unsympathetic, for she directed her next plea to the shaman. "Surely you can tell that my brother means no harm. He died before his time. Now he acts as my protector."

The shaman's eyes softened. When she spoke, it was with a rough sympathy I hadn't expected. "I know," she said. "Many ghosts linger because they were taken before their time. That injustice chains them to the realm of the living. It's my duty to help them reach peace and move on to the realm of the dead."

"No, no," Min moaned. "That's not what we want at all."

This time I wasn't paying attention to Min, though, but to her ghostly brother. He crouched at Min's side, the ends of his black legs dissolving into that wavering smoky haze, just as they had in human form. Unlike Min, he didn't look aggressive, just tired and uncertain.

"Maybe she's right," Jun said, his ears drooping.

I scarcely knew him, or how he'd come to die, but my heart

ached to see him so beaten down. No one should be reduced to that state, not even a ghost.

On the other hand, maybe the best thing for Jun would be to move on and take his place with the revered ancestors. He wouldn't be gone forever, after all. Rather, he'd dwell in the underworld with all the other ghosts. His family could perform the ancestral rites to reassure him that he was remembered. At least, I assumed that even foxes bowed to their ancestors' graves and made offerings of food and wine. But foxes might do things differently.

If Min was Jun's only remaining family, I could understand why she wanted to hold on to him so desperately. I tried to imagine losing my parents and Aunt Sooni, what it would be like if even Uncle Hwan were taken away from me. Just contemplating the possibility pierced my heart.

Min whined again. But the fight hadn't entirely gone out of her. "You promised you would see every one of the Thousand Worlds with me, Jun!" she said. "I'm not giving up on you that easily!"

Sena's expression hardened. "Your loyalty to your older brother does you credit." She almost sounded as though she meant it. "Think, though, of the rest he deserves. As long as he lingers in the world of the living, he will bring bad luck to you and everyone around you, no matter how good his intentions."

Sena pulled out a tiny sheet of paper that twinkled like a slip of starlight. I strained to see if anything was written on it, but it seemed to be blank. She snapped her fingers and the paper started to burn with a white flame, white for purity.

A soft moonish glow started up around Sena. It made her shine like a dream of faraway nights. I found I couldn't tear my eyes away from her.

The glow strengthened, and the shaman began to hum. Despite the lingering pain, my breathing slowed. Calm descended upon me.

I wasn't the only one affected by the ritual. Out of the corner of my eye, I could see that Hwan's face had gone slack. Even Shield had dropped what remained of his treat—not much—and was flat on the deck with his mouth agape.

And Jun—the target of this ritual—drifted in Sena's direction like a fish to a lure. He was a handsome fox, larger than his sister, his eyes gleaming in the shaman's moonlike glow. He started to fade from the outside in, as though someone had taken an eraser to him.

Min barked and leaped for the shaman. Even stripped of Charm and shape-shifting, she still had her teeth and claws. But Shield lunged for her. They fell to the deck together with the dog's fangs buried in Min's flank. She screamed.

The shaman lowered her hand, and the slip of paper stopped glowing.

Jun roused from his trance. "Min!" he cried, and stopped drifting toward the shaman. Although he remained translucent, his color brightened, and his outline became more distinct. He shook his head in confusion. "What . . . what . . ."

"You tricked my brother!" Min shrieked. "All that time you were pretending to talk to *me*, you were trying to exorcise him!"

The shaman smiled thinly back at her. "It wasn't a trick," she retorted. "That's what awaits your brother if you don't cooperate. Anyway, what were you expecting, singing and dancing and chanting like in the old days?"

That was exactly what I'd thought she needed to do to move Jun along. My few glimpses of shaman rites back home had involved people dancing while in elaborate, brightly colored

costumes and speaking with the voices of the gods that pos-
sessed them. But I also knew that there were different kinds of
shamans, and had been even in the old days, when their practices varied from region to region. Plus, the rites must have
evolved over the centuries since we'd left our home planet to
settle the Thousand Worlds.

Min glared at the shaman.

Sena continued, "My role is to ease the ghost's passage
to where he belongs. *With the dead.* If that means soft words
rather than a traditional dance, then so be it. But you can earn
a respite for him—if you work with us."

Jun looked from Sena to Min and back again. His outline
flickered, reflecting his uncertainty. "Min . . . ?"

"You see," Hwan interjected, "the shaman can guide your
brother to his rest at any time." Despite his smooth tone, it was
clear that he was making a threat.

Min wasn't done. "You had the shaman's dog neutralize our
magic to the point where we can't even appear in human form,"
she pointed out. "There's no way I can call on Charm to brainwash people to do your evil deeds, Hwan."

"You might ask yourself," Hwan said, his voice deceptively
pleasant, "why they're 'evil deeds' when you use Charm on my
behalf, but they're purely innocent when you use your corrupt
powers to control people for your own gain."

I shook myself, remembering how she'd used those powers
on *me*. Who knew how many people she'd Charmed during her
travels, and how much damage she'd caused along the way?

Instead of spitting back a retort, Min fell silent and lowered
her head.

"The dog will retreat enough for you to exercise your powers," Hwan said. "But if you show any sign of resistance, the

shaman will banish your brother. Behave, and she'll leave him alone. Are we clear?"

A strange realization pierced me. For all that Min had done to me earlier, right now I was more afraid of Uncle Hwan than her. Sure, I wasn't comfortable with Min's powers, but she'd thought I was a traitor. She might have believed that she had justification for Charming me to find out about his plans. And one thing I did know was that I wouldn't want to be Uncle Hwan's enemy.

Are you making excuses for a fox? I asked myself.

I didn't have to see Min's wide eyes to detect how frightened she was. The smell of her terror was overpowering. Even Shield whined in sympathy, and he was her natural enemy.

"I'll cooperate," Min said. She spoke softly, with none of the spunk she'd shown earlier. "Promise me that you'll leave my brother alone if I . . . if I do what you want."

Hwan nodded gravely, with the courtesy he would have shown any honorable opponent. "I swear it," he said, "on the honor of the Juhwang Tiger Clan."

I was relieved to hear the oath. It reaffirmed his belief in the importance of the clan, and of honor. After all, I told myself, blackmailing a fox wasn't *really* wrong. There was no other way for Uncle Hwan to ensure our safety from her wicked magic.

I felt a sudden sharp pang in my forehead, where I'd been blasted, and groaned involuntarily. Hwan's attention instantly fixed on me. "Sebin," he said. His obvious concern warmed me. "Are you all right?"

Rationally, I knew that I hadn't taken any lasting harm. And Uncle Hwan, with a predator's instinct, would have prioritized subduing any source of danger—Min, in this case—before checking on my welfare. It made tactical sense and was exactly the kind of decision-making that my upbringing had prepared me for.

Still, a part of me wished that he had asked a little earlier.

"That special investigator got away," Sena noted, her brow creased in displeasure.

"We'll take care of Yi in due course," Hwan said with chilling nonchalance.

I struggled to my feet, remaining in tiger form. I would be more formidable this way if something went south.

Hwan had returned his attention to Min. "Take me to your compatriots, then," he said. "Captain Chaewon."

Min blanched. "She's in sick bay," she said, her voice wavering. "She didn't react well to whatever you did to her. They were supposed to put her in a medi-coma." Min had recovered enough of her courage to glare at Hwan again. "Even if I Charmed her, she wouldn't be much good to you."

Hwan didn't say a word. Instead, he inclined his head at the shaman. Sena brandished the slip of white paper again.

Before today, it would have never occurred to me to describe a simple bit of paper as *menacing*. Here, however, it signified that the shaman was about to cleanse herself in preparation for a ritual. I wasn't sure she needed to do it again so soon after the last time, but it worked as a threat.

Min's tail was firmly tucked between her hind legs again. "All right," she said in defeat. "But you need to let me resume human shape. I'm no good to you if the *Haetae*'s crew shoots me for being, well, a fox."

I smelled the sharp acid flare of Hwan's distrust. For a moment I was afraid he would have Sena banish Jun anyway. But for all his suspicion, Uncle Hwan could see reason. He nodded curtly, without looking in Sena's direction. He didn't have to.

"Can your dog, er, turn off whatever it's doing?" Min asked.

I'd been wondering that myself.

Sena nodded and whistled to Shield. The dog pricked his ears. His mouth lolled open and he licked his chops suggestively.

I was impressed. Shield wasn't just the shaman's companion—he had a deal going with her. If I had the ability to stop a gumiho in her tracks, I'd milk it for all the treats I could, too. Especially since my rumbling belly reminded me that I was still hungry and unlikely to receive a decent meal, or even a terrible one, anytime in the near future.

"Really?" Sena asked with a sigh that made her look like an ordinary human again. "Now?"

Shield lifted a paw in an unmistakable *feed me* signal and barked twice.

Sena's eyebrows lifted. "*Two* treats?"

Shield wagged his tail.

Min was eyeing the dog as though she had decided it could be bribed. The thought had occurred to me, too.

"Fine," Sena said, sighing again. "You are the most spoiled dog in the Thousand Worlds, have I ever told you that? And I let you get away with it." But I could tell from the rueful indulgence in her voice that she loved the creature. She fished out two treats, which smelled at once disgusting and tasty.

I was tempted to lunge for one of them, but I didn't want to embarrass myself. Besides, who knew if the dog had supernatural powers against tiger spirits, too? I didn't know the extent of a Sapsali's abilities.

I'm not evil, I thought. Still, that didn't mean the dog knew that.

Before I could ponder this any longer, Shield made a peculiar whuffling sound and tore apart his first treat. I caught myself holding my breath as he did so, partly wondering what would happen next, and partly to keep from inhaling any more of the tantalizing odor.

At last Shield finished both treats and licked his chops again. Then he tilted his head back and uttered a mournful howl. The air around him shimmered as though obscured by secretive mists. Or, more accurately, as though mists that I hadn't noticed descending were now evaporating, leaving my vision clear.

As I blinked, Min's shape flickered in a way I found familiar from my experience of watching other shifters. When I looked at her again, she had resumed her human form: a teenage girl, her gray uniform slightly creased by everything she'd been through. This time I could smell a faint whiff of fox about her, no doubt due to the dog's protective influence. My nose hadn't been able to detect her true nature earlier.

"Lead on," Min said. Her mouth compressed into a tight, unhappy line. Despite the fact that she was my enemy, I couldn't blame her.

"Sebin, you know the way?" Hwan asked.

I was eager to prove my usefulness to him. Thank goodness I'd had a chance to pore over the map of the ship's layout earlier. "Yes, sir."

Min's eyes narrowed, but she didn't say anything.

Judge me if you want, I thought. If she hadn't abused her powers, Hwan wouldn't hold a grudge against her, and she wouldn't be in this fix. Someday I hoped to find out more about their shared history—I bet she'd done some absolutely terrible things—but now wasn't the time.

Like a dire parade, we proceeded toward sick bay. I disliked having the others at my back. At this rate I would develop a permanent itch between my shoulder blades. Still, I had to concede that I was the most expendable member of the group.

Uncle Hwan had command experience, to say nothing of being a full-grown tiger. Min's supernatural powers were more formidable than anything I could summon up. I wondered if her brother, Jun, retained his gumiho abilities even as a ghost. Shaman Sena's magic kept us safe from anything Min might try. Even Shield, with his anti-fox and anti-ghost properties, was more important than I was.

Another cadet might have found this disheartening. I did have to admit to a twinge of resentment. But I reminded myself how hierarchy worked, whether on a battle cruiser or in a situation like this one. A starship couldn't thrive with a captain alone, after all. It relied on everyone working together.

Great, we're working together, I thought with an edge of hysteria. *We're even about to "persuade" the real captain to work with us.*

We rounded a corner, and the hatch was before us. A sign with the round symbol for *longevity* told us that we had arrived at sick bay. I shifted back into human form. "This is Cadet Sebin," I announced, trusting that the intercom would convey my voice to whoever was inside. "I need to enter, please." Best not to get too specific.

My memory told me that the hatch should have opened automatically so as not to impede first responders. With some injuries, even seconds could mean the difference between life and death. On his past visits home, Uncle Hwan had told me about some hair-raising emergencies. Disembowelments, burns, amputations, the works. I'd never been certain whether or not he was exaggerating to keep me from getting overconfident.

I guessed that whoever lurked inside sick bay had reprogrammed the hatch to remain obdurately shut in case of intruders. In all fairness, there *were* intruders. Ones that Uncle Hwan had snuck aboard—which still made me uneasy because they weren't family, so I didn't know how reliable they were. What were the mercs up to now?

"They're not opening up," Min said, stating the obvious. "I hate to break it to you, *Hwan*, but I can't do anything to anyone through a closed hatch."

"I'm aware of that," Hwan said, a distinct edge to his voice. "Once you do act, however, you will make sure to spare Sena, Sebin, and myself from the effects of your Charm."

"I'm not sure I can—"

"You'd better figure it out." Then he added, "Sebin, everyone. Stand back."

I obeyed immediately. I recognized that tone, even if the others might not. The one that meant *Do as I say or I won't be responsible for the consequences.* I had heard it from time to time growing up, usually from the Matriarch or my parents.

This time, when Hwan transformed, it didn't take place instantly. He burned like the dense white heart of a star, hard to look at and impossible to look away from. His human form evaporated, revealed as a temporary shell, and stretched into the massive, muscled form of a white tiger.

Then he sprang at the door, claws flashing, and shredded the hatch off its hinges.

FOURTEEN

The metal screamed as the hatch was wrenched from the bulkhead. Hwan surged through the opening, which was scarcely wide enough for his bulk. After a shocked pause, blaster fire bombarded him. I smelled the scorched reek of his fur. But it wasn't enough to take him down.

"Now!" Hwan roared, full-throated, as he bounded toward the shooters. They started to scatter and hide.

I panicked for a moment, thinking he was ordering me to follow suit, but Hwan hadn't been addressing me. Min strode up behind him, her face white but resolute. "Sorry about that," she said to the people holed up in sick bay, speaking almost as rapidly as Special Investigator Yi did. "We're all friends, right? I'm just here to check on Captain Chaewon. Put your blasters away. You can come out now. It's safe."

A few people straightened and crept out from behind cover. I could still detect the residual stink of their terror, rapidly replaced by an unnatural calm. Their heartbeats slowed, their breathing steadied. All because of one fox spirit. The reminder of her unnatural power made me feel sick all over again.

I hid my dismay as I counted the small number of non-patients present. Only four wore the insignia of the medical corps. The rest were people I recognized: Ensign Hak, Jee, Namkyu, and Euna. Their arms hung slack at their sides. I was surprised to realize that there were only three blasters for the entire group. It had felt like more when fire had rained down on Hwan. Euna still had her glare pistol, but she must have elected not to use it so she wouldn't blind her own side as well.

I saw no sign of the special investigator. Had something happened to Yi, or had they managed to hide somewhere else? I decided to keep my mouth shut rather than distract my uncle, who was changing back to human form. He'd deal with Yi in his own time.

My own pulse was still racing, this time because my old comrades *weren't* defending themselves. *Make up your mind,* I told myself irritably. *You can't have it both ways!*

The shaman, who had hung back, finally entered with her dog. People gave Shield strange looks. I supposed it wasn't every day you saw a pet on a battle cruiser.

I had to calm myself so I could follow what was happening. Min was still speaking. She was good at talking people down, but her magic probably made the actual words irrelevant.

"C-Captain Hwan is here to take charge," Min went on. Her voice quavered only a little when she said his name.

Namkyu studied her with a puzzled line between their brows, as though they were looking at two plus two and wondering why they added up to spleen. I remembered that sensation, and my heart ached for Namkyu.

Uncle Hwan's plan had sounded so simple, so straightforward, when he'd explained it to me. Secure the ship. Turn

Min's powers against his enemies. Take the *Haetae* in search of glory for the clan.

But those "enemies" were my comrades. People like Jee and Euna—and Namkyu. I'd only known the other cadets for a day, and it wasn't like we were close friends, but they'd done nothing wrong. Like me, they'd come here for training and gotten embroiled in a lethal situation simply because of bad timing. Also, I knew how awful it felt when Charm wore off. Maybe Hwan had a history with Min, but using her against other people couldn't be right. . . .

I regarded the wounded. The thrilling prospect of joining Hwan against the universe seeped away. I couldn't go through with it, not at this cost.

My stomach roiled. My uncle had gone too far—and I'd gone along with him.

I should have known better. But maybe it wasn't too late to act.

"It's true that Captain Chaewon has a broken arm," Namkyu said, their brow furrowed. "But that doesn't mean she can't—"

"Captain Hwan needs to secure the crew's cooperation," Min said. I had to admit she was smooth. "Captain Chaewon could be suffering lingering effects from the knockout gas, so it's better for Hwan to take charge. We don't want there to be any confusion about the chain of command, do we?"

Namkyu's face cleared. "No, of course not."

"Glad that's settled." Min bit her lip, then asked, "Where's the XO?"

Looking back, I'm not sure of the exact moment when my plan shifted from working with Hwan to defying him. Maybe it was when I realized how far he had gone in his plot against the *Haetae*. Or when I saw how ruthlessly he used Min's regard for her older brother against her. Wasn't loyalty to family above all the great virtue that had been drilled into me?

Except, perhaps, when your family acted like this.

I stood frozen as Ensign Hak pointed out the XO, Commander Ae, resting on a pallet, their face pale and damp. Someone had hooked them up to a medical unit and covered them with a blanket. I couldn't see any obvious injuries, but throughout the sick bay I could smell blood and bile. These wounded must have been the unfortunate victims of the explosions I'd heard.

I'd never encountered those smells in association with people, only small prey like rabbits or voles, which we'd hunted to keep our reflexes sharp. (Also, the Matriarch enjoyed a good rabbit stew.) But we'd always dispatched our prey quickly so they didn't suffer. Here, agony permeated the air.

While Min talked, Hwan spoke in a low voice into his wrist communicator. Within moments, I heard footsteps, although those in the sick bay seemed oblivious. But the noise couldn't be denied forever.

A squad of eight mercenaries appeared at the hatch that Hwan had clawed open. My guts knotted at their presence. While the mercs' smell was more or less human, there was an alien quality to the reek of their armor. I still couldn't believe that my uncle had teamed up with mercs because he was so desperate for troops. That should have been my first clue that something was wrong.

I should have given Min the benefit of the doubt when I'd had the opportunity—even if she was unlikely to have let me join her, given my relationship to Hwan. I'd missed my best chance of making a difference.

And the odds of it ever happening kept getting worse and worse. I should have tried to free Min and Jun earlier, *before* the squad of mercenaries arrived. I may have been well-trained as a warrior, but clearly I lacked the tempering of real combat and good decision-making.

Aunt Sooni always liked to say that a good plan at the right moment was better than a brilliant plan two hours too late. I'd never dwelled on her advice before. Now I saw the wisdom in the saying.

"We acknowledge you as our new captain, sir," Ensign Hak said to Hwan as though nothing were out of the ordinary.

Hwan didn't waste time gloating. "Excellent," he said. "You will also defer to my personal guard." He gestured at the beetle-like armored mercs.

"Of course, sir." For a second, doubt flickered in Hak's eyes, but it subsided as Min turned a brilliant smile in her direction. I could smell Min's overpowering guilt. She was a convincing actor, but she couldn't control her scent as readily, not with Shield's magic inhibiting hers.

"Now to deal with loose ends," Hwan said, turning to me.

For a terrible moment, I thought he was going to have me killed, even though I'd been on his side up to now, even though tigers couldn't read minds—nobody could.

Hwan's mouth quirked in sardonic acknowledgment. As the apex predator present, he could scarcely help noticing my apprehension. "Special Investigator Yi is still at large," he said.

I bit down a curse. So he'd noticed after all. Yi's freedom might be our best chance of resistance.

"Sebin, I want you and Six to hunt down Yi and bring them to me." He picked up a slate from one of the nearby tables, tapped some commands into it, then handed it to me. "I've assigned you a higher security clearance so you can track Yi through the surveillance system."

One of the mercs detached themself from the group. Their helmet was painted with a curious hexagon symbol. This must be Six. They smelled like an older teen, perhaps a few years older than I was. I supposed that if the Thousand Worlds had thirteen-year-old cadets, mercenaries from the Sun Clans could have younger soldiers, too.

"I'd like to bring Cadets Jee, Namkyu, and Euna along, too, if I may, sir," I said, thinking quickly. "They each have a specialty that will be useful." The one I needed most was Jee, but it might make Hwan less suspicious if he thought I just wanted the company of my friends.

Hwan considered the matter. "And those specialties are . . . ?" he asked them.

"Communications," Jee said.

"Medical," Namkyu said, holding up the medkit they still carried.

Euna raised her head defiantly. "Weapons." She looked down at her glare pistol, then flushed. "I'm good with a blaster, too, but there weren't enough to go around."

"You're too useful here, Cadet Namkyu," Hwan said to them. "But Jee and Euna will accompany Sebin."

I winced at the implication that Jee and Euna weren't *useful* to Hwan. From the wry twist to Euna's mouth, she'd noticed, too. But she didn't say anything. For his part, Jee looked uncomfortable at being teamed up with me once more.

Besides, what mattered wasn't that Jee and Euna might be useful to my uncle, but that they were useful to *me*. Euna could back me up against the young merc named Six. I was pretty sure Six's job was to keep an eye on us. But I'd seen Euna's aim during our first confrontation with Hwan, and I was positive that my uncle was underestimating her.

As for Jee, he was the linchpin to the rest of my plan. Once the ship exited the Gate, we could send word to the nearest station, or any other ships in the area, and ask for help. The fact that Uncle Hwan had trusted me with Jee meant that he considered me reliable. Turning against my uncle didn't feel great, despite my new resolutions. But I had to snatch any advantage I could.

"We'll be off, sir," I said to Uncle Hwan with a painstakingly correct salute. I hoped he was too preoccupied to detect the thumping of my heart, or the nervous sweat that was trickling down my back and collecting in my armpits. I was going to need the world's longest shower when all this was over.

"Go," Hwan said with an affable nod.

We left him giving instructions to Min as the shaman stood like a statue by his side. I would be haunted by that image of the three of them later: Hwan at the height of his power; the shaman his willing accomplice, as I had been; and Min cowed into becoming his pawn.

I will fix this, I promised the world at large as we headed out into the corridor.

I didn't know how long Min's powers would continue to affect Jee and Euna, but I had to be careful around the entire squad, including Six, that Hwan had entrusted to me. If I made an obvious move against their new captain, the three of them might attack me.

As soon as we were out of earshot of sick bay, I turned to the merc and asked them, "Is your name really Six . . . ?"

The merc responded in a gruff voice. "You couldn't pronounce my name, Cadet Sebin." They had a slight accent, but I could understand them easily enough. They had no trouble with my name at all. Then Six added, "My name literally means *sixth-born*, so it's not far off."

I smiled uneasily at Six, wishing I could see their face. Then again, if I were aboard an enemy ship, I'd want a helmet for protection, too. I would have welcomed one right now. In training with Aunt Sooni, I'd always hated how a helmet impeded my peripheral vision. But here, outnumbered three to one and without any weapons but my claws and teeth in tiger form, I was starting to change my mind.

"I'd like to try to say it anyway," I told Six. Working with someone without even learning their name would be disrespectful in the extreme, even if they were a foreigner. I didn't know whether Six was an elder, but I didn't know that they weren't, either.

"Rokuro," the merc said, "but really, Six is fine." I couldn't read their voice at all. It was very nearly a monotone. "My people don't use those pins that your people do, but you may refer to me as *they*. It will be simplest."

"Rokuro," I repeated. Not so difficult.

"Quite good," Rokuro conceded. "Where was this Special Investigator Yi last seen?" If the merc resented having to follow another cadet's lead, they showed no sign of it.

I choked down my gratitude. I couldn't give in to weakness

and trust any of them, no matter how much I wanted an ally. At least Rokuro had asked a question I knew the answer to.

I checked the slate Hwan had given me. It showed me an overview of all known personnel and their locations. I handed the slate to Jee. "See if you can figure out where Yi has gone now," I said, "and don't let them know that we're coming. Just think of what you'll be able to do with the security clearance that Captain Hwan gave us!"

Jee brightened. "There's Yi," he said after inputting a whirlwind of commands that I couldn't follow. I was glad he was still under Min's thrall and working with me, not against me. "Do you want me to jinx the doors to keep Yi from moving about?"

"What have Yi's movements been during the last couple of hours?" I asked.

Jee accessed the ship's records, humming tunelessly under his breath. "That's odd," he said, looking up at me. "Yi's heading back to the bridge."

"That can't be good," Euna said.

"Yi won't like the surprise awaiting them there," Rokuro remarked. "Our leader, Captain Uchida, will have secured it for Captain Hwan's use."

I wished desperately that I could have asked Min to stall for time. Any attempt at communication with her would only have aroused Hwan's suspicions, however. I had to trust that Hwan was going to be busy for a while using Min's unnatural powers to secure his control over the crew. In the meantime, his mercenaries would guard the bridge until he could show up personally.

"We'll have to get there before Yi does," I said.

Rokuro cocked their head. "Yes, and team up with my comrades. We'll have this Yi person surrounded."

Great, so I could be even *more* outnumbered. But I couldn't say that.

Further conversation died as we made our way to the elevator.

Where is Yi now? I mouthed to Jee as we got in.

Jee held out the slate so we could crowd around and take a look at the map. The investigator had slowed to a halt just shy of the bridge. I bet they'd done some scouting, whether electronically or in person, and realized that they couldn't simply charge in there.

"We'll have to split up," I said, "and cut Yi off from either end."

Rokuro's voice was flat. "I don't like this."

"It's the best way," I argued. "Jee, come with me. Euna, back up Rokuro." I hoped it wasn't obvious to the others that I was trying to get Jee alone. "Jee and I will take the north end. Rokuro, you and Euna cut Yi off from the south."

"Time for some action," Euna said eagerly. "Even if no one wants to give me a real weapon."

"If you insist," Rokuro said, sounding displeased. Rokuro and Euna conferred briefly before heading off together. My plan was working!

We crept through the *Haetae*'s corridors toward the side passage where Yi awaited. I couldn't tell what the investigator was doing. Jee obligingly hacked one of the cameras using the higher access that Hwan had given us, but it didn't reveal anything illuminating.

Yi appeared to be digging through the contents of one of

the emergency lockers. The image did nothing to disguise their tousled appearance: hair hanging around their face in straggly locks, clothes rumpled, streaks of grime marring their skin. Even the distinctive yellow utility boots looked as though they were ready to wilt off Yi's feet.

I frowned. "What's Yi looking for? They can't think there's a secret weapon in there." Maybe they were searching for a personal shield against blaster fire?

"Not our problem," Jee said. He was looking at me for direction.

Was this what it felt like to be a captain, except with even more people depending on you?

It should have been a heady moment, small as it was. Unfortunately, it was marred by the knowledge that I was keeping secrets from Jee. Even if I had very good reasons. Then again, Uncle Hwan must have thought he had very good reasons for doing the things he did, too.

"Let's go," I said roughly.

We reached the end of the corridor, tiptoeing as quietly as we could. My head was starting to ache again.

Yi was nowhere in sight. Frantically, we rechecked the video record. It showed the special investigator still fussing with the closet.

We'd been had.

"I hate to point this out," Jee said, clearing his throat. The noise was shockingly loud, and I was about to chide him for it. "But there's something beneath—"

Too late. My foot came down, and the world exploded around me.

FIFTEEN

I came to slowly, as though my head had exploded into puzzle pieces and someone was reassembling them haphazardly.

". . . coming to," a voice said. It sounded familiar, but everything hurt so much I didn't want to open my eyes and face the world. I tried to reclaim the soothing blanket of darkness that had descended upon me, rather than give way to the massive jabbing headache that threatened to shatter my skull from the inside.

More puzzle pieces made themselves known. I could feel the slight stirring of air as it circulated around me. It had the characteristic metallic tang of the atmosphere on a starship, flavored unpleasantly by sweat and the stench of exhaustion. I realized that some of the smell came from me. Okay, most of the smell.

I opened my eyes, then cringed from the light. I couldn't hide from reality forever, headache or no headache. Even when it seemed like a really good idea.

I was being held in a small office, or maybe someone's quarters, if that someone had the personality of a puddle.

Containers held spare styluses, while messily stacked emergency kits littered the single desk. I rested on a cot, bound to it by restraints that didn't budge when I strained against them experimentally.

"That trap hit you harder than I intended," Special Investigator Yi said. They stood above me, their expression bemused. At least one thing about the video feed had been accurate. Yi was, in fact, rumpled and badly in need of a change of clothes.

I had a hard time following the investigator's rapid speech, but I forced myself to concentrate. I couldn't afford to pass up any clues they might drop.

A *trap*. That explained how I'd been knocked unconscious. I remembered now. Yi had jinxed the surveillance system so it *looked* like they were digging around in the locker, all to lure us into that corridor. And Yi had had plenty of time to mess with wiring or rig something with a disassembled blaster or whatever they'd done. I'd been stupid, falling for the trick.

All the same, while the special investigator had me where they wanted me, I had Yi where I wanted them. I smiled up at them, even though it made my head pound worse. It probably came out as a grimace. "Where are the others?"

"If you mean the cadets and the merc," Yi said, scowling, "they escaped. I assume they've been coerced by Hwan."

I had so many questions for Yi, I figured I might as well start asking them. "How long have you known," I shot back, "that your assistant is a gumiho?"

Yi didn't flinch. "It's never been a secret to me."

"So you brought Min here deliberately, knowing that she'd use her powers on people. On *me*."

Yi sighed. "That obviously backfired. When did you figure it out?"

"When her powers wore off me," I said. "I know *some* of the old stories." Who didn't?

Still, that wasn't the only answer I needed. "She's in a nasty predicament now," I continued. And Jun, also. Did Yi know about the ghost? I wondered again. I didn't want to bring down more trouble on Min, so I didn't mention her brother. And anyway, I had more urgent things to discuss. "Hwan threatened her into using Charm on the crew, including the other cadets. He's going to have her brainwash everyone so he can make off with the *Haetae*."

Yi's eyebrows flew up. "You're concerned?" They made no attempt to conceal their disbelief. "And why aren't *you* affected?"

I held back an impulse to snap at Yi. I'd have the best chance of persuading them I was on their side if I didn't lose my temper. "Hwan thought I was on his side at the time. He had Min Charm his opponents, but not himself or me or the shaman who's working with him."

Yi paused to consider, then indicated that I should continue.

"After Min left me in the brig," I said calmly, "Hwan showed up and offered to free me if I agreed to cooperate with him. I didn't want to be stuck in a cell with the ship sabotaged. And I thought . . . At the time, I thought he was in the right to work against a fox spirit. When he blackmailed Min and started using her powers for his own ends, I realized he was in the wrong."

"Hmm" was all Yi said. "An interesting story. Almost plausible."

I winced. I could have protested that I was telling the truth, but if Yi didn't believe me, what difference would that make? And my threatening Yi from this prone position would be ludicrous. Pleading or begging seemed unlikely to work, either. Besides, I was well aware that my confession didn't paint me in the best of lights.

"Listen," I said after several uncomfortable moments, "Hwan may be my uncle, but he's up to no good. I realize that now. I wish I'd seen it earlier. I don't know what happened to cause him to turn his back on his duty, or what history he has with Agent Min." I swallowed. "But I'm part of the Space Forces." *Even if I haven't sworn the oath yet.* "My first duty is to the Thousand Worlds entire, not my family."

The scar on my hand hurt so badly I thought it had started bleeding again.

"I think you're telling the truth," Yi said, frowning. "Which puts me in a very uncomfortable position."

"What do you mean?" I asked.

"I was hoping Hwan would follow you here." Yi left the statement hanging.

My mind went blank. Then the implications flooded in. "You used me as *bait?*" I demanded in outrage.

"Yes," Yi said heavily. "But you weren't the only one." As if that made me feel any better. "He eluded us for some time, disappearing in the Ghost Sector—we thought he'd died there— and then resurfacing, always a step ahead of us. We knew he had a grudge against Min because she'd foiled him in his search for the Dragon Pearl, but he had gotten wise to her powers and kept avoiding her. We also knew that your family is quite . . . close-knit. So we pulled some strings and dangled you in front of him as a possible coconspirator. That finally brought him out into the open."

I wondered what they'd been about to say in place of *close-knit*, but I didn't want to interrupt.

I thought back to how happy I'd been to receive word that the Space Forces had admitted me as a cadet. And how Captain Chaewon had been called away before carrying out my oath. Was all of this fake, down to the uniform I wore?

"I'm not a real cadet, am I?" I said, my voice shaking. "Just a pawn so you could catch Hwan."

"No, no," Yi interrupted, their face crumpling in distress. "Your acceptance was real. Your application was what gave us the idea for the scheme in the first place. Unfortunately, we failed to stop him before he carried out his plan for Min."

"The emergency with Norandol . . . Was that real?" I asked.

"Real enough," Yi said. "Ordinarily, you and Jee would have been left behind for orientation while the *Haetae* sped to its destination. In the past, Hwan hadn't shown any sign of wanting to take on a fully staffed starbase. But a ship—oh, he remembers being a captain, all right. He'd risk himself for a ship."

I stared at Yi. "Well, your plan for *me* worked," I said bitterly. Uncle Hwan must indeed have learned about my assignment and decided that the *Haetae* made as good a hijacking target as any other battle cruiser.

"We've been monitoring your family for a long time," Yi said, which didn't ease the pain in my head. "The Juhwang Tiger Clan's Matriarch, in particular, has a reputation for ruthlessness and underhanded dealings. Her influence reaches throughout the Thousand Worlds. But she's always been too clever to be caught doing anything incriminating. And until his desertion in the Dragon Pearl incident, Hwan, too, always made sure he stayed on the right side of the regulations."

Hearing all that only made me feel worse. Was my entire family rotten to the core? Even my parents and Aunt Sooni?

I thought back to my childhood. The constant insistence that we had to be prepared for enemies, even though none ever showed up. The martial drills. The emphasis on loyalty to family above all else. The Matriarch's high-handedness, as Admiral Hasun had put it, and the mysterious parcels that came to her. Circumstantial evidence, perhaps, but it all fit.

I could have demanded proof, but I knew. I knew.

Yi must have read my thoughts on my face. They said, more gently, "I misjudged you, Cadet. If I'd worked with you, instead of assuming that you were tainted by association with your family . . ."

"It's not too late," I said, despite the way the investigator's words had stung me. Time to lay everything on the table. "You know that Min travels with her ghost brother?"

"I do," Yi said. They eyed me, then added, "I'd better release you from those restraints."

As Yi did so, I rapidly explained how Hwan had blackmailed Min into Charming the crew for him by using Sena and Shield. "I was coming to ask you for help," I said. "Unfortunately—"

Yi straightened and held a finger to their lips for silence. They hadn't finished freeing me.

I quieted instantly. I'd gotten that much out of my childhood, at least—discipline. There were times for argument, and there were times when you had to follow orders.

The hatch swished open. I'd been so intent on Yi that I'd

lost track of sounds coming from outside the office. I cursed myself for my inattentiveness.

The special investigator swore and ducked behind the cluttered desk. Their reflexes weren't fast enough to save them, however. Blaster fire of a type I'd never encountered before— livid purple instead of the usual red of Thousand Worlds blasters—arced through the air and outlined Yi in sizzling light. The investigator choked out a word I couldn't understand, then dropped with a *thunk*.

My heart hammered as I struggled to free myself from the remaining restraints. With a snarl, I shifted into tiger form and snapped the cables with a surge of raw strength. I was grateful that had worked. It would have sucked to lose a leg because I'd foolishly shifted while in a restraint too small for me.

Rokuro, Euna, and Jee burst in. The merc was brandishing a pistol of some sort, and purple sparks still danced around its muzzle. Uneasily, I wondered how deadly it was. What if Rokuro had killed Yi?

"There you are!" Jee exclaimed. He smelled overpoweringly of anxiety. "I'm so glad we got to you before Yi killed you or whatever."

Euna, unfazed by the fact that most of the office was taken up by an adolescent tiger, knelt and picked up one of the broken restraints. "Was Yi *torturing* you?" she demanded, her voice rising in outrage.

If I'd had any question as to whether Jee and Euna, and possibly Rokuro, were still Charmed, that settled the matter. I was amazed by the range and longevity of Min's magic. I tried to turn around in the tight quarters, then shifted back. My wrists, ankles, and ribs ached. At least my headache was receding.

"Is Yi alive?" I asked, looking over at them.

Rokuro knelt to check Yi's pulse. "Yes," they said in their flat voice. They hoisted up the special investigator and trussed Yi to the cot where I'd been a prisoner just minutes ago.

Sorry, I thought at Yi. But I couldn't think of a good excuse to stop Rokuro. If I aroused suspicion, the merc might lock me in here as well, and I couldn't risk that happening.

"What now?" Euna asked. She was covering the hatch with her blaster.

"Great thinking," I told her with a nod at the hatch, and she gave me a jaunty smile, the edges of her eyes glowing faintly. At least someone was having fun. "I want to check out the bridge." I felt bad about leaving Yi behind, but I trusted they wouldn't inconveniently expire while I figured out my next steps. That thought made me ask, "Rokuro, does that weapon of yours do any lingering damage?"

The merc sounded almost offended. "The stunner will leave your special investigator incapacitated until it wears off in one or two of your hours. But Yi will suffer no lasting harm. If they had been hit at close range, on the other hand . . ." Rokuro shrugged.

Useful to know. "Thanks," I said.

This was going to be the most difficult part of my plan to pull off, not least because I had to assume that everyone I met was hostile. Either they were working for Uncle Hwan, and they would try to prevent my attempts to send out a signal for help, or they hadn't yet been Charmed by Min, in which case they might think I was on Hwan's side and would attack me on sight. An interesting pickle.

"Shouldn't we report back to Captain Hwan?" Euna asked,

wrinkling her nose at Yi's slumped form. "After all, we've achieved our mission."

She had a point—if I had any intention of following Hwan's orders.

"I'll send him a message," I said.

"Here's the slate," Jee said, obligingly passing his to me.

When he did so, I angled my body so he couldn't see what I was doing. Of everyone here, he was the one likeliest to catch me faking the report. I hated lying to him and the others, but until I could rescue Min and get her to undo the effects of her Charm, I didn't see an alternative.

Maybe Min would rescue herself and save me the trouble. Unfortunately, I couldn't count on that. *Always plan for the worst,* my family used to tell me. That had turned out to be excellent advice for this cruise. Ironic that I was using my family's advice against my uncle. Besides, Hwan had utterly alienated Min. The moment he let his guard down, she'd be at his throat, and in the literal sense, too. So that was no good.

Quickly, I typed in an abbreviated account of our success, then left the message in draft mode instead of sending it to Hwan. If Jee happened to double-check later, I hoped he would think I'd made an honest mistake.

My palms were sweating. "While Captain Hwan has so much going on," I said, trying for an authoritative tone, "we can save him some trouble by checking the captain's office." This was the kind of reasoning I might legitimately have presented to a squad of my own if I weren't a jumped-up cadet.

There were so many things that could go wrong. Whatever mercenaries guarded the bridge might tell us that they'd already searched the office, or refuse to let us in. I was betting, however, that they hadn't been given instructions to ransack the place, but simply to secure it.

Judging from Rokuro's behavior, the mercs might be by-the-book types. I hoped the ones guarding the bridge didn't include any unruly individuals. Surely Rokuro's Captain Uchida wouldn't be the sort to smash everything in sight? Probably not, if Uncle Hwan had done his job right. He would have given that task only the most reliable of warriors.

I wished I could see Rokuro's face. "If you insist," they said in that maddeningly neutral voice.

"Sounds good to me," Jee said, although he eyed me uneasily.

"Lead on," Euna said briskly. "I'll bring up the rear."

Wordlessly, Rokuro dropped back to join her.

Euna rolled her eyes, then winked at me when Rokuro's head was turned. I did, in fact, feel better knowing that I wouldn't have a complete stranger at my back. Even if I didn't know Euna very well, either. It was hard to believe I'd only been on the *Haetae* for a day. Less than a day, even.

My heart rate remained elevated as we made our way to the bridge, as if we might be attacked at any moment. It didn't help that Jee startled at every small clank and groan that emanated from the ship. I had no way of knowing if the remnants of the crew had escaped and were planning an ambush. Especially since the fact that we were accompanied by one of the mercs made our allegiance clear.

We arrived intact, and the bridge looked entirely different this time. No fallen bodies, no miasma of combat and despair. Even the flashing red lights seemed less intense.

Four mercenaries stood watch. Their leader sported a

different helmet than the others, with a mask in the shape of a grimacing ... ogre? Demon? Regardless, it had a ferocious scowl and gleamed bright red. *This must be Captain Uchida,* I decided.

Rokuro thumbed their breastplate. I tensed and nearly transformed into a tiger, then rocked back on my heels as the other four mercs mimicked the action. This must be what passed for a salute among them.

They conversed in their own language. I had no way of knowing what they were saying, and I tried not to fidget. I cast a glance sideways at Jee, wondering if his training had included this language, or if he could get me a machine translation. Jee caught my eye and shook his head. No such luck, then.

Then I noticed Euna darting significant looks in my direction, trying to get my attention. I cocked an eyebrow at her. She mouthed a single word. I frowned at her in confusion. She did it again, then her face stilled into an impassive mask when one of the mercs looked her way.

I wished I could decipher her warning, but I wasn't good at lipreading. I added it to the list of life skills, like ethics, that my family had failed to teach me. Clearly, the next time I saw the Matriarch, I would have to suggest some changes to the curriculum.

"State your request," Rokuro said abruptly. "I'll translate for you and Captain Uchida."

I hadn't realized that not all the mercenaries spoke Hangeul, the language of the Thousand Worlds. Uncle Hwan must have chosen Rokuro for their fluency, although whether that was to make communication possible or so Rokuro could spy on anything Jee, Euna, and I might say to one another was unclear. Maybe a bit of both.

"We're here to check on the captain's ready room and make

sure everything is in good shape for Captain Hwan's takeover," I said, doing my best to project confidence. I faced the ogre-masked merc.

"'Acceptable,'" Rokuro translated for Captain Uchida. "She says you must surrender your weapons. We can assure your safety."

Euna's mouth was set in a mulish scowl. She didn't like this. I didn't, either—it suggested that *someone* already found us suspicious—but I saw no alternative.

"We'll get them back on the way out?" I asked, my tone challenging.

"'Of course,'" Rokuro said for Uchida. Was it my imagination, or was Rokuro's voice more toneless than usual?

With a sigh, I nodded at Euna. She handed over her glare pistol and chuckled darkly at the mercs' baffled expression. It appeared they'd never seen anything like it, either.

"Your knife," Rokuro added, surprising me. How did they . . . ?

I'd completely forgotten about the knife that Aunt Sooni had given me. It hardly counted as a weapon, but I was reluctant to part with it. Even if I couldn't trust my family anymore, I missed her. Giving it up felt like giving up one of the last things that tied me to my family.

Sighing again, I gave Captain Uchida my knife.

"Thank you for your vigilance," I said to Uchida, fighting to hide my worry.

I'd learned the hard way that even a tiger can go down if they're unlucky. And I didn't want anything bad to happen to Jee or Euna, neither of whom had so much as a personal shield. But we were outnumbered, and the best way forward was to cooperate. For now.

SIXTEEN

The ready room was outside the office, but they were both marked by similar signs. It reminded me that I'd been to the captain's office once before, when I'd tried—and failed—to have myself sworn in to the Thousand Worlds Space Forces. When I'd tried—and failed—to warn Captain Chaewon that I'd detected my uncle's scent mark. I was haunted by the thought of how much would have turned out differently if I'd at least succeeded in the latter.

Still, I couldn't alter the past. I just had to make sure of a better future.

I tried the hatch to the ready room. No luck. I assumed Hwan had the overrides, but I didn't blame him for not handing them out, not even to his hand-picked guards. And it would definitely arouse his suspicions if I called him for access now.

"Jee," I said, "can you get us in?" I did my best to sound casual.

"No problem," Jee said with his usual cheer.

"You've got to teach me how you do that," Euna remarked, watching as Jee pulled up a decidedly nonstandard program on his slate. "My parents didn't approve of me fooling around with computers. Granted, that was because I spent all my time playing shooters. And I might have, uh, rewired my nini's food processor into a makeshift glare pistol once or twice. For some reason my family and friends *hated* that."

"It's not hard," Jee offered, "but you do have to know a lot about the protocols that they've coded into the system. Tell you what—if you show me how to rewire hardware, I'll teach you some of my tricks."

He continued talking amiably in geek jargon as his fingers spidered over the slate. There came an audible *click*, and the hatch whooshed open.

"Good work," I told him, and he beamed at me.

"Impressive," Rokuro said, a note of surprise in their voice. And to Euna: "You must show me some of those shooters sometime."

"I could use someone to stand watch," I hinted to Rokuro before they got too distracted. Even so, I felt a pang of envy. Aunt Sooni had been the only one in my family who played video games, usually the kind where you mauled hordes of the undead. Once in a while she'd let me sneak in a game, though she knew my parents disapproved.

"No one will get past the guards," Rokuro said forbiddingly. "Or Captain Uchida."

"How did she meet up with Hwan, anyway?" I asked as the others preceded us in.

"He spared her in battle," Rokuro said, even more forbiddingly. "She pledged our clan's loyalty to him in gratitude."

Huh. Rokuro sounded like they didn't entirely approve. That could be useful.

We crowded into the captain's ready room. Given its size, it accommodated all four of us comfortably. There were only chairs for two people on this side of the desk. The captain's seat was empty, of course, and I grimaced ruefully.

I listened to the *swoosh* of the hatch closing behind us, careful not to betray any sign of my anxiety.

For this to work, I needed to have as few witnesses as possible. Jee had to be here, because he'd make everything possible, and he and Euna were still Charmed. But I'd failed to get rid of Rokuro. The real problem was going to be whether I could fast-talk my way past all three of them—not one of my notable strengths.

"Jee," I said, as nonchalantly as I could manage, "could you check to see if the top-priority messaging system is active?"

I held my breath. Normally, the captain or acting captain was the only one who could send top-priority messages. In theory, once we exited the Gate, it would broadcast an encrypted communication to everyone in the area. Any Thousand Worlds station or ship in the area that received it was obligated to relay it to Space Forces High Command.

It would be easier to send out a general distress call, but I was sure Rokuro would put a halt to that, even if Yi's original briefing was accurate and there wasn't any help nearby. I also didn't want any enemies or pirates lurking in the area to be aware of our weakened state.

On the other hand, I was gambling that Rokuro didn't know the emergency protocol. Which left the question of how long Jee and Euna would go along with me. I didn't have a good sense of the limits of Min's powers.

Indeed, just then Jee was shaking his head and mumbling, "What . . . what . . . ?"

Oh no! Min's Charm was wearing off—at the worst possible

moment. I was confident of my ability to wrestle down Jee, but Euna had a fighter's reflexes. In any case, I didn't want to fight either of them if I could help it.

Rokuro barked something in the foreign language and drew their stunner.

Jee's mumbling had given me just enough warning. Could I take Rokuro down before the guards outside heard signs of a struggle and intervened?

I flowed into my native tiger shape, gathered myself, and leaped for Rokuro, all in one smooth motion. Euna brought up her blaster but wavered with uncharacteristic indecision. She smelled strongly of confusion.

Where did she get that? I had a moment to wonder. Hadn't she surrendered her glare pistol to the guards? I had to deal with Rokuro quickly, before Euna came to her senses and took me out.

I crashed into Rokuro and landed partially on top of them. Ouch! All those spiky protrusions on their armor hurt even through my thick layer of fur. And I still hadn't entirely recovered from being knocked out by Yi's trap.

Rokuro got off one shot anyway, and scrambled out from beneath me. A tiger makes for a large target, and the purple bolt caught me in the hind leg. My entire limb went numb, and I collapsed to the deck with a *thud*. So much for secrecy.

Then Rokuro wheezed something that sounded like "Reflex, didn't mean it," and went quiet.

How good is the soundproofing in here, anyway? I wondered. We were about to find out.

"Sebin!" Euna cried as I attempted to move my paralyzed leg. She shoved an alarmed Jee behind her to the cover of the desk, crouched, and fired not at Rokuro themself, but at their stunner.

Whatever her reasoning, it was the right decision. The stunner melted, running down Rokuro's gauntleted hand in a foul-smelling ooze. It dripped down onto the carpet, leaving equally nasty-smelling scorch marks.

That gave me the opportunity to reach out with one of my forepaws—tigers are incredibly stretchy—and sweep Rokuro's legs out from under them. The mercenary went down.

I shifted back to human form. "Secure Rokuro," I said, surprised at how remote my voice sounded. "Euna, where did that blaster come from?"

"I was trying to tell you earlier," Euna said breathlessly. "That brainwashing trick stopped working on me a while back. I figured I'd wait to see what you were up to and back your play, or not, as necessary. As for the blaster—please. I always have a spare in a hidden holster. You think I'd let the mercs take my only weapon?"

Jee, the only one who hadn't been involved in the brief combat, was shaking. "Sebin," he said plaintively, "what's going on? Are you with Hwan, or—"

"Wait," Rokuro croaked from where they'd fallen. Not unconscious after all.

Euna turned her blaster on them.

I held up one paw—no, hand—for silence as I strode to the hatch and pressed my ear to it. I didn't hear anything. Was that a good sign or a bad one? Belatedly, it occurred to me that excellent soundproofing could work against us, too.

"Okay," I said to Rokuro. "Speak."

"I don't want to be your enemy," Rokuro said. "Hwan has

gone too far. I didn't realize how powerful the fox's magic was. If Captain Uchida knew Hwan was brainwashing people like this, she would turn against him, too. I hope."

Jee's eyes flickered from Rokuro to me. "Fox's magic?"

"We can trust Rokuro," I said to Euna. "They smell sincere. Give me a second, Jee, and I'll explain. Rokuro," I went on, "why didn't you tell your captain about what Hwan did?"

Was Rokuro *squirming*? "I thought you were under the fox's thrall," they said. "I didn't want to have to fight you when it wasn't your fault. I'm glad the enchantment wore off."

All right, I couldn't argue with that logic.

Euna raised an eyebrow but nodded and pointed her blaster at the hatch again.

I could have asked Jee to turn on a camera feed to the bridge so we could see what was going on out there, but I needed his attention on more urgent matters. "I only have time to go over this once," I said, "so listen. . . ."

I told the others my connection with Captain Hwan and his plot to hijack the *Haetae*. That Min was a gumiho, and she'd used her Charm not only on me, but on everyone else after Hwan blackmailed her. I didn't mention that Yi had used me as bait. It felt too personal, and anyway, it wasn't relevant to the present situation.

Jee blanched. Euna merely looked grim and commented, "If this were a shooting game, I'd be having the time of my life, but as it stands . . . No one's going to believe us when we tell them we were on a hijacked ship during our training cruise. And it'll be classified anyway, so I can't draw a webcomic based on it. . . ."

I rifled through the captain's desk for anything that might

be useful, feeling like an impostor. I didn't find anything in my cursory search.

"What are you doing?" Jee demanded. "Do you know how much trouble—"

Euna had already figured it out. "We need every resource we can get," she said. "Right? If we're lucky, we'll find more weapons."

"I must agree," Rokuro said, a tinge of worry coloring their normal monotone. "You can always apologize to your captain later. Euna, you should continue covering the egress. I will help with the search."

"Sure," she said, after a glance at me to make sure I approved.

I nodded agreement. "I imagine we're not the first crew members to improvise," I said dryly. I didn't look forward to explaining this to Captain Chaewon. "Jee, I have something more important for you to work on." I willed him to focus on my voice so he wouldn't become even more rattled.

Whether it was my steady tone or he'd found some inner oasis of stability, Jee drew a deep breath, then nodded, biting his lip. "What can I do?"

"We need to get word out over the relay to Space Forces High Command." To anyone who would believe us, really. "We can't count on having access to the relay until we exit the Gate, so we'll need to queue up the message."

If anything, Jee paled further. "Who's going to listen to a bunch of cadets?"

I grimaced. "One of the admirals is a relative of mine. Admiral Hasun. They *might* pay attention."

"You must have a *lot* of relatives," Euna observed in

fascination. "Like my family, except we're mostly grunts, not flag-officer types." Her grin took the sting out of the words.

"Anyway," I said with a rueful nod at Euna to acknowledge the comment, "I don't know how to work the ship's comms. Not to send a priority-one distress message to Command over the relay. But you do, Jee."

Jee gulped. "I'll—I'll do my best."

I stifled my frustration. We all depended on each other. There was no other way we could succeed. "I've seen you at work, Jee," I said, doing my best to project confidence—in him. "We'll guard the office so you can concentrate."

Jee swallowed again and then nodded, his mouth firming. "I'll do *better* than my best."

I left Jee muttering to himself. "Rokuro," I said, "can you feel out your captain by telling her about Hwan?"

"I can do that," Rokuro agreed.

"Euna, are you able to get us a video feed of the bridge?" I asked. "I want to keep an eye on what's out there. Rokuro, signal us if you need help."

Euna's eyes crinkled. "I'm second choice for this technical stuff, aren't I?" she said. She holstered her blaster. "But I get it. We can't risk Hwan taking anyone unawares. I mean, he has control of a real live Space Forces battle cruiser, and it wouldn't be hard for him to spoof Captain Chaewon's likeness over an outgoing video feed."

A counterfeit image? That possibility hadn't even occurred to me, but with modern computers . . .

"One would hope they'd have countermeasures for such things," Rokuro observed as Euna navigated several menus on a slate she'd pulled from the captain's desk. "Where I come from, people caught faking video footage are stuffed and mounted as museum exhibits."

I shuddered. "Remind me not to go on vacation there."

"Just kidding," Rokuro said, deadpan.

I blinked at them. Was that a joke? Too bad I couldn't see their face. I wondered how human they looked beneath that helmet.

"I guess no one's perfect," Euna said, ignoring our byplay. "Hackers get more and more clever, and you should see some of the stuff digital artists can come up with. Anyway, let's have a look before we send you out there, Rokuro—" She cursed at the interface, then brought up a view of the bridge.

No one was there.

"Rokuro, can you call Captain Uchida?" I asked.

Rokuro nodded and spoke into a wrist unit. We heard Uchida's voice speaking sharply, and Rokuro's response, even more monotone than usual. The captain was still talking when they cut her off.

"What did she say?" My stomach clenched tight with dread.

"She said to remember the blood-debt the clan owes Hwan," Rokuro said. "I wasn't there for that battle—I was too young at the time. But this . . . This can't be right." They sounded queasy. "In any case, it seems Captain Uchida and her squad have been called elsewhere."

"Remember," I said, trying to fight my unease, "we thought Special Investigator Yi was in that corridor, but they'd jinxed the video feed. And now Uchida suspects us—she may be alerting Hwan even as we speak. We need to check the bridge in person."

Euna wrinkled her nose at me. "I suppose. At least I still

have my blaster. You might want one too, Sebin. And one for Rokuro, since I managed to melt their weapon . . ."

We performed a quick search of the office. I could add it to the charges that would be leveled against me at my inevitable court-martial. I was pretty sure desecrating a captain's office counted as *some* type of vandalism. Even if the circumstances were desperate.

To our relief, we located two emergency blasters. One of them had an empty power cell, which would have made me question Captain Chaewon's competence, except it also sported deep scratches and shattered optics. Power cell or no, I doubted it worked. She'd obviously kept it as a memento, perhaps from some former battle, rather than a functioning weapon. At least the other blaster looked all right.

"Rokuro, you'd better take this," I said, giving them the good one. "I've got fangs and claws."

To my relief, Rokuro handled it expertly, making sure not to point the muzzle at anyone as they tucked it into the holster that had formerly held their stunner. It more or less fit.

"I'm going to take tiger form," I told Euna and Rokuro. "I'll crouch down so I don't impede your field of vision or lines of fire."

Euna gave me a jaunty salute. I wasn't sure I merited one, under the circumstances, but I didn't protest. Right now, anything that kept our morale up was welcome. Rokuro merely nodded.

"Here we go," I muttered, and shifted. It came as a relief, honestly. Everything became more vivid, including the pain in my hind leg, to my tiger form's sharper senses. But it was the impetus I needed to remind me how much was at stake.

Euna triggered the hatch, since the computer quite under-standably wouldn't respond to orders in tiger roars. Too bad, because it would be convenient if it did.

The hatch hissed open. I rushed out of the office, trusting my reflexes to warn me if there was an attack incoming. Euna and Rokuro would guard my back and, more importantly, Jee, who was doing the important work of hacking into the relay system.

For a brief moment, I wondered if this was how my relatives felt when they had to depend on someone else to do some-thing they couldn't. Not that I could see Uncle Hwan admitting weakness. Yet even he had allied with the shaman to deal with Min, because Sena had capabilities he didn't.

Captain Uchida was gone, and she'd taken one of her guards with her. That left two, I assumed to keep us bottled up while they fetched reinforcements. My heart sank. I'd hoped the reason that everything remained so quiet was the cabin's soundproofing.

Taking advantage of my reflexes, I charged the two guards, knocking one into the other. They went down in a tangle of limbs. With the others' aid, it was soon over.

"They're not dead," I said to Rokuro after I shifted back.

"Thank you," Rokuro said. I could smell their gratitude. "They might have felt obligated to fight us. This way is better."

Euna and Rokuro helped me drag the two fallen mercs out of sight. "They left the bridge in pristine condition," Euna remarked. "Too bad we can't ask them to take over our chores for the rest of this voyage. Should we scout this level and figure out where the other mercs went?"

I hesitated. "It's tempting, but we shouldn't leave Jee

unattended," I said. "For all we know, they're hoping we'll venture out of this area, even though we're defenseless—or so they think. After all, there are more of them than there are of us, and they're bigger, too."

In tiger shape I would have been larger than any one of the warriors. And Euna's blaster made her smaller size irrelevant, other than allowing her to hide behind cover more readily. I couldn't imagine those massively armored mercs successfully hiding behind anything, except maybe one another.

Euna opened her mouth, then stopped dead. Rokuro and I did, too. We'd all heard a distant *thunk*. Had someone gotten careless, or was it a trick to draw us out to investigate?

I realized that we should have been speaking in whispers or in signs. I cursed myself for my laxness. Still, it wasn't too late to start taking precautions. I dropped my voice to a whisper and said, "We'd better—"

The *thunk* came again. This time it sounded closer.

"Let's close the bridge hatch," I said. "That will slow them down."

I was worried they'd soon get to us anyway. I remembered the dismaying sight of Captain Chaewon and the bridge crew knocked out by Hwan's earlier attack. I didn't want to oversee a reprise.

Get back to the ready room, I mouthed to the others.

I didn't have to explain my reasoning. Euna and Rokuro nodded.

We hastily retreated. I tapped on the hatch to the office. "Jee!" I said in a fierce whisper. "It's Sebin. Let us in."

There was a distracted oath from inside—soundproofing *definitely* wasn't the office's strong suit, good to know—and then the hatch swooshed open to admit us. We hurried in. I caught myself counting the seconds until it closed again.

"How are things going, Jee?" Euna asked.

"Shh!" Jee hissed, and I prodded Euna to get her to shut up.

She was either more easygoing than I'd realized, or she recognized the importance of Jee's task. She nodded.

Jee's slate blinked once, twice, and then he straightened, pumping his fist in triumph. "I'm in! Uh—what are we going to tell them?"

"Let me." I knew exactly what I wanted to say.

Jee handed me the slate. I typed in the necessary salutations, even though I fretted about wasting time. But I couldn't risk the message failing to go through because of *protocol*.

Former captain Hwan of the Juhwang Tiger Clan has hijacked the Haetae *with the aid of Sun Clan mercenaries,* I wrote. *He has blackmailed Special Investigator Yi's assistant Kim Min into assisting him.* I wondered whether to mention she was a gumiho, then decided that the authorities must already know. *Captain Chaewon and the senior officers are in critical condition. We require assis—*

Euna and Jee yelped at the sudden *bang* as an enormous dent formed in the door. Even Rokuro stiffened. How could the mercs have gotten past the bridge hatch so quickly?

We were under siege.

SEVENTEEN

Drat! I'd been hoping we'd have more time than *that*. I closed the message with my name and rank, such as it was—*Cadet Juhwang Sebin of Space Forces Battle Cruiser Haetae*—and hit SEND. My heartbeat jackhammered as I waited for the indication that the message was queued to go out as soon as we exited the Gate.

"Done!" Jee said in triumph when the slate flashed its acknowledgment.

"Folks, we need to get out of here," Euna said, her gaze flicking to the door. We could see it vibrating as whoever was on the outside slammed something against it like a giant battering ram.

"They're just doing that to intimidate us," I said, which may or may not have been true.

"I don't think that's the only reason," Rokuro noted.

It wasn't the most *efficient* way to break through a locked hatch on a ship. That would have involved blowtorches to cut the hatch out of the bulkheads, something I'd heard about from Uncle Hwan himself. I *assumed* the room was reinforced against even supernaturally or magically enhanced attempts to break in, but the growing dents in the hatch didn't reassure me.

"Now what?" Euna asked, keeping her blaster pointed at the hatch.

I doubted a single blaster would help us much, but if it made her feel better, fine. I wouldn't have minded a comfort blaster of my own.

I squeezed my eyes shut, visualizing the ship's layout. "We need to get to the engine room," I said. "From there we can disable the ship so that Unc—I mean, so Hwan can't take the *Haetae* on a rampage, or escape before the cavalry arrives. If we can drain the Gate drive's crystals, he won't be able to jump again after we emerge—that'll buy us some time."

"What if he takes it out on the crew?" Jee said, his voice trembling. He was probably thinking back to sick bay and its crowd of casualties.

I couldn't scrub those images out of my head, either. But then, I didn't want to. They served as a reminder of what was at stake.

"Hwan's already done that," I said soberly. "C'mon. We can't go back out the way we came, that's obvious. We'll have to escape through the ventilation shaft."

Euna gulped. "I don't like enclosed spaces."

Interesting phobia in a spacer, I thought, considering that a starship was nothing but a giant tin can. I had enough sense to realize that pointing this out could prove disastrous. "You'll be fine," I said. "We'll be with you."

I pointed up at the grate in the ceiling. "We're going to be court-martialed for dismantling this office, but since that ship has already sailed . . . Euna, can you shoot out the screws holding that in?" I remembered how easily she had destroyed Rokuro's stunner. We might as well put her amazing aim to use.

"No problem," she said, her eyes brightening. "No one is *ever* again going to tell me that playing shooters is a waste of time!"

Any worries I might've had about her ability to perform under pressure dissipated when she made a series of flawless shots, reducing the screws to molten slag. Still, the grate remained stubbornly stuck. All the while the pounding on the hatch grew louder and louder.

I growled and shifted, then leaped up and hooked my claws into the grate, pulling it down. Some of the molten metal singed my fur, and I couldn't help but hiss.

Jee's hands flew up to his mouth and he made a stifled noise of dismay. Still, the grate fell with a clatter, and I sent it to the side of the room with a swipe of my paw.

I lowered myself to the deck and tried to purr in a friendly fashion, although this was something that, like all tigers, I'd never mastered. It came out as a chuff instead. I crouched down and raised a paw invitingly.

It was too bad the captain's desk was bolted into place away from the grate's opening. I doubted we'd be able to budge it. Fortunately, I had another solution.

Euna figured out what I meant immediately. She climbed onto my back, and then I reared to my full height, allowing her to scramble up and into the ventilation shaft above.

"Careful of the edges," she called down to Jee and Rokuro. "They're still hot in places."

Jee winced. "Too bad I'm not suited up for this," he muttered, "but there's no time." He patted my flank. "Sorry about using you as a stepladder, Sebin! I'll make it up to you later."

I chuffed again for good measure.

"My armor will be an impediment," Rokuro said, sounding displeased.

While Jee clambered up after Euna, Rokuro's fingers danced on a cleverly recessed control panel on their arm. Their armor sprang open like a sarcophagus—*Don't be morbid,* I thought hysterically—and the merc stepped out. It should have come as no surprise that they looked like they smelled: a human only a few years older than the rest of us, with black hair rumpled from being stuck under the helmet, and tawny skin. Their uniform beneath the armor was a simple yellow jumpsuit. They hurriedly stowed the armor under the captain's desk.

I didn't think the hatch was going to last much longer. It had bulged inward so much that it looked like a giant's tongue. *Thanks for that gross image,* I informed my brain.

"You two should hurry up!" Jee called down, his voice muffled and echoing strangely in the enclosed space.

Because they were taller than the rest of us, Rokuro needed little assistance from me. I was relieved I didn't have to bear the weight—or spikes—of all their armor.

My turn. I crouched down, then sprang upward. The ventilation shaft hadn't been built to accommodate a tiger, even a juvenile like myself. So I had to shift back to human form at the apex of the leap. I almost had the timing right, but I ended up clinging by my fingertips to a perilously hot, ragged edge. I yelped.

Rokuro caught hold of my wrist and tugged. With their help I was able to make it the rest of the way up and into the shaft.

"Sounds like the hatch is going to crack any minute now,"

Jee fretted from ahead of me. I wished he would stop saying things that reminded us of how much danger we were in. But that was his way of dealing with anxiety, different as it was from mine, and I was hardly in a position to scold him. It wouldn't have eased his mind anyway.

"Euna," I said, "do you know where you're going?" This was going to be a hundred times more awkward if I had to navigate for us from the rear.

"I do," she said. In the confined space, I could smell that she sounded more confident than she felt. However, of the four of us, she had served longest on the *Haetae*, even if only by a few months, and we had to start somewhere.

"Lead on, then."

We crawled through the shaft. I was of two minds as to whether to be grateful that the ship's artificial gravity hadn't been affected by all the chaos. If it hadn't been on, we could have easily floated along the shaft as far as we needed to go, instead of laboriously crawling. I was in good shape, but I could tell that my knees and elbows would sport bruises at the end of this.

"The only advantage of being a kid," Euna said in a stifled voice, "is that I'm not too cramped in here."

"This is one time I wouldn't mind being a few years younger," Rokuro agreed. Their broad shoulders were hunched uncomfortably.

I grimaced my agreement, then remembered that Euna couldn't see me. Not only was I behind her, but Jee and Rokuro were between us. Breathing the miasma of their stress and sweat wasn't pleasant, but I wouldn't have dreamed of complaining. After all, I stank pretty badly myself.

"We're going left at the juncture ahead," Euna whispered. This agreed with my mental map of the ship.

We could still hear the irregular thudding of the battering ram, or whatever it was, behind us. It didn't raise my confidence. How much longer would it be before they figured out where we'd gone?

Worse—and this thought made my breath catch—what if they were banging on the door just to rattle us while they sent someone to intercept us by a faster route? Not only did Hwan have enough troops that he could afford to divide his forces, it was the kind of devious thing he'd do. That he would once have taught *me* to do.

Unfortunately, we were committed to our current course of action. I didn't see any better alternatives. The *Haetae* was a big ship, but we couldn't simply go to ground, even if we had plenty of hiding places. That would give Hwan a free pass to do as he pleased. We *had* to stop him.

And I needed to start planning for what we did *after* we sabotaged the Gate drive. There was no question of *if*. We didn't have any choice but to succeed.

Under Euna's leadership, we climbed several narrow shafts and emerged in new passages. Taking these would lead us directly to the engines. Hwan would be aware of that as well, and I expected he would have the engine room under guard.

The ship was full of unsettling noises I hadn't noticed before. Granted, my stint aboard the *Haetae* had involved so many nonstop emergencies that I hadn't gotten much opportunity to listen to the ship's normal sounds. I wasn't particularly musical, but there was an odd sort of melody to its moans and *thunk*s.

Here, in the ship's very spine, I heard the ship murmuring

and sighing to itself. It wasn't *soothing*, exactly, although maybe an engineer who knew the *Haetae*'s characteristic sounds would have found it so. There were long, metallic groans, as though the ship's structure were under an unseen tidal stress, or the distant percussion of footsteps, or an occasional alarming *ping*. I wished I knew how to interpret those sounds.

Maybe, the thought occurred to me, *I'm happier not knowing.*

"Stop," I breathed to my comrades when a new noise intruded on my awareness. More footsteps, except these were approaching us—well, *beneath* us—and they were marching in perfect cadence. Call it cynicism, but I hadn't seen any evidence that Captain Chaewon's crew practiced that kind of lockstep motion. The Space Forces were disciplined, but they didn't adhere to infantry practices.

The foreign mercenaries, on the other hand . . .

Rokuro stopped still. I could only assume Euna and Jee had as well.

I hadn't realized earlier how stifling the air was. Was it my imagination, or was the temperature getting warmer in here? People thought of space as cold, and that was true to a certain extent. One of the things Great-Uncle Myung had emphasized, however, was that space was also an excellent *insulator.* The climate control in a starship had a lot to do keeping the vessel from getting too *hot*, because dumping excess heat was difficult, and masking it from local detection was impossible without magical aid.

Please don't let them find us, I thought, like a prayer to the heavens. I wasn't sure whether I meant the mercs marching beneath us or pirates patrolling the bleak depths of the void. Maybe both.

I strained to hear the mercs' conversation from my position. Their voices came to me as though from an undulating distance, distorted by the strange acoustics of the space we were trapped in. Then it occurred to me that I needn't have bothered to listen. I hadn't miraculously learned their language, after all.

I couldn't see Rokuro's face from my position, but I heard their intake of breath. "They have been ordered to block access to all the escape pods," Rokuro whispered.

Did Hwan really believe I was so cowardly as to abandon ship—and my comrades—the moment we exited the Gate and it became safe to do so? I'd never do that, even to comrades who had once locked me up in the brig. I realized I was growling and made myself stop. It wouldn't do to give our position away.

Of course, I thought darkly, even worse would be to allow people to cast off from the *Haetae*—and then for Hwan to open fire on the defenseless pods. It would be monstrous. But if I'd thought of it, so could my uncle.

I held my breath until bright spots floated in front of my eyes and the world seemed to spin around me. Just when I thought I would pass out, the footsteps receded. I exhaled, then inhaled deeply, almost coughing as some dust caught in my throat. The ship's filters must not be doing their job properly. Still, I sighed in relief.

"Let's keep going," I said when I realized the others were waiting for a signal.

It seemed as though we'd been crawling for an eternity. In my imagination, we had become a clandestine settlement of creatures scuttling through the ship's ducts, like an invading disease. Not far from the truth, if you took Hwan's viewpoint. What if he trapped us here and we lived out the rest of our mayfly lives in the shafts, growing stunted and wan?

Get a hold of yourself, I said to myself. *He hasn't defeated us yet.*

"Sebin." Jee's voice floated back toward me some time later.

"Yes?" I asked when he didn't elaborate.

"How are we going to keep the Gate drive from recharging for another jump, anyway?"

Thanks to the monotonous work of moving my arms and legs, I'd had plenty of time to think about the problem. "We're going to rig the drive to disconnect from its power core *after* we safely exit the Gate."

I could practically hear Jee blanching. "Are you sure that's safe?"

"Nothing about this operation is safe," Rokuro said.

"Safety is for losers," Euna agreed jauntily.

"We can do it safely," I said, which was more wishful thinking than anything else, but it seemed to satisfy Jee. "Disconnection by itself is standard engineering procedure, anyway. They have to take the drive offline to perform certain repairs." One more thing I'd learned from Uncle Hwan's stories.

This time Euna had a question. "How do you know all this, anyway? You've barely been on the *Haetae* a day!"

I smiled ruefully, glad she couldn't see me. "Military family, remember? I grew up hearing all the tales."

"I just bet," Euna said. "*My* family mostly liked to gross me out by talking about the terrible food!"

"Are we close to the site yet?" Jee asked. "I'd check, but there's no room to get my slate out."

"Don't turn it on!" I warned him. "Hwan might be able to track the signal!"

"Like I'd be caught that easily," he said, but I caught a whiff of his uncertainty.

Tactfully, I didn't mention it. We were all doing our best. "If I've been keeping track of all the intersections correctly," I said, "it should be left at the next juncture. Euna?"

"That's right," Euna said, pleased. "I'll be grateful to get out of here. My back is going to hurt for a year at this rate."

Privately, I thought we'd be lucky to escape with nothing worse than backaches. I had one, too. Going around on all fours was one thing when I was a tiger, but it felt awkward in human shape. At least the fact that this shaft had been designed to accommodate human adults meant it wasn't as cramped as it could've been, even if it wasn't exactly roomy, either.

"Good thing that menace Hwan hasn't tried to gas us or flush out the atmosphere in the ventilation system," Euna said. "He can't do that without shutting off the air circulation in the rest of the ship, and it'd be a risky way of getting to us. I'd survive, but the rest of you . . ."

"I'm so glad I don't have your imagination," Jee mumbled.

"Imagination is a detriment," Rokuro agreed. I couldn't tell whether this was another joke.

All too soon we neared the juncture. "Slow down," I suggested, my voice barely a breath. "We don't want to alert any sentries."

"Good call," Euna agreed.

The slowness of our approach made me agonizingly aware of how precarious the odds were. Did we have a chance against battle-hardened mercenaries under an experienced captain's command?

"We're here," Euna whispered in the darkness.

She needn't have said anything. I could smell the mercs below us. There were eight of them, and to get to the Gate drive in the engine room, we would have to take them out.

EIGHTEEN

"What do we do now?" Jee whispered back.

I didn't want to voice my thoughts, given that it would increase the chances of the sentries overhearing us, but I had no choice. "Someone pass me a blaster so I can open the grille. I'll toss it back after. I'll drop down, draw their fire, and then Rokuro can follow. Jee, see if you can get the maintenance robots on our side. Euna, you snipe them from above."

"Sounds good," Jee said, and Euna murmured acknowledgment. Their agreement eased a knot in my chest I hadn't been aware of.

"One thing," Rokuro said suddenly. "Please avoid killing my comrades. Some of them may listen to reason and turn against Hwan. Just try to push them back—their armor will offer them some protection."

"All right," I said. The fewer dead, the better.

Jee was more useful for hacking than in hand-to-hand situations, whereas Euna would be deadliest firing from behind cover. I felt bad about asking Rokuro to join me in close combat, especially against their own, but if it bothered them, I couldn't tell. Even their smell didn't tell me anything about their mood.

This was going to require tricky maneuvering in the tight confines. I wished that I hadn't been the last one into the shaft, but there was no helping it. I'd needed to be a tiger to boost up the others.

Everyone scooted down the shaft in what would otherwise have been a comedic fashion, like a parade of ants. At least there wasn't anyone else to witness the scene. When we reached the grate, the others squeezed themselves against the wall to let me by, and then they stayed in a cluster right behind me. As much as I hated having my personal space encroached on, I understood why they were doing it. The closer Rokuro was, the more quickly they could scramble down after me.

I took a moment to peer down through the grate. The narrow slats limited my field of vision. I could only see a single sentry from my vantage point. Fortunately, I wasn't limited to the sense of sight. My nose told me we were downwind from at least four of the mercs.

Rokuro passed me their blaster. *Here goes nothing,* I thought. Taking careful aim, I fired at one screw after another. The backwash of heat stung my eyes, and I heard someone below rapping out orders in a shrill voice.

I slid the blaster back to Rokuro. Then I lifted the grate and handed it to Euna, drawing back from the edge of the opening now lit by the violet lightning of the mercs' stunners.

Some of the violet nimbus grazed my hand. Two fingers went numb. On my right hand, too—the dominant one. I was tempted to squeeze my eyes shut against the sudden lack of sensation. Even pain would have been preferable.

I had to act. I inhaled sharply, then dove into the path of fire, willing myself to shift as I did so. I wasn't sure whether it would work while I was partly paralyzed by the stunners. There was only one way to find out, so I took it.

I fell out of the opening like a stone, taking the brunt of the stunner fire. Everything turned to static, and for a panicked moment I wondered if I would still be able to breathe. Then I remembered that Special Investigator Yi hadn't seemed paralyzed to quite that extent.

Still, it was hard to keep dread from overwhelming me as I landed heavily on the deck, trapping a merc beneath me. They squawked, then fell silent. I couldn't find it in myself to feel sorry for them. After all, they were the reason I was slumped on my side like a giant shaggy lump. I felt like the world's most useless carpet.

Come on, I told my inert body. *You weren't hit that hard. Get up!*

Try as I might, though, my body wouldn't respond. Meanwhile, Euna exchanged shots with the warriors, who were trying to get a good angle of fire up into the ventilation shaft. Euna either had uncanny luck or amazing reflexes, because she hit two of them in the hand and kept returning fire.

The only thing that assuaged my growing surreal sense of horror was the fact that an unpleasant tingling sensation had returned to my whole body. Sort of how it might feel if my skin had been covered by mosquito bites, and never mind that it would take a persistent mosquito to penetrate my shaggy fur.

The battle continued around me. I hated being unable to contribute. Jee still hadn't had any luck summoning robot reinforcements, but a sudden, agonizing thump on my back told me Rokuro had taken their chance to move. They dove past me into a partly protected niche and quickly forced the defenders back by coordinating their fire with Euna's. Four down, four to go.

My heart lifted when I finally saw maintenance robots swarming out of the vents and crawling up the remaining warriors' backs like deranged insects. Despite the robots' unfortunate resemblance to overgrown cockroaches, I couldn't help grinning as the warriors yelped and flailed at the unexpected attack, trying futilely to claw the robots away from them. I was relieved that Jee's hacking had triumphed once again.

Focus. I had to concentrate on what *I* could do. I twitched a muscle carefully as more sensation returned. Yes! I could move again.

I wasn't completely foolhardy. I remained still, feigning helplessness while I waited for the right moment to counterattack. It would be bad if my muscles failed me when I finally took action.

Then I heard a cry from above. "Sebin, they're trying to flush the atmosphere out of the vents!" Jee said. "I'm not sure I can override—"

"Get down where there's atmosphere and take cover behind Sebin," Euna said. "I'll stay up here."

I heard a buzzing alarm. "Warning," the computer said in an eerily serene voice. "All personnel must exit vents. Ventilation system is being sealed due to depressurization."

Jee scrambled out of the vent and dropped down just before a clear membrane sealed the opening in the ceiling. It would harden in place to prevent atmosphere in the ship proper from being sucked out as well. "Euna's trapped up there," he whispered.

She would be all right. I had to believe that. There had only been time for one person to escape the vent, and Euna could survive in a vacuum, while Jee couldn't.

I sprang up, gathering my hind legs beneath me in a crouch, then leaped forward in a powerful pounce. Jee's robots had the sense to scatter. My bulk slammed into three of the remaining four mercs. *If only they weren't so heavily armored,* I thought as we went down in a tangle of flailing limbs. The spikes and ornaments on their armor dug painfully into my hide.

Unluckily, I hadn't counted on my body betraying me again. My hind legs buckled, and I landed more heavily than I'd intended. I let out a completely undignified yowl.

Still, even if I couldn't move from my current position, I could bat at the mercs with my forepaws. I bowled over the last one with a mighty swat. The merc shrieked as they toppled, then fell silent.

The unpleasant tingling started in my forelimbs as well. I wondered how long the aftereffects would last.

I shifted back to human form when I was certain all the mercs had stopped moving. "It's safe!" I called up to the now-sealed opening, wondering if Euna could hear us through it. Sound didn't travel through a vacuum, but maybe she could feel the vibrations. "Are you okay?"

There was a long pause. Euna pressed her face against the membrane, her mouth moving. "I got winged." Her voice drifted down, distorted and barely audible. "But I'll be all right." I could hear the note of pain in her tone.

"I'd help you get down," I said wryly, "but . . ." My legs folded under me again as I made another attempt to stand up.

"Do we dare break the seal?" Jee asked.

"We can't leave her stuck up there," I said. "Besides, even

Hwan wouldn't be so crazy as to remove the atmosphere in the whole ship. The air might get thin, but we'll be all right." At least I hoped this was true.

Rokuro climbed up on my back—ouch!—and sliced through the membrane with a knife. The air hissed as it was sucked into the opening. Rokuro reached up and helped Euna down. She was glowing all over now, like an untidy star.

I cast a worried eye over her. She held one of her hands gingerly. "It's fine," she said, noticing my look. "I've gotten worse cramps drawing cartoons."

"Jee," I said, "there's no hull breach, is there?" A little localized vacuum was one thing. With the seal broken, the pressure would eventually equalize. But a hull breach—*that* would be a problem even I couldn't solve.

"Nope," Jee said after checking his slate. "Thank goodness."

Rokuro regarded me. "Judging by the fact that you were able to move earlier, Cadet Sebin, it should be only five or six minutes before your full function is restored."

Did we even *have* five or six minutes? I wished I could check, but the countdown that mattered was measured in the ticktock beats of my uncle's ambition.

Rokuro checked on his merc comrades to ensure that they had only been stunned unconscious. By the time Rokuro had finished, sensation had fully returned to my arms and legs, although I suspected I shouldn't exert myself too much in case I had another collapse.

"How's everyone doing?" I asked. "Anyone need medical attention?" Better to find out now than in the middle of the next fight. And if there was one thing I was certain of, it was that more confrontations were coming.

"Singed but okay," Euna said.

Jee held up his slate. "I've got some of the maintenance robots scouting for us, so we'll—"

Just then, we were interrupted by a menacing growl over the intercom. I nearly shifted, and I suffered the stomach-churning nausea of a stifled shape-change. Euna moved her finger to the trigger of her blaster but stopped short of firing. Jee ducked behind the nearest cover, which happened to be Rokuro. The merc was the only one who didn't flinch, and I envied them their stoicism.

"Greetings, Sebin." Hwan's voice came out as a distorted snarl, and my hackles rose. "I see you have chosen to be a dis-appointment to the family."

Euna's gaze cut sideways. She was clearly worried about how I'd react.

The scar on my palm felt as though a blade of ice had cut all the way down to the bone. I clenched my jaw and said noth-ing. My uncle wasn't wrong. I doubted the Space Forces would want me after this escapade concluded, even if I survived it. And my family wasn't going to welcome me back with open arms after screwing up both as a cadet *and* a member of the Juhwang Tiger Clan.

"You took advantage of my trust," Hwan continued. "Very clever."

Jee swallowed audibly and clutched his slate to his chest as though it could protect him.

"But do you think a mere cadet has any hope of success?"

My thoughts came back into focus on the word *cadet*. I might have the Thousand Worlds' shortest service record after today, and I might be the lowest of the low. But I still had a duty, and I wasn't going to let *my own uncle* prevent me from doing it.

"Listen," I snapped at the others. "We've got to get into the engine room and prepare it to go offline. Jee, there has to be a section in the ship's manual for this. Find it. Euna, Rokuro, you'll be responsible for guarding Jee. My uncle might think he can intimidate us with his words, but every moment he spends talking is a moment he's not focused on what we're doing."

I considered taking the time to figure out how to tie up Uncle Hwan's unconscious mercs, then decided against it. Every second mattered. Once we were inside the engine room, we could barricade ourselves against any intruders. I trusted that no one would be so foolish as to mount a full assault on the area with the most sensitive and vital machinery.

Jee looked up from the manual on the slate and groaned in dismay. "This hatch might take some extra work to hack my way past, Sebin."

"Better get started, then," I replied.

He groaned again.

Euna and Rokuro patrolled together in one direction, while I went in the other, alert to any changes in the air or smells that wafted in our direction. The absence of definite clues was more frustrating than an imminent threat would have been. I knew how to fight. But waiting—now *that* was hard.

"Did it!" Jee crowed after what seemed like forever. I could hear the engine room's hatch sliding open before I turned my head.

"Everyone in," I said. "And hurry!" My sensitive hearing detected a faint tread. Had Hwan's reinforcements reached us?

Jee smelled only too glad to retreat to some form of haven.

Rokuro was next, while Euna backed into the engine room so she could fire out if necessary. I went last.

The engine room might as well have been another world. I almost felt as if I'd stepped into a miniature garden. It formed its own oasis within the ship, with banks of consoles and their reassuring gauges and soft blue lights. The whole place hummed quietly, like music from a faraway dream. I allowed myself a moment to stand there and let the soothing atmosphere wash over me.

Never mind that none of its personnel were present. Hwan's forces must have taken them out earlier. I tried not to think of what might have happened to them. I had to focus on the task at hand.

"I wish I'd brought a sketchbook for this," Euna remarked in a hushed voice. "Too bad my pencil's useless in a blaster fight."

I let out my breath in a quiet sigh and hoped the others hadn't heard me. As much as I wished I could stand here and meditate, I couldn't pretend forever that we had reached safety. We had work to do.

It took me a moment to realize what had gone wrong. Mainly because it was an *absence* of sound rather than an actual noise. "Jee," I said, "why isn't the hatch closing?"

Jee's face was pinched. "I don't know!" he said as he jabbed frantically at his slate. "It's not responding to my commands anymore."

Uh-oh. Time for a backup plan. "Rokuro and I will guard the opening," I said, "and be ready to ambush anyone who tries to get in." Rokuro took the left, so I took the right. "Euna, be prepared to shoot anything that makes it past us. Jee, you've got the hard part."

"On it, sir," Jee said. I glanced back at him in surprise at the address and saw his shaky smile. "I think I see how to do it, now that I have physical access." He set the slate to one side and took up a position at the largest console. "It's not that the procedure is difficult—it's hacking my way past the security watchdogs, and for that I'm going to have to . . ." His voice trailed off into intent muttering.

"We have a bigger problem," Euna observed. "If the hatch here, specifically, won't close, it's because Hwan knows where we are and what we're trying to do."

"Why do you think we're preparing for—" I began, then dropped silent when stunner fire arced through the doorway. I flattened myself against the bulkhead so the halo of paralytic light didn't catch me.

Hwan's voice resumed haranguing me over the intercom. "When I do catch up with you, *Cadet*," he growled, "rest assured that you will be thoroughly punished for defying me. I will regret having to report your failure to your parents, but it's not as if they would mourn losing such a clearly unworthy specimen. Better that you go to your rest than sully the clan rosters."

I couldn't read Rokuro's expression at all, but I heard a small gasp from Euna. "That's cold," she said from behind me. "He's your *uncle*."

I didn't need the distraction. All the same . . . "Yes," I said, trying to cover the desolate hole that Hwan's words had opened inside me.

Was he right? Would my parents take his side, instead of agreeing with me that Hwan was a dangerous renegade who had to be stopped? I had imagined that duty would always provide a compass to guide my actions. Now, it only left an aching hollow where my heart should have been.

"If Hwan's coming for us," I said, "he has Min with him. We need some way to protect ourselves from Charm."

Rokuro colored. "I have a headset with me. I'm not supposed to bring it on a mission, but it cancels noise."

"It's worth a try," I said.

Rokuro fished in their jumpsuit, then handed the set to me. "You take it. Hwan is likely to target you first."

I only hesitated a little. "All right." I put it on.

I had expected our attackers to rush the doorway after that first salvo. Though I couldn't hear anything, I saw Jee crouch down behind the console where he'd been at work.

There was a flash as Jee triggered something that shouldn't have been there. None of us had thought to check the engine room for traps, because we'd been so stressed and desperate that we'd seized upon the place as a safehold. I had just enough time to form the thought that we'd fallen right into Hwan's trap, and not enough to holler a warning.

NINETEEN

A concussive blast boomed through the engine room. The headset didn't prevent me from hearing *that*. The noise was deafening. I shifted instinctively, without conscious control over the impulse. My body knew that my tiger shape could endure more punishment than the human one. In the split second before everything went white, I wondered whether the others had reached cover in time.

Red afterimages floated in front of my entire field of vision. I staggered sideways, then realized that I was curled up behind one of the consoles. Unfortunately, even a juvenile tiger didn't comfortably fit in that little space, and my rear limbs were left exposed.

All thoughts of self-preservation fled as I remembered my comrades. I had to find out if they were okay. I blinked rapidly in an effort to clear the afterimages. It didn't help.

I resumed human form, wishing that as a tiger I could speak in a way that non-tigers could understand. *Report!* I signed. It was one of the words I knew in the military tactical sign language.

Euna waved. I could see the steady sizzling of her blaster as she fired. Rokuro copied her.

Even in my half-stunned state, I could do math. If Euna, Rokuro, and I were all right, that left . . . "Jee?" I bellowed, hoping he hadn't been deafened and could still hear me.

But my nose, which I should have relied on when I realized the afterimages were a problem, told me the answer. I smelled blood—Jee's blood. My heart almost stopped. "Jee?" I asked again.

No answer.

This couldn't be happening.

I couldn't believe Hwan was desperate enough to plant an explosive trap *inside* the engine room. Who even knew if anything was functional anymore? The smell of smoke clogged my nostrils.

It came to me that I'd misjudged the effects of the grenade. I assumed it had been a flash grenade—good for distracting or blinding people, but unlikely to do lasting harm. Unless you landed right on top of it.

Jee had been right on top of it. I didn't know what to do about the sick, roiling sensation in my gut. He had to be okay. I hadn't known him long, but he'd proven himself again and again. Besides, I was the one who'd gotten him into this situation. I was responsible for making sure that he emerged intact.

The afterimages dimmed enough for me to note where everyone had ended up. Everyone but Jee had assumed positions on either side of the engine room so we weren't in immediate danger of taking fire. Euna, with her eye for angles, had sheltered in a nook and only occasionally poked part of her head and her hand out to take potshots at the enemy.

Hwan's voice kept booming over the intercom, audible only as a faint buzzing through my headset. By now, I'd grown numb to his insinuations, which I could figure out even without being able to distinguish his words. Yes, I knew that I was a disgrace to the Juhwang Tiger Clan. Yes, I knew that the Space Forces didn't want me, either.

If I stopped long enough to think about either of those things, I'd never start moving again. So I balled up the messy feelings about my family, the home I'd never see again, and even my uniform and shoved the wad into the back of my mind so I could refocus on the task at hand.

"Rokuro," I said loudly, fighting to keep my voice steady, "check on Jee. I'll hold the entrance in case they rush us." I didn't know how to say something that complicated in sign language—something I wanted to remedy if we got out of this alive—and besides, I didn't know if Rokuro understood Thousand Worlds military signs.

The merc gestured their acceptance. A moment later, they mouthed, *Injured.* Not dead, then.

I wished I dared a peek to see who was out there. I reminded myself that I could rely on my sense of smell instead. What little I could hear through the headset suggested that our attackers were keeping their distance, although I didn't like relying on my ears, not when Min was still a threat. So far, stalemate.

Then Euna's fire stopped.

I met her eyes. She grimaced. "I hate to break it to you, Sebin," she yelled, "but I'm out of power!"

Battery? I signed.

Euna's mouth twisted, and she shook her head no.

I groaned. "We need time to rig the Gate drive to go offline,"

I told her, hoping I was enunciating clearly enough. "I'm going out there. Do whatever it takes to close the hatch after me. Shut down the intercom. Don't trust me if I ask to be let back in." I knew Min was still working for my uncle, after all. I couldn't expect her to sacrifice her brother's ghost to defy him.

Euna nodded.

Suddenly Hwan's harangue over the intercom shut off mid-word. I heard his voice anew—this time from right outside the engine room. He bellowed so loudly I could hear him even through the headset.

"Very good," Hwan said. "It was a valiant effort. Worthy of a tiger." His coldness receded a fraction, replaced by grudging acknowledgment. "It's too bad you picked the wrong side."

Cautiously, I peered out to scan the area. Uncle Hwan was there, flanked by an honor guard of those mercs. The shaman and her dog, Shield, stood to his left. She held a blank slip of paper in her hand, already incandescent with magic, while Shield's mouth lolled open in a fierce doggy grin. I wasn't sure which of them I was more afraid of.

My attention narrowed to the one who mattered, the one who could change the balance of power: Min. Despite her humanoid shape, she had sharp, foxlike features and amber eyes, perhaps a result of the dog's influence.

Hwan had scarcely finished speaking when I shifted and gathered myself to leap toward Min. I had to buy time for Jee to recover, or failing that, for Rokuro or Euna to finish what he'd started.

I knew going in that I'd only have one chance. Hwan would order Min to Charm me, and after that I'd be his pawn. But even Charm couldn't outweigh the laws of physics. Once I launched myself in tiger form, it wouldn't matter if I became Min's puppet.

I cursed myself in mid-leap. I'd been an idiot. I should have taken out the *shaman*. But it was too late.

Hwan nodded sharply at Min.

She straightened. "Sebin!" she sang out, like I was an old friend she'd spotted in a crowd. "Sebin, come to me. There's been a misunderstanding."

I knew better than to listen to her, except I'd miscalculated. When I shifted into tiger form, I didn't retain any clothes— including the headset. Nothing protected me from her Charm.

I desperately tried to avoid crashing into her, newly worried that I'd hurt her. Min was nimble, though, and she stepped aside when I landed heavily. She rested her hand on my back and stroked my fur. I chuffed contentedly.

Up close, she smelled out of place on this starship—her scent was of windy, star-strewn nights, and labyrinthine pine forests, and the distinct animal odor of fox. I craned my head back and saw that her eyes gleamed bright fox-yellow. While she herself didn't sport a fox's tail, let alone the nine tails of the most powerful gumiho, her shadow was the silhouette of a fox sitting upright, its ears pricked forward and its bushy tail thumping against the deck.

She's very definitely a fox, the rational part of my mind noted. I couldn't shake the conviction that this was a key fact, but I couldn't for the life of me figure out why it mattered. Besides, she was patting me as though I were an overgrown house cat. Normally this would have offended me—a tiger is *not* a pet— except I didn't want to do anything that would keep me from basking in her presence.

Min leaned down so her mouth was next to my ear. "Sorry, Sebin," she whispered, so quietly I was sure no one else had heard her.

I moaned in confusion, but she wasn't done.

"Do me a favor," she said. I could hear my uncle rapping out orders, but I wasn't interested in them. Min's wishes were the only ones that mattered. "Things are about to get messy, and I don't want the dog to get hurt. Get him far away from here and keep him away—got it?"

Then she straightened, pale but determined, and I knew it was my turn to act. I didn't like leaving her side. Still, she was my friend, and she'd asked a favor of me. She wouldn't have requested this if it weren't important.

I sprang forward and grabbed Shield's ruff in my mouth, careful not to break his skin with my sharp teeth. The dog howled, but by then I was off and running. I heard Hwan roaring behind me—whether human or tiger it didn't matter—and then the clash of combat.

Shield clawed at my face. I resisted the urge to spit him out, considering how gross his fur tasted—like cloying strawberry shampoo. I closed my eyes and navigated by memory as I ran. While I normally had an excellent sense of my surroundings, it was hard to concentrate while the dog was attacking me. And I didn't dare shake him or do anything to protect myself. Min had emphasized how important it was to keep Shield safe.

Still, it occurred to me as I scraped against a bulkhead and then corrected course, Min hadn't said that I couldn't come back. Surely she'd expect me to secure Shield, then return to assist her. Yes. That was what she'd meant, even if she hadn't gotten a chance to tell me her plans in detail.

I skidded to a halt and looked around. Shield was still struggling and howling. *Stop that,* I wanted to tell him, except my mouth was full of his awful-tasting fur, and I wasn't sure dogs, even Sapsalis, understood tiger-speak, anyway. We'd wound up far forward of the engine room, near a series of bunkrooms.

I backtracked, wishing I could still hear what was going on in the engine-room fight. One of Shield's flailing paws caught and tangled in the thick fur of my own ruff, and his howling changed into a pitiful whine as he realized his claws were stuck.

Thank goodness no one is watching us, I thought, longing to spit out the dog and take a drink of something, anything, to wash away the taste. I had to find a place to deposit Shield, and soon.

Aha! I came across a bunkroom that had been left open. A hastily scrawled sticker said that the door was jammed and needed repairs. I sequestered myself in the room, then shoved my head and shoulders under a desk and let go of the dog. He was still stuck in my fur. He dangled there, barking in aggravation.

I shifted back into human form and lunged for Shield's ruff again, barely managing to pick him up. He sank his teeth into my arm. "I'm doing this for your own good," I informed the dog through a clenched jaw.

My maneuvering dislodged the headset, which had reappeared on me along with my uniform, and it fell to the deck. I ignored it. It wasn't important, anyway.

"Come *on*, Shield."

The dog's expression was distinctly jaundiced.

How on earth was I supposed to keep him here? "Listen," I said to Shield, who was still attached to my arm, "this doesn't have to be unpleasant." How had I ended up bargaining with a dog, far away from the action?

Shield growled. His jaw slackened enough that I could pry him off me. He sprang at me with a snarl, but I dodged him, thinking furiously. It would be embarrassing if I couldn't outwit a dog!

As I circled the room, dodging the dog's attacks, I caught a whiff of . . . Was that a *field ration*? My family had served them once a week, more often if there was a training exercise. *To prepare you for the rigors ahead,* Mom liked to say. At the time I'd considered it a minor badge of honor that I could choke down the barley hardtack and dried meat without complaint. Even the chocolate-and-marshmallow-cream pies that served as dessert became tedious when I ate them over and over again.

I remembered the dog's greed for its stinky treats. "Hey, Shield," I said after dodging another lunge. "I'll make you a deal." The dog stopped attacking and whine-growled suspiciously.

"There's *food* in here," I said. I could tell I had his interest. "It may be out of reach for *you*, but *I* could retrieve it and give you some."

Shield's tail twitched, then began to wag. His eyes crossed as he tried to maintain his fierce attitude, even as his desire for tasty snacks betrayed him.

I edged along the side of the room, following the smell of the meal. Now that I wasn't fending off an angry canine, I could tell that it was japchae, a dish of stir-fried beef, vegetables, and glass noodles that was normally served on holidays. The version that appeared in field rations, with its stringy meat and grayed-out greens, could *ruin* a holiday, but I wasn't about to mention that to the dog.

Aha! Someone had stashed the ration under their pillow, whether to save it for later or because they couldn't figure out a better way to get rid of it, who knew? Gingerly, I flipped over the pillow, then retrieved the ration in its sealed metal tray. In theory the seal should have kept any of the odor from seeping out, but either it was faulty or my nose was too sensitive. I'd never encountered a field ration this smelly before.

The battle's going to be over by the time you get back there if you don't hurry up, I thought.

I opened up the tray. The pungent odor of the preserved japchae within almost made me gag. Shield lunged again, but I held the food high out of reach.

"Not so fast," I said. "I don't know where your loyalties lie—"

I interpreted Shield's eager bark and tail-wagging as *To my belly, what did you think?*

"—but I promise not to hurt your shaman. My quarrel is with Hwan." *My uncle.* But the dog wouldn't care about that detail. "All you have to do is stay here and enjoy this, er, tasty meal. Can we agree to that?'

The dog hesitated. Another whine escaped him, though, and I sensed his resolve was wavering. He crouched low on his belly, mouth opening as he drooled over the prospect of more food.

I clamped my own jaw shut when I realized that I, too, was starting to drool. When was the last time I'd eaten? Or even had a snack?

Shield glowered at me. Just as I could smell his hunger, he could smell mine.

"If you do as I ask," I added, inspired, "you can have the *whole meal.*" I glanced hastily at the tray. Sure enough, one corner included the coveted chocolate-and-marshmallow pie. "Except for this," I added, retrieving the dessert.

Shield curled his lip at me.

"Chocolate's poisonous to dogs," I chided. Min would be upset if I allowed the creature to die of food poisoning! "After all"—I did my best to lower my voice into a coaxing purr, horrified that I sounded not unlike my uncle—"you'll have the rest to feast on. Surely an ample meal for a loyal dog such as yourself."

The dog wriggled shamelessly.

Using the food, I lured the Sapsali into the bathroom. I tossed the tray on the floor. Shield jumped toward the contents, shoving his muzzle into the japchae with the air of someone encountering a New Year's feast out of season. *Lucky critter,* I thought, as objectively disgusting as the ration was.

Hastily, I closed the hatch behind Shield, trapping him in there. Fortunately, this door was functioning just fine. Hopefully it would keep the dog safe until the action was over.

Time to find Min and offer her my support. As I broke into a run, I tore open the chocolate-marshmallow pie's wrapper with my teeth and jammed as much of it into my mouth as I could fit. The sweet chocolate coating and gooey filling were the best thing I'd ever tasted. This would have to sustain me in the fight to come.

TWENTY

I expected to find a bloodbath by the time I returned, out of breath from sprinting, to the engine room. The smells of blaster and stunner fire hung heavy in the air. But instead, I found no one—no one but Min and a closed engine-room hatch.

"Min!" I exclaimed, glad to see her there, apparently unharmed. Then I noticed her glum expression.

"Sebin," she said, and my heart almost seized at the anguish in her voice. Her eyes unfocused for a second.

I wondered if she needed medical attention. Then a fog I hadn't been aware of lifted from my thoughts, and memories came flooding in. She'd Charmed me again—but to remove the dog that impeded her powers, not to attack my friends, as I'd feared.

Tempted as I was to seize and shake her until she gave me some answers, I had to acknowledge that she had freed me. "You have three seconds to tell me what's going on," I growled.

Min lifted her head, mouth firm. "It was the only way I could keep my brother safe from the shaman," she said. "Once the dog was gone, I was free to Charm Sena."

I didn't like the sound of that. "Where is she now?"

Min made a face. "Hwan figured out the threat as soon as you left with Shield. He turned into a tiger, grabbed her, and ordered the mercs to retreat with him. Unfortunately, I only had time to give Sena one instruction before he made off with her. Jun is safe from her, but the rest of us . . . not so much."

Great, so now we had to face a shaman's magic as well. "And everyone else?"

"Holed up for safety," Min said. "I figured you'd return here. We need to track down Hwan and put an end to his shenanigans."

I looked at her steadily. "We could have been working together from the beginning," I said, "if only you and Special Investigator Yi had trusted me more."

Min sighed. "You're not entirely wrong, but we don't have time for this right now."

"Are the others okay?" I asked. I choked up for a moment, then added, "Is Jee—"

"I ran a remote diagnostic," Min said. "The Gate drive's powered down, although the crystals still hold some charge. Someone's been working in there—I think it must be Jee."

I felt myself pale despite my relief at the fact that Jee had survived after all. He must not have been able to drain the crystals yet. "Then Hwan still has a chance to take over the ship, power up the drive, and escape before anyone can stop him."

Min was right. Our best hope, now that Jee was ensconced in the engine room, was to confront my uncle directly.

"Do you know which way Hwan went?" I asked.

She held up a slate. "We can locate him with this."

"Then we'll cut him off," I said grimly. "One moment." I

had to see if I could reach Jee, anyway. "Cadet Sebin to engine room." The computer chimed to let me know that the intercom was on. "Jee, this is Sebin."

"How do I know it's really you?" Jee's tinny voice responded. "That you're in your right mind?"

I sagged in relief. Even though Min had told me he had to be alive, it was good to hear his voice. "Min has freed me from her Charm," I said. "Believe me or don't believe me, but keep working on the Gate drive."

"Uh, okay," Jee said, nonplussed.

We started toward Hwan's last known location according to the computer.

Unfortunately, the interruptions weren't over. "Uh, Sebin?" Jee's voice came from the intercom again.

"Yes?" I asked without slowing down.

"Bad news," Jee said. "I had some programs monitoring the ship's systems. Hwan just disabled all the escape pods."

Min and I exchanged glances. She looked as green and ill as I felt. Hwan meant business. This was far worse than just blocking access to the escape pods. If anything went catastrophically wrong on the *Haetae*—besides a renegade tiger trying to hijack it, that is—none of the crew would be able to get to safety. We were trapped.

It was a monstrous thing to do. I hadn't thought any captain—or ex-captain—would contemplate such an action. All the ship's protocols I had learned specified that the escape pods must always remain available in case evacuation became necessary.

"Sebin, are you there?" Jee asked.

I couldn't smell his fear over the intercom, but I could hear it. "I'm listening." I'd slowed down a fraction, trusting that Min would keep an eye out for any threats.

"Do I keep working on the Gate drive?" Jee said. "Or do I try to get around whatever Hwan did to the escape pods?"

It wasn't a choice. "Fix the pods," I said heavily. "We can't afford to take the chance that Hwan won't gas the ship or release a toxin or do something equally horrible." For all I knew, he was willing to take the rest of us down with him. "After that, counteract the locks on all the hatches. People need to be able to get to safety once they regain consciousness from that knockout gas."

"Uh, Sebin . . ." Min said.

"One moment," I said, trying to figure out what other instructions to give Jee while I had him on the line.

"No, really, *Sebin*." She shoved me, hard.

She was too slight to knock me over, so I recovered my balance easily, a retort on my lips—which died when the stunner bolt arced past my ear, missing it by a scant inch and forcing me to fall.

Min was already scuttling backward like a crab. I reflected that it was too bad battle cruisers didn't feature crates lying around, or rocks the way we had on planets, for cover. I levered myself back up and shifted into tiger form, landing in a defensive crouch.

My gaze immediately fixed on Hwan, who had arrived, maintaining his human shape. Even as a man, he exuded confidence—and danger. My lip curled back in a snarl when I spotted the blaster that he was carrying. He had it aimed not at me, although that could change easily enough, but at Min.

Worse, Hwan was accompanied by six mercs, all armored,

all wielding stunners. Chief among them was Captain Uchida with her ogre helmet. There was no sign of the shaman, Sena. Hwan must have decided that he couldn't rely on a Charmed ally.

"We don't have to settle this through fighting!" Min yelled at Hwan. She ducked around a corner.

Hwan gave no sign of having heard her. Instead, he fired over me toward Min's last location.

My eyes narrowed, and I stared at his ears. Aha—he was wearing earplugs. Real ones, not like the headset I had tried to use against Min's Charm not so long ago.

Jun materialized in his human form and launched himself at Hwan, fingers extended like talons, lips peeled back from sharp, distended teeth. Even though he had no substance, the icy wind that unfurled before him and the otherworldly menace he exuded were enough to foul Hwan's aim as he fired again toward the corner where Min had retreated. Jun passed *through* Hwan, causing him to shake his head as ghost-substance momentarily clouded his vision.

"It's up to you now, Sebin!" Jun cried. "I can't stray far from Min." Indeed, he was already withdrawing to the same corner, mists billowing around his nowhere feet.

Time to take advantage of the opening the ghost had given me. I roared as I sprang at Hwan, determined to wrest the blaster from him before he hurt Min or me. I had a scant moment to feel foolish. If he couldn't hear Min's voice, I doubted my roar was getting through, either. Besides, an adult tiger was unlikely to be intimidated by me of all people.

Hwan didn't take on his own tiger shape, to my disappointment. A primal part of me wanted to fight him for dominance—for control of the ship. Never mind that I had forfeited all hopes of a future captaincy. The part of me that was a tiger knew only that it had a challenger, and that I had to defeat him to save everyone.

Instead, Hwan rolled out of the way, unbelievably agile for such a large man. He came up firing, this time at me. Worse, his mercs kept up their stunner fire. They, too, seemed unaffected by Min's shouted pleas, and I guessed that they'd also protected themselves with earplugs.

I didn't dare let any of the shots land, but a tiger makes for a large target. *What am I going to say to Aunt Sooni and my parents?* I wondered as I dodged by the expedient of shifting from tiger to human, human to tiger, combined with unpredictable movements so they couldn't tell where to aim. Aunt Sooni had trained me in this technique, and I was good at it. But it had the unfortunate disadvantage of burning up energy reserves. If I survived this fight, I was going to need to sleep for a year. Too bad that meal tray had only contained a single chocolate-and-marshmallow pie. I resolved never to complain about rations again.

As I weaved and dodged, I considered my options. Sooner or later, Hwan and his mercs were going to wear me out. The edges of my vision were already graying ominously. *I can't give up now,* I thought.

Even so, tempting visions flashed through my mind. I imagined feasts of barbecued pork, and a sunlit bed to sleep in. My stomach growled. I wouldn't be able to ignore the distraction of hunger much longer. I caught myself swaying dizzily. How could I defeat Hwan if I gave in to weakness?

My uncle had the advantages of height, mass, and years

of experience. Not to mention numbers, since he had the six mercs on his side. He'd even neutralized Min—

That wasn't entirely true. Hwan had ensured that neither he nor his mercs could be Charmed. Which was fine as far as that went.

He hadn't thought about what Min could do with *me*.

I shifted back into my human form and nipped around to the corner opposite Min's. I only had seconds to convey my message. "Min," I whispered. "Charm *me*."

Her eyes widened. "What? Sebin, I—"

"*Order me to win the battle.* No matter the cost."

I was grateful she didn't argue. Her eyes glowed fox-amber, and that woodland smell wafted from her again as her fox nature asserted itself. "The only thing that matters," she said in a voice that rang like bells, "is defeating Hwan. You won't feel anything else."

In a dim corner of my mind, I doubted that magic would overpower the effect of the stunners. But it was worth trying. Energy filled me from the heart outward as Min's magic took hold.

On the past occasions, Charm had resembled a fog creeping over all the crevices of my mind, dulling thought. This time, though . . . This time was different. I had put myself under Min's influence willingly, as part of a mission I needed to fulfill.

This is what duty should be, I thought in the moment before I rejoined the fight. Loyalty freely given, rather than obedience coerced. It was something I'd had to learn for myself, because my family had never taught it to me.

This time I did not roar, or pounce. Instead, I marched out

from behind cover at a steady pace. Not slowly, but not quickly, either.

Hwan could have taken me down easily. Instead, he gestured with his free hand, and the mercs' stunner fire ceased. He continued pointing his own blaster at my head. If he hit me there, squarely between the eyes . . . Well, even a tiger spirit's hardiness had limits.

I didn't bother growling at him in the language of tigers. Even if he'd been able to hear me, it wouldn't have mattered. I raised my head.

Look at me, I willed him. I didn't crouch down in a submissive or placating posture, but neither did I threaten to attack. Just gave him that look, inviting him to remember that we were family.

If he really wanted the *Haetae,* he was going to have to go through me to get it.

Captain Uchida signed at him, her annoyance evident, then raised her stunner threateningly.

Hwan snarled, lips peeling back from his teeth.

I shifted back to human form, then pointed at my ears. *Take out the earplugs and we'll talk.*

He scoffed.

"Min," I called, "I can take it from here." I wondered if Hwan could read lips, even if I hadn't been trained in the skill.

"Sebin . . ." Min's voice from behind me was distinctly worried.

"Let Sebin handle this," Jun said. "They'll be fine."

"Retreat," I said, confident that this was the way to reach Hwan. I couldn't talk him down while he was wary of being mind-controlled by a well-meaning fox spirit. "Walk past us and out of hearing range so he can see you doing it."

Min emerged, scowling, with Jun drifting in her wake. Her hands were up, which struck me as funny until it occurred to me that maybe she could Charm people by using sign language and not just her voice. I decided not to ask her about it in front of our enemies, earplugs or not.

Min kept walking, shooting wary glances behind her at the tableau as she did so. Her footsteps receded into the distance, like an agonizing countdown. I waited until I couldn't hear her anymore, then gestured at my ears again.

Hwan's dark eyes searched mine. Then he nodded slowly and removed the earplugs. "Sebin." He said it like a curse.

I couldn't see the mercs' faces from beneath their helmets, but I could smell their confusion and distrust. They continued to hold their fire, though, much to my relief.

"Min's out of range now," I said, which I hoped was true. I had as good as promised that she wouldn't involve herself further, and honor still meant something to me. "If you want to take the *Haetae*, you will have to kill me."

"Sebin," Hwan said, and this time he sounded weary. "If you had ambushed me, it would be one thing. But you are alone and outnumbered. You've foolishly sent away the one ally who could have made a difference—if you can count on a treacherous fox at all. I know how you were trained, because it's how I was trained. It would be trivial for me to take you apart in a fight."

Ordinarily his words would have caused me to tremble, for they were true. But the resolve that Min had given me burned in my heart. Hwan was measuring victory in the language of claw and fire. Those weren't, however, the only weapons I had against him. And I could tell from the fact that he hadn't yet shot me—that he was *still talking*—that he knew it, too.

As he spoke, I took one step toward Hwan, then another. Daring him to attack me. If he failed to stop me, I would subdue him and bring the fight to an end.

It didn't take a tiger's senses to detect Hwan's agony. He had tensed up, despite his earlier relaxed arrogance. His lips were compressed into a flat, unhappy line, and he reeked of frustration and another emotion I couldn't quite identify. Regret, maybe.

Hwan's finger moved to the trigger of his blaster. My heart sank. I knew he wouldn't do so unless he were willing to fire. I'd been trained the same way in firearms usage. He was too far gone for me to reach him after all. My gambit had been for nothing. I was going to die at my uncle's hand.

"I admired you for so long," I said to my uncle. "All I wanted was to follow you into the service and become a captain like you. Maybe an even better one."

His finger shook, then steadied. His stare bored into me, implacable, unreadable.

"Every time I trained with Aunt Sooni," I went on, trying not to fret about the blaster pointed at me, "I thought about how hard I needed to work to make you proud of me. You were my guiding star. The Matriarch told me once that 'the compass that guides you must be the way of the clan.' For me, that compass was *you*."

I took a deep breath. Hwan still hadn't budged. "We're family," I said, so that at least I would die with those two words lingering in his ears like a curse. I had never heard that tiger spirits could curse people, but it seemed worth a try.

Hwan hissed a particularly vile oath under his breath. His

finger withdrew from the trigger. He holstered the blaster.

"I can't do it," he said bitterly. "Of all the people they could have sent to stop me, it's not the damned gumiho. I had ways to deal with her. It had to be *you*. My own blood." His eyes were haunted.

I stepped forward, ready to take him into custody.

I'd been so intent on Hwan that I had allowed his mercenaries to slip my mind.

Captain Uchida, seeing the threat to the man who had spared her life before, raised her stunner to fire at me.

Hwan, displaying his unbelievable reflexes one more time, shifted into his tiger shape. He wasn't quite fast enough to prevent me from taking stunner fire. But he roared so loudly I thought the entire ship would vibrate with it, and he took out all the mercs—including Uchida—with swipes from his mighty paws.

For a second, my dazzled eyes saw not Hwan, but a different, immense white tiger, its pelt glowing like star-fire—the White Tiger of the West, coming to my defense. My scar throbbed in response.

I thought I heard the White Tiger speaking to me, in a voice like storms. "Pay the price for breaking your oath," it said, "but pay it willingly."

It's over, I had time to think before the darkness claimed me.

TWENTY-ONE

For a long time I drifted in pleasant dreams. I was drowsing in a sunbeam—what feline doesn't like a hospitable sunbeam?—at the estate. My dreams never had much in the way of smell, curiously, but I could hear the splashing of the carp pond and its fountain, and the wind rustling teasingly through the azalea bushes and the grass. It would have been pleasant to linger there forever, even though I had the vague sense that I had work to do.

Then a smell intruded on my dream. Normally this wouldn't have bothered me, except it didn't match my agreeable surroundings. It wasn't the sweetness of sun-warmed grass, or the nearby water, or pollen drifting upon the wind. (I was lucky I didn't have allergies like Aunt Sooni.) It smelled like . . . fear? And not in the appetizing manner of prey, either.

My eyelids cracked open. The light was wrong, too, the sterile, carefully balanced white of artificial light, rather than the warmer glow of the yellow sun I'd grown up beneath. "Where's my sunbeam?" was the only thing I could think to mumble.

A face came into focus. Two faces. It took me a moment to identify them—Jee and Min.

"You're awake!" Jee cried, and then crushed me in a painful hug.

My entire body ached, as though I had pulled all my muscles. I squawked in protest. "Sunbeam?" I asked wistfully. And why did my voice sound so weak?

Min's eyes widened. The alarm wafting from her intensified. "Oh no," she groaned. "Where did that medic go?"

"I was dreaming about a sunbeam," I said, realizing that she thought I was befuddled or worse, had a brain injury.

Then memories of what had happened before I lost consciousness swept over me. I struggled to sit up and had to be restrained by Jee and Min. "Hwan!"

"It's all right," Min said rapidly. "He brought you to sick bay himself, then turned himself in. Captain Chaewon had just about recovered by then, so she and her security detail locked him up in the brig. And there he'll stay until the *Haetae* can hand him over to the authorities for his court-martial."

Hwan had taken down his own coconspirators to save me. Or, perhaps more accurately, in revenge for them attacking me. Only he knew the truth of it. It wouldn't redeem him in the eyes of the court. But at least I knew that the uncle I had grown up loving and admiring wasn't entirely dead, even if I never saw him again. That would have to suffice.

"Is he . . ." I swallowed, gathered myself. "Is he physically all right?"

Jin looked at me strangely. "Sebin, he *attacked* you. More than once."

"He's still my uncle," I said. And he hadn't been able to kill me after all.

To my surprise, Min nodded, and I felt an icy breeze brush my face as her ghost brother manifested for a moment, like a shape unfolding out of shadow. "I know what that's like," she said. In the harsh light her face was sober. "Even—even people like Hwan have families. I never stopped to think about that before."

She'd been about to say something other than *people*. Maybe *monsters*, or *villains*. Not so long ago, I would have described Min as one of those myself. It was funny how experience turned things inside out, and not always in comfortable ways.

"I'm glad you still have yours," I said, looking at Jun.

He smiled and ducked his head.

"Thanks to your help," Min agreed. "As well as Shield's greediness. When we found him locked in that bathroom, he had licked that ration tray clean."

I laughed a little, and it hurt. "What about the ship?" That should have been my first question. I imagined it was the primary thing Captain Chaewon had inquired about after she came to, although I doubted I'd ever get to ask her about it.

"Jee messed up the Gate drive so thoroughly we're undergoing repairs," Min said wryly.

"It's what you told me to do, Sebin!" Jee protested. "The captain said I have a future in sabotage. It . . . I'm not sure it was a compliment." His mouth pulled to the side in a rueful half smile.

"You did the right thing," I said. "It was a desperate situation." Another thought occurred to me. "What happened to the shaman and her dog?"

Min's expression turned sly. "For *some reason* she's obsessed with reciting bad limericks over and over. At least it keeps her out of trouble. And everyone's taking turns feeding Shield. He practically has a fan club."

"The *Haetae*'s not in danger now, is it?" I asked.

A shadow fell over me. I turned my head to see its source and my eyes widened—Captain Chaewon, her arm in a sling. Jee saluted, somewhat sloppily. I'd never gotten a chance to show him how to do it properly. Min bowed deeply, which still bothered me even though she wasn't a member of the crew. I struggled once more to sit upright.

"At ease," the captain said dryly. "You're injured. You look like they've started digging your grave and they're just waiting for you to roll into it."

Her bluntness took me aback. Did I really look that awful? "Yes, sir," I said.

"Tell me in your own words what happened," Captain Chaewon said. "From the beginning, for the record."

Of course. The captain would want my statement not just to evaluate my conduct—I winced just envisioning the consequences to come—but to aid in the court-martial of my uncle. I doubted any of the mercs would cooperate, assuming they'd survived, and the shaman didn't fall under their jurisdiction. Besides, other than Hwan and the mercs, I'd been the only eyewitness to that final confrontation.

My mouth had gone dry. I gulped. Before I had a chance to ask for a glass of water, Captain Chaewon gestured to someone standing to the side, and they brought me one. I murmured my gratitude and drank deeply, using the time to gather my thoughts, then began recounting everything from the beginning.

Partway through the account, my stomach growled loudly. I couldn't remember the last time I had eaten anything but that purloined chocolate-marshmallow pie. How much time had elapsed since I was last conscious? It seemed like a bad time to ask, though. Heat rushed to my face as my belly continued rumbling. I ignored it as best I could, knowing that I had a duty to give the captain my full report no matter how ravenous I was.

At last, Chaewon asked, "Do you avow that this is your full and accurate report of your service aboard the *Haetae* and your actions regarding the traitor Hwan?"

"I do," I said, as firmly as I could. I fought down a surge of nausea. *You've just ended your career.*

Even if I hadn't sworn the oath to the Space Forces, though, I had a duty. And I was going to complete it. I could find another future. I didn't know what that would look like—I'd always assumed that I would follow in my uncle's footsteps—but I'd have a lot of time to figure that out.

Captain Chaewon looked me up and down, her face unreadable. Then she nodded. "Get some rest," she said, as if I hadn't already been doing just that. She turned on her heel and left.

I stared at her retreating back, numb. Was that it? What was to become of me during the rest of my time aboard the *Haetae*? Granted, it didn't sound like I'd disgraced myself so badly that she was going to drop-kick me out of an airlock. I suspected I'd be offloaded as a witness when she handed over Hwan to the authorities.

Jee's voice interrupted my glum musings. "Hey, Sebin," he said, waving a hand in front of my face until he had my attention. "Everyone in sick bay can hear your stomach growling. You want me to get you something to eat?"

I was too hungry to turn him down. "Yes, *please.*"

He hurried off.

Min patted my shoulder. "You should have told him to get you *real* food, not the rice gruel that they feed invalids."

"I don't care what it is as long as it's edible," I said fervently, then wondered if I was going to live to regret my words.

"As long as you don't eat *me*, I don't care." She winked.

"How are the others?" I asked.

"Euna had some blisters from standing in the way of too much stunner fire," Min said, "but the medic applied synthetic skin and gave her painkillers. She's already been discharged. Jee you know about. He was smart enough to barricade himself in the engine room—he got the hatch working again—and not come out until Captain Chaewon personally ordered him to stand down."

"Namkyu?"

Just as I spoke the other cadet's name, they swept into view, bearing a tray that smelled tantalizingly of seaweed soup and rice and gimchi. Jee accompanied Namkyu, smiling broadly. I restrained myself from lunging for the tray.

"I hear someone's hungry?" Namkyu asked. They placed the tray easily within reach. "I've been kept busy assisting the medics. It's the best hands-on training I could get, really. Even if they told me I couldn't keep Guts where the patients could see it." They chuckled.

I had already shoveled some rice into my mouth. I chewed hastily, swallowed, then asked, "How long *have* I been out?"

"No one told you?" Namkyu asked, fixing Min and Jee with a disapproving stare. "You were out for three days. We were starting to worry. Those stunners are nasty business if they hit you at close range. You got lucky."

Come to that, my fingers and toes did feel stiffer than usual.

Namkyu saw me struggling to hold the spoon, and their mouth curled into a sympathetic smile. "You'll need some physical therapy," they added. "The good news is that, if you're disciplined about it, you should recover in time."

It could have been worse. I could be dead if Hwan hadn't changed his mind, or if he hadn't intervened against his own mercs. Besides, I'd spent all my life doing exercises of one sort or another. Physical therapy wouldn't be much different.

"Thank you," I said to Namkyu, and meant it. "What about Rokuro?"

Namkyu looked puzzled, but Jee knew who I meant. "Rokuro surrendered," he said. "I vouched for them, so Rokuro's under arrest in one of the guest cabins. They swore on their honor not to try to escape. When Captain Chaewon learned that Rokuro had helped us against Hwan, she agreed that they didn't need to be tossed in the brig. She said that if they turn evidence against Hwan and renounce their clan, they might be able to claim asylum in the Thousand Worlds."

I nodded my understanding, relieved that our ally didn't have to suffer too much. I remembered my own stint in the brig, however brief, all too vividly. It hadn't been so much the discomfort as the shame. If I was honest, it pricked at me still.

I was busy stuffing my belly, but Min, Jee, and Namkyu lingered, keeping me company. For a time I was content to relax in their company, and let my worries about the future fall away for later consideration.

Euna showed up not long afterward to check on me as well. I couldn't tell she'd been injured at all. She passed me a hand-drawn card featuring a ridiculous cartoon tiger with a blaster in each of its four paws. I recognized her art style. "This is for you," she said.

I opened the card. Inside it said, *Get well soon.* Okay, it may not have been the most original of messages, but still, it warmed me. All the cadets had signed it. "Thank you," I said.

Euna studied me with a small frown. "You look worried."

By then I had finished everything on the tray. I wouldn't have minded another one. "Shouldn't I be?" I blurted out. "I don't know what's going to happen to me."

Everyone fell silent. I regretted my outburst. I'd thought I had better self-control than that, but the last few days had been difficult. I was more tired, more worn down, than I'd realized.

"Captain Chaewon is strict but fair," Euna said. "You haven't gotten to know her yet, but she'll give you a chance." She patted my shoulder. "You did a great job leading us, Sebin. She's got to recognize that." The others nodded their agreement.

I wasn't so sure, but I tried to look optimistic for their sakes.

I heard frustratingly little about Captain Chaewon's decisions for the rest of the voyage once the ship was repaired enough to continue onward. Then again, that would have been the case anyway. It wasn't as though captains ordinarily confided in cadets.

If nothing else, I wasn't under arrest the way Rokuro was. The captain allowed me to return to the cadets' bunkroom. I started classes on the ship's functions, which were so *ordinary* they almost made me long for the adrenaline rush that had come with fighting for my existence.

Is that how it began for my uncle? I worried. Did I share whatever flaw had corrupted him? I wanted to believe that the honorable man I'd thought I'd known hadn't been a mirage. That he'd existed once upon a time. But Hwan himself was the only one who knew for sure.

I ran into Special Investigator Yi once in the mess hall. We'd dropped out of a Gate a day ago and were recharging the crystals. Yi had recovered from the drubbing they'd taken at the hands of my Charmed friends, to my relief. The investigator signaled for me to come over, so I did.

"I owe you an apology, Cadet Sebin," Yi said.

I shook my head. "I didn't always make the best decisions." All the same, I wouldn't have had to endure the hijacking of the ship, and what came after, if it hadn't been for Yi's distrust.

"You did when it counted," they said. "That's what mattered. You stood up to your uncle, and you helped put his partner out of commission."

"What's going to happen to Shaman Sena?" I asked. "I understand that the Space Forces don't have jurisdiction, but she has to pay for her part in this, doesn't she?"

"You can set your mind at rest on that score," Yi replied. "Shamans regulate themselves, and I will be bringing charges against her on behalf of Domestic Security as well. It's likely that she'll have her shaman status revoked by her peers just in time to stand trial."

I nodded, relieved that Sena wouldn't be running around causing more trouble. Especially for Jun.

Finally, I decided to ask the question that had been eating at me all this time. "Special Investigator, why *do* you wear those yellow utility boots?"

Yi lifted a foot and waggled the toe of their boot, grinning.

"Undignified, aren't they? I wore them on my very first assignment for Domestic Security, a hair-raising affair involving a curse, and it netted me a promotion. I figure the boots bring me good luck."

"Of course," I said. I smiled, but I was reminded of how I'd lost the knife that Aunt Sooni had given me. Had that been an omen?

I ran into Min several times as well. "How can you tell when something's right and when it's wrong?" I asked her once. "When you do what you do?"

We were alone in the ship's recreation room, placing black and white baduk stones on a board without making much pretense of paying attention to the game. Jun kept us company, amusing himself by putting his hand *through* the board. The chilly wind that accompanied him almost felt restful, like a reminder of winter's repose.

She didn't pretend not to understand that I was asking about Charm. "Believe it or not," Min said, picking her words with care, "I never used to think about that. If I saw a way to get out of trouble, I used it. Sometimes it's creative problem-solving, and sometimes it just makes the trouble worse."

I considered that. "I guess it's no different than being good at hacking, like Jee, or being stronger than humans, like goblins or us tigers, or having a medic's skills, like Namkyu," I said. "It's all in how you use it."

"I guess," Min echoed. She fidgeted. "I'm not used to trusting people, but maybe everything would have gone better if I had. You . . . You're not like your uncle." Her mouth turned down at the corners, and she cast me an uncertain glance.

"That last time, when you *asked* me to Charm you . . . That was really different."

I nodded, not trusting myself to speak. I remembered that glow of inner certainty and how it had helped me face down Hwan. In a way, I wished I could have it back. But it wouldn't have been right to ask her for it, not for selfish reasons.

"There's nothing about it," Min said, "in the lore of—of my people." Her eyes darkened with thought. "It gives me hope that maybe I can help others . . . and I won't always have to hide what I am."

Three crew members entered the rec room then, and it was no longer safe to speak. I smiled at Min. I'd never considered what it was like for a gumiho, even a well-intentioned one, to live in secrecy at all times. I had hated the stigma against my family because of my connection to Uncle Hwan. It must be a hundred times worse to have to conceal something so fundamental about yourself. I'd have to remember that, even if I might never again be in a position to do something about it.

The days blurred into each other. I showed up for my physical therapy sessions on time every day. The medic who worked with me declared that she'd never seen anyone so *diligent* about it. I didn't mind the exercises, which involved relearning fine motor control in my fingers and doing weird stuff like writing out characters with my toes. But I didn't exactly want more of them, either, so I smiled and said I appreciated the help.

I went to my classes and studied with a single-mindedness that surprised even me. I'd always had good focus, but every time I looked out a viewport or walked through the starship's corridors, I was reminded that this might be the last time I spent aboard a battle cruiser. I had to make the most of it while I was here.

Sometimes, when I was washing vegetables from hydroponics for the ship's cook or scrubbing a bulkhead—tasks that the medic had approved—I thought about what I could do instead with my future. I didn't want to give up entirely on my dream of serving on a ship. There were independent traders and miners. It wouldn't be the same as being in the Space Forces, but I tried to convince myself that I could be content with life aboard a ship, any ship.

At the same time, I tried to avoid thinking about my family. Despite my efforts, my thoughts went to them anyway. Would I ever see them again? Even Uncle Hwan, though I knew what fate awaited him? And would Captain Chaewon allow me to say good-bye to him?

Worse, even if I did return to my family, would they want me anymore?

It came almost as a shock when I received a summons from Captain Chaewon. I'd known intellectually that we were approaching the main starport of Madang, fabled for its gardens, but it hadn't quite sunk in that my time aboard the *Haetae* was nearing an end. I stared at the notice on my slate, then left the other cadets without a word and headed toward the captain's office.

I saluted the captain and waited, silent, for her to address me.

"We'll be docking in twelve hours," Captain Chaewon said, regarding me with that imperturbable face. "I will be sending you to the base with an escort"—she must have seen me flinch, though I tried to cover the reaction—"for your own safety. After everything that's happened, it's necessary to take precautions."

"Yes, sir," I said. There really wasn't any other response I could have made.

"Sebin . . ." She hesitated. "The admiral in charge of the investigation will have many questions. Just answer honestly, the way you spoke to me, and everything will be all right."

I wasn't sure I believed her, so I merely said, "Yes, sir," again, and left it at that.

TWENTY-TWO

Ensign Hak escorted me off the *Haetae* after it docked. I had my duffel bag, and I took comfort, however scant, in the cadet uniform I wore. I wondered when I would be asked to remove it and resume civilian clothing.

I'd said my farewells to the other cadets and to Min already. There hadn't been much to say. But I held the warmth of Jee's good-bye hug, Namkyu's and Euna's bows, and Min's solemn nod to me like talismans.

The base unfolded around me in origami splendor. This starport featured sleek geometric buildings composed of faceted triangles, so that I felt like I was walking into the heart of a glittering jewel. Even the high windows and gleaming support pillars and buttresses, also faceted, added to this impression.

"Where's Unc— Where's Hwan?" I ventured to ask Ensign Hak. I hadn't seen a sign of him, or the shaman and her dog, or the mercenaries.

"Offloaded already," Hak said, subdued, "along with the shaman. Captain Chaewon ordered special precautions. We thought it would be less of a fuss if you debarked separately."

She looked sidelong at me. "The shaman will face a tribunal of others in her profession, and I doubt they'll treat her kindly. You do know what will happen to . . . to your uncle."

I nodded jerkily. Hwan had committed capital crimes, and they wouldn't let him go unpunished for them. That decision, at least, was out of my hands.

I hadn't dared to ask to see my uncle while he was in the brig of the *Haetae*. But I'd wanted to. I wanted a chance to say good-bye, despite what he'd done. And I wondered now if I'd ever see him again. For the rest of my life I would remember that final sight of him taking down my attackers, even at the cost of his own fate, and that unearthly vision of the White Tiger of the West.

We marched through the base, a dolorous procession. After what felt like months on the *Haetae*, even though it had only been weeks, I was overwhelmed by all the people passing us and by their chaotic, intoxicating smells as well as the tantalizing hints of greenery and pollen from outside that the environmental filters hadn't managed to remove. I welcomed the distraction.

At last we reached a waiting room, where Ensign Hak turned me over to a sharp-nosed clerk who sat at a cramped desk. He bade me sit and added, with a perfunctory smile, "You may have to wait a while. Feel free to get yourself tea from the dispenser if you want it, and the restroom is two doors down the hall on the left."

I marveled that I didn't seem to be under arrest even now. Still, I was thirsty, so I poured myself some green tea. I scarcely tasted it, which was probably just as well. Someone had over-steeped it to the point of astringency.

Maybe the wait was long, maybe short. I lost track, instead doing physical-therapy exercises to occupy myself since I figured I might as well make good use of the time. I was in the middle of a particularly tricky exercise for my toes—hidden by my boots, of course—when the clerk cleared his throat.

"They're ready for you now, Cadet Sebin," the clerk said. I didn't correct him for addressing me by a rank I had never actually achieved. He smiled and indicated the door behind him. "You may proceed. They'll tell you what to do."

That was good, because my nerves had returned and I was so rattled that I had forgotten everything that the handbook said about how I was supposed to conduct myself during an inquiry. I flushed, then put the cup in the recycling receptacle and made my way to the door.

The chamber it opened into wasn't as vast as I had expected, although it could easily have accommodated thirty people. An admiral sat at a table at the head of the room. Captain Chaewon and Commander Ae had just retaken their seats at a facing table. There were other officers present, none of whom I recognized.

I did recognize someone else, though—my uncle, shackled and under guard, seated in a section of his own. There was no sign of Sena.

I couldn't help wincing when I saw him. No one had told me he'd be at my hearing! It meant he was going to bear witness to my testimony. Would he try to intimidate me into lying? Would I crack under the pressure? I was tempted to turn on my heel right then and there.

Hwan met my eyes with a steady gaze. I saw no fury in his face, no malice or desperation. He acknowledged me in a way he'd never done before—with a nod ... as though we were equals. Then he pointed his chin at the admiral, as if to say *Pay attention, Sebin. Do your duty.*

I stopped in my tracks and saluted the admiral, which seemed to be the right thing to do.

"Sebin," said the admiral, who had almost no hair, and whose face was a maze of wrinkles. I read her name tag: ADMIRAL AN MUN-HEE. Still, her eyes were sharp, and I knew better than to assume that age had dulled her wits. "I understand, from Captain Chaewon's account, and from the confession of the accused traitor, that you were a witness to the hijacking of the *Haetae*."

"That's correct, sir," I said.

"We will hear your testimony now," Admiral An said. "Please come forward."

I could see the spot on the floor where I was meant to stand, scuffed from footsteps past. I did as ordered, then faced the admiral and saluted again.

"At ease," An said. "Swear that you will answer our questions fully and honestly, to the best of your ability."

"I do so swear," I said in a strained voice. I drew a ragged breath and stared at Admiral An. Tried to quell the wobbling of my knees. I would have liked to sit down, but that was quite impossible.

She asked a great many questions about what had happened during the hijacking. Despite being painfully aware of Hwan's presence behind me, I answered them fully and honestly, just as I had sworn. The answers didn't always say the best things about my character, but that wasn't what was important. Uncle Hwan had betrayed the Space Forces, and he had to face the consequences, just as I would in my turn.

I still didn't understand what had motivated my uncle. Had

the Dragon Pearl—or the shaman—addled his mind somehow? Losing him as a hero was more painful than any injury I had received.

After a long time, Admiral An nodded and dismissed me. I took a last long look at my uncle, who was now answering questions of his own and had no attention to spare for me. I went back out into the waiting room and had more tea.

Even later, the admiral herself came into the waiting room. I was surprised to see her there, and I scrambled to my feet to salute her.

"Do you know why I am here, Cadet Sebin?" Admiral An asked.

I shook my head. "No, sir."

"What we are concerned with is what should happen to you, Cadet Sebin."

The air in my lungs turned to ashes. Nevertheless, I choked out, "Yes, sir."

"How do you evaluate your own conduct, Cadet?"

I couldn't read anything in her voice, only a certain detached curiosity. "I did the best I knew at the time," I said, "and it wasn't enough. The *Haetae* was endangered because I failed to warn Captain Chaewon when I had the opportunity. And I fell under Uncle Hwan's sway because of my reaction to being Charmed by Min." My eyes burned, and I fought back tears. Later, maybe, I'd have a good cry, but not now, while I faced the admiral's judgment.

"It's true that in a perfect world, we would all have perfect judgment," the admiral agreed drolly. "An earlier warning would have enabled a more effective defense against Hwan. But it *is* also true that Gate transitions cause hallucinations, so it's understandable that you hesitated. And your actions after that were ultimately to the benefit of the *Haetae* and its crew. You worked with Special Investigator Yi's assistant after you resolved the misunderstanding regarding her particular abilities. After Hwan freed you and showed his true colors, you turned against him when the time was right. You faced him down and persuaded him to end his treasonous actions at the risk of your own life."

I gaped at her. "Sir?" She made it sound as if I had *planned* all that. It hadn't felt like that at the time. Mostly I remembered an ordeal of moment-by-moment decisions, each one precarious.

Admiral An lifted an eyebrow. "Ex-captain Hwan gave testimony to that effect. The blood relationship between you two would ordinarily make his words suspect. However, the *Haetae*'s computer systems recorded everything that happened, so we have external confirmation."

I never thought I'd have cause to be grateful for the pervasive surveillance aboard the *Haetae*. *Thank you, ship*, I thought in what I hoped was its general direction.

"Sir," I whispered, starting to hope in spite of myself. I willed my heart to stop hammering so hard in my chest. There was a dull roar in my ears. I wanted to make sure I heard every word the admiral said.

"In my opinion," Admiral An said, the corner of her mouth lifting, "you acquitted yourself . . . not flawlessly, but certainly with merit for a thirteen-year-old cadet *on their very first day*. A more than usually calamitous first day at that. I hope that you will continue to be an asset to the Space Forces."

I sagged in shock. Fortunately, my legs didn't buckle beneath me. I silently thanked the medic back on the *Haetae* and the recuperation period I'd had for enabling me to recover from the fight against Hwan.

The admiral paused to let me take that in, then added, "That being said, your first *real* cruise should take place under less outlandish circumstances, and after you've had a chance to recover more—psychologically as well as physically. The *Haetae* needs further repairs anyway. You will have a medical leave of absence during that time. Use it wisely."

I recovered my voice. "And after that, sir?"

The admiral smiled at last. Unlike that of the clerk here in the waiting room, hers reached her eyes. "You're still a member of the *Haetae*'s crew, Cadet. You'll ship out with her on her next mission. I trust that this satisfies your ambitions."

"Yes, sir!" I breathed.

"See to the cadet's disposition," Admiral An said to the clerk. And to me: "Dismissed."

The day before I was to report for duty to the *Haetae* again, I received a letter from Admiral Hasun, my uncle. It came on formal cream-colored paper, although without the seal that would have marked it an official communication from the Space Forces. A personal letter, then.

To be honest, I had given up all hope of hearing from my family again. I was in my temporary quarters, sitting on my bunk in the barracks, when I opened the letter. I'd waited until I had a moment alone for this.

Cadet Sebin, the letter said, *I regret to inform you that the Matriarch has disinherited you. It was one of the last statements she left on file with the Yonggi authorities. Of course, I'm not sure how much it matters. She and the entire Juhwang Clan have abandoned their estate and are on the run. Hwan's capture has caused a great many of the Matriarch's schemes to unravel. It may take years for Domestic Security to figure out the extent of her meddling.*

I shook my head in disbelief. I couldn't imagine anyone dislodging the Matriarch from her beloved, well-kept estate. But then, tigers were survivors.

I am afraid, it went on, *that this means your parents have left you behind. Legally I am now your guardian, as the nearest relative who isn't a fugitive.*

My eyes pricked. Hasun hadn't mentioned Aunt Sooni—they didn't realize that I'd been close to her—but I could read between the lines. She'd left me, too. Losing the knife she'd given me had been an omen after all.

The White Tiger had told me, *Pay the price for breaking your oath, but pay it willingly.*

"There's only the Space Forces now," I whispered to myself. "Make it your home, Cadet."

Captain Chaewon welcomed me back onto the *Haetae* the next day. Ensign Hak escorted me to her office. "It'll be all right," Hak said awkwardly. By then everyone knew what had happened, and what my role had been. "You'll be all right."

"Thank you, sir," I said.

Once more I stood before Captain Chaewon in that beautifully appointed office. Thankfully, there were no remaining signs that we had ransacked it. "You've been through a lot, Cadet," she said, not without sympathy. "Are you ready to swear the oath?"

"I am, sir," I said. I couldn't stop my voice from trembling, or take my eyes off her ring-pommeled sword.

"Swear to serve the Thousand Worlds, and defend its people, and respect the chain of command, and serve your superiors," Captain Chaewon said, her voice ringing. "From this moment on, you will be part of the Space Forces, an institution greater than yourself, dedicated to serving others."

My gaze fixed on the sword. "I will serve the Thousand Worlds, defend its people, respect the chain of command, and serve my superiors." The words stung me on the way out of my mouth, but they tasted sweet. Perhaps that was the way it had always been, if I had but realized it earlier.

"Your right hand, please," the captain said.

The one with the scar. I held it out.

The sword flashed as she brought it down. Whether by coincidence or intent, she slashed the old scar open. There would be a new one in its place after the cut healed. I stared, engrossed, at the welling blood.

"It's done," Captain Chaewon said in a more normal voice. "Report to the bunkroom—the others will fill you in on your new duties. You'll be with Cadets Namkyu, Euna, and Jee, as before."

"Yes, sir," I whispered, overcome with emotion. I saluted her, then passed out of the office, following her orders.

On the way, I stopped at one of the viewports. The sight of the stars was as glorious as ever, perhaps even more so now that I knew the cost of serving in space. But I wouldn't have traded it for anything. I had a future in the Space Forces after all. I could still pursue my dream of becoming a captain.

"Cadet!" a sharp voice said from behind me. "Don't you have somewhere to be?"

I snapped to attention and about-faced, saluting hastily. "Sorry, sir!"

The officer, a lieutenant, looked me over, his eyebrows rising when he saw my name tag. "Ah, you're *that* cadet." He paused for a moment, and then asked, "Coming from the captain's office, are you?"

"Yes, sir."

"Good for you." He gave me a meaningful glance. "But don't expect that to be a regular occurrence, Sebin. She has more important things to do than waste her time with cadets who are probably overdue for latrine duty. Now, on your way."

"Of course, sir. Looking forward to it, sir." I saluted again, and then quickly headed toward the bunkroom, my friends, and my next assignment.

PRONUNCIATION GUIDE

(Pronounce all syllables with equal stress)

Ae: eh
Baik Jee: behk jee
Borasaekbam: boh-rah-sehk-bahm
Chaewon: cheh-wuhn
chima: chee-mah
Chin-Mae: cheen-meh
Euna: yoo-nah
gumiho: goo-mee-ho
Hae: heh
Haetae: heh-teh
Hak Bada: hahk bah-dah
hanbok: hahn-bohk
Hangeul: hahn-gool
Han-gyeol: hahn-gyuhl
hanja: hahn-jjah
Hasun: hah-soon
Hwan: hwahn
Jamjari: jahm-jah-ree
japchae: jahp-cheh
jogori: joh-goh-ree
Juhwang Sebin: joo-hwahng seh-been
Jun: joon
Jung: juhng
Jung-Soo: juhng-soo

Kim Min: geem meen
Myung: myuhng
Namkyu: nahm-gyoo
nini: nee-nee
Norandol: noh-rahn-dole
pungsu jiri: poong-soo jee-ree
Rhee: ree
Rokuro: roh-koo-roh
Sapsali: sahp-sahl-lee
Sena: seh-nah
Sooni: soo-nee
Ssang-yong: ssahng-yohng
Uchida: oo-chee-dah
Yang: yahng
Yonggi: yohng-ghee

ACKNOWLEDGMENTS

Thanks to my wonderful editor, Steph Lurie, and to Rick Riordan, both of whom made this book possible. Thanks also to Jennifer Jackson and Michael Curry, and to my agent, Seth Fishman.

Thank you to my beta readers: Cyphomandra, David Gillon, Tina Gilman, Helen Keeble, and Yune Kyung Lee.

Thank you to the following people for their support: Dhampyresa, Eller, Stephanie Folse, Isis, Sonya Taaffe, Vass, and Ursula Whitcher.

Special thanks to Reason for naming the shaman's dog.

And finally, last but not least, thanks to my husband, Joseph Betzwieser, my daughter, Arabelle Betzwieser, and my sister, Yune Kyung Lee, for putting up with me while I was writing this.